Heartfish & Coffee

Kimberly Soesbee

TOUCH
PUBLISHING

Published by Touch Publishing
www.TouchPublishingServices.com

Contact the author through her website:
www.KimberlySoesbee.com
Twitter: @AuthorSoesbee

Author photo by Tyler Case
@tylerjcase

This book is for Cooper.

It is also for the staff of Claro, 2013:
Sherri-Ann, Jennifer, Michelle, Wayne, Chelsea,
Chelsey 2.0, Ben, Laura, Darryl, Paula, and Jeremy.

Finally, this book is for
Joe Hellmig and Rene Garcia.
Thank you for being Cooper's best friends.

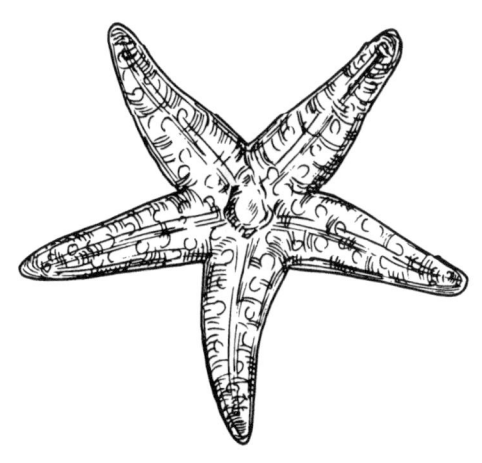

PROLOGUE

She willed the mound of dirt to move. Squinting. Searching for signs of life. There was none, save for the teeny green insect that decided the knoll held no reason to linger. Her eyes tracked it as it flew away.

"No, little bug. There's nothing for you there," she said weakly. "Nothing at all." A shoulder-slumping sigh escaped her lips.

"Come on, Joey," her husband coaxed, pulling her gently to her feet. "Let's go home for a while."

"I—can't leave her," she whispered.

"She's not here anymore, sweetie. She's with Jesus," he said softly. He ran his thumb over his wife's cool hand before pulling it to his mouth and kissing it. "They're going to close the cemetery soon. We can come back tomorrow if you'd like."

Joey knew she would have to leave. She knew the tiny body they buried that afternoon would be there tomorrow. And the next day. And the day after that. She also knew that when her daughter was lowered into the ground, Joey's heart was lowered with it, covered by black earth and hidden from the world. Craig knew it, too. He only hoped it wouldn't remain buried forever.

1

Part One

JOEY

FIVE YEARS LATER

Craig! I need you!" she screamed as loudly as she could. She listened. Nothing. She called out again with even more urgency. Her husband's footsteps could be heard bounding up the stairs, and a moment later he appeared in the bathroom where he found Joey, frozen in an awkward lunge position. Her back was to the door, so she caught his eye in the reflection of the bathroom mirror. She obviously dared not move.

"Baby, what's wrong?" he breathed. He looked around for a spider or (heaven forbid) a mouse.

"Quick! I need you to get the clear nail polish from under the sink. I have a run in my nylon, and this is my only pair! I don't have time to stop at Walmart. If I move, it will go down my leg. It's there on the right."

Breathing a sigh of support, Craig found the polish and handed it to his desperate wife. She dabbed a generous amount at the stop of the run and then traced it upward along its sides for good measure. Only then did she breathe out her own relief.

"Phew," she stood and pulled her skirt, straightening it. "Can you see it?"

Craig stepped back and eyed his wife's lovely legs. "Nope. You averted the danger."

"Do people even wear nylons anymore?" she wondered for the tenth time. "I don't want to look like an old lady."

"Whether you wear panty hose or not, they're going to love you. Any school would be blessed to have you as a teacher." Craig came forward and kissed the top of Joey's head.

"I do know that no one says, 'panty hose' anymore," she scolded. She wrapped her arms around her husband. "Am I doing the right thing?"

Craig hugged her tightly. "Oh, baby. Don't fret. You're going to make a wonderful teacher. You are the smartest woman I know, and I am sure the school will see it, too." Craig's encouragement of her ambitions was one of the things she loved most about him. He was a rock—always confident of her abilities. He gave her one last squeeze and released her. It was time for her to go.

Thirty minutes later, Joey stared at the large white letters affixed to the front of Black Bear Creek Middle School. She was fifteen minutes early and preferred the comfortable enclosure of her minivan to the unknowns inside the building. The Eagles' *Desperado* strummed sweetly from the radio speakers. The weight of this interview was palpable. Once she opened the car door and went inside, there was no going back. Whether she got this job or not, this interview marked another turning point in Joey's life. Not nearly as big as the one that came five years prior, but it was most assuredly an indication that whether she liked it or not, she had to keep putting one foot in front of the other.

Her feet had moved in baby steps over these years. It took ten full months until she could even walk through the children's building at their church without tearing up. It took another nine before she could resume her Sunday School teacher responsibilities. And deciding to go into teaching full time? Well, that was something God laid on her heart two years ago. She enrolled in an alternative certification program to accompany her bachelor's degree from North Carolina State; thirty online courses and forty classroom observation hours later, here she was.

Sleepless nights enveloped her often with doubt. Twice she broke down and told Craig she couldn't go through with it. But she plodded on, sending resumes and praying for a response. The summer was excruciating as long, hot days rolled by with no response to the applications she submitted to nearly every school in her county and the next county over. With the national news persistently talking up teacher shortages and post-COVID learning loss, she couldn't understand why no one had contacted her for an interview.

Loaded with faith, Craig kept assuring her that

the opening she was meant to have just wasn't available yet. But when school started, she'd given up hope of landing a job this year and conceded that perhaps God didn't really want her to go into teaching; perhaps she'd heard Him wrong. So, when she opened the e-mail in her inbox yesterday asking if she'd be interested in a position with the Exceptional Children at Black Bear Creek Middle School, she was shocked. For two straight hours she bounced back and forth in her head, not even wanting to tell Craig, as she knew what he'd say. In the end, she accepted the interview.

Gathering her handbag, she left the safety of her car. A young girl, perhaps all of twenty-two, exited the school as Joey entered. Joey wondered if she was the competition. She smoothed her skirt and took a deep breath.

"Hi. I'm JoAnn Russo. I'm here for a meeting with Mr. Matthews," she said as calmly as she could to the woman at the front office desk.

"Have a seat, please," she smiled. "He'll be right with you."

Joey sat gingerly on one of the orange fabric-covered chairs that lined the wall. She crossed her right leg and noticed that the run on her nylon had made another go of it. "Shoot," she thought grimly and wished she'd tossed the nail polish into her purse. She was about to ask the location of a restroom so she could remove her insolent nylons, when the receptionist's phone buzzed.

"Ma'am? He'll see you now." The woman indicated a hallway to her left. "Go down that hall to the first door on the right. It's our conference room."

Joey walked as if on eggshells, begging the tear in her stockings to keep still. Mercifully, she was able to position her handbag in front of her thighs as she shook hands with the principal of Black Bear Creek. He was a tall gentleman who was likely not much older than Joey's forty years. A neatly trimmed mustache and beard framed a wide smile.

"Mrs. Russo?" he inquired. "I'm Darryl Matthews. Nice to meet you. Please have a seat." He walked around the conference table. She waited until he sat, then took her own seat directly across from him.

"There will be one other person joining us," he explained. "Mrs. Dunne from our Exceptional Children classroom will be here in a moment."

"No problem," Joey said, noticing a slight shake in her voice. She cleared her throat. "Would you like a copy of my resume?" Joey had prepared a tidy, bradded orange folder (the school's colors were orange and white) complete with her resume, newly acquired teaching certificate, and letters of recommendation. She offered it proudly to the man who might become her new boss.

"Thank you very much," he said, taking it warmly and setting it on the table. He didn't even open it. "I've looked over the resume you submitted online and–" The door opened, and a rotund woman pushed her way into the room. Her face was as red as the sweater she wore, both of which reminded Joey of a rubber four-square ball. She did not smile as she took the seat at the head of the table, resting forward onto dimpled elbows. She breathed heavily and looked to Mr. Matthews. He continued, "Ah. Mrs. Dunne. There you are. This is Mrs. Russo."

"Nice to meet you," Joey said brightly. Mrs. Dunne nodded in reply, her eyes not even turning to meet Joey's.

"Mrs. Russo, the school year started two weeks ago," Mr. Matthews said, getting right down to business. "A teacher in one of our classrooms started the year but due to some personal health matters is unable to continue. This has opened a position in our Exceptional Children department. The job is in our highest-needs classroom. It is a classroom that contains nine children at the moment. All of them are identified as having special needs that are not best served in the general education classroom. The number in the room may fluctuate during the year. There are three teachers in there, plus Mrs. Dunne, who oversees the learning activities."

Mrs. Dunne nodded her head and explained dryly, "These kids can't handle being in a general education classroom. Some have behavior issues, and being in quarantine during COVD made it worse. Their disabilities–mostly autism–prevent them from learning in a regular general ed class. We do the best we can in our specialized room." She made it sound about as much fun as picking burrs off a donkey–something Joey grew up doing on her grandparents' farm.

"It isn't an easy job," Mr. Matthews said firmly. "Do you think you could handle such a position?"

His question took Joey completely off-guard. They had no questions about her qualifications? No wonderings why she is entering the education field after working in a dental office for all those years? Nothing about her schooling or grades? His question appeared careless. She thought carefully before answering. "As a first-year teacher, there are a lot of things I am unfamiliar with in regard to school policy, lesson planning, and all of that," she began.

Mrs. Dunne cut her off. "Oh, you don't have to do any lesson planning. I take care of all that for our room. We'll get you up to speed on the routine and what to do. You've got the licensure for exceptional students, right?"

"Yes. I passed the K through 12 exceptional children exam and have my license for middle school grades 6 through 9," Joey affirmed proudly. "For the past two years I've worked in our Sunday School at church with a boy who has Down syndrome. I've really connected well with him. I'd like to help kids who need extra support." She wanted desperately for them to ask her, "Why? Why are you here?" But they didn't ask.

"That's good. You need to have the special education designation to teach in our class. Without it, we could list you as a paraprofessional, but it is much better for you to have the full designation," Mrs. Dunne said more to herself than to Joey.

"Mrs. Russo," Mr. Matthews said, "as I mentioned, this isn't an easy job. There are seven boys and two girls in the class, and the boys keep things—how should I say—quite busy. It isn't for the faint of heart. Eleven- to thirteen-year-old boys are a handful as it is, and when you add special needs to the mix, well, it can make for a challenge. I would hate to see you take a job then find out later that it is too much to handle. I'd want you to be sure you are up for it."

Joey struggled to envision the kind of difficulties of which he could be speaking. This was a public school, after all. "Mr. Matthews, this would be a new experience for me. But I can assure you that I know how to teach, and I would do my very best for the kids you entrust to me." Her voice got stronger as she spoke. She sat back and smiled.

It was the easiest interview she possibly could have imagined. After assurances from Mr. Matthews that they would make their decision as soon as possible and that the job could start as early as the next week, the interview was over. Her confidence was high as she raced home to share it all with Craig.

In 1873, Mark Twain and Charles Dudley Warner penned a novel titled *The Gilded Age: A Tale of Today*. The satirical work poked fun at the lustful drives that permeated post-Civil War Americans, whose wealth far surpassed their morality. The title of the story stood the test of time. The term *The Gilded Age* came to define that entire period in America's development—greed, political corruption, and luxuriousness. America's labor wages soared during this period and the economy boomed. Driven to make good showy use of his own wealth, in the late 1880s, George Washington Vanderbilt II commissioned the building of a new and extremely grand summer home: The Biltmore Estate in Asheville, North Carolina.

Between the architecture reflecting stately chateaus of the French Renaissance and extravagant décor presenting the best of the Victorian Era, the Biltmore Estate is breathtaking— incomparable to any other home in the United States. The grounds cover more than eight thousand acres; landscape having been designed by Fredrick Law Olmstead, whose work also included Central Park in New York. Not only is it Asheville's most prestigious tourist attraction, but thousands of locals regularly frequent the property to loll away the day. Craig and Joey became season's pass holders years ago and used them whenever possible. Better than any city park, Biltmore offers endless opportunities either to get lost in a crowd or find solitude.

The day after her interview, Joey took her journal and a novel and spent the better part of the afternoon in the Rose Garden. Despite her own black thumb, she held as much appreciation for the flowers, bushes, and trees of Biltmore as any seasoned horticulturist. In her mind she designed exquisite gardens. In reality, the best she could hope for is that her rose bushes would flower and the azaleas would open. The Biltmore landscape contributed as much to Joey's spiritual healing following Emily's death as any of the therapy sessions she attended. The hand of God traced every leaf's curve. She stroked the softness of her daughter's skin again with each touch of a gentle petal, the aroma of the roses soothing her soul. George Washington Vanderbilt II knew it not, but when he built his opulent estate, his efforts were not all for his own glory. More than one hundred twenty years later, his legacy provided a place of healing, where a grieving mother found the glory of God.

Around 2 p.m. Joey left the sanctuary of the Rose Garden for a stroll to the Biltmore Bake Shop. An afternoon coffee was greatly needed, and the Bake Shop served a hazelnut blend that never failed. Warm brew in hand, she took a seat at an outdoor table and had just started chapter seven of her novel when the buzz of her phone interrupted her thoughts.

"Hello?" she queried.

"JoAnn Russo, please," a man's voice requested.

"This is Joey," she said. Her heart pounded as she recognized Darryl Matthews's voice.

"Mrs. Russo, this is Darryl Matthews from Black Bear Creek Middle School. How are you today?"

"I am well, thank you. And you?" she asked, the quiver in her voice making another appearance.

"I'm just fine, thank you. Listen, we had a couple of candidates for the teaching position at our school, but after deliberating with Mrs. Dunne, I would like to offer you the job that you interviewed for yesterday. The one in our high-needs classroom," he clarified unnecessarily. "If you accept, we would really like for you to start on Monday, if possible. Human resources said they would get you in tomorrow to complete your paperwork, and we can orient you to the school and the routine next week. You seem like a fast learner, so I am sure you'll get up to speed pretty quickly."

She appreciated the compliment, but wondered how on earth he could have deciphered that she was a fast learner from the brief interview that asked no question of any real difficulty? She wanted to ask him for time to think about it but feared any hesitation would move him along to the next candidate.

"Mrs. Russo?"

"Yes, sorry, I was just thinking," she said. Craig would tell her to take it. She spoke quickly to leave no room to change her mind. "Yes, I would very much like to come work at your school. And yes, I can start on Monday." Phew. She repeated "yes" one more time to keep the word "no" confined to her fears.

"Well, that's just great!" he said. Was it happiness she detected in his voice? Or relief? "We're glad to have you. I will text you the address of our district offices and they will expect you around 9:30 tomorrow, if that's OK with you. Then I will see you on Monday morning, eight o'clock. School starts at eight forty-five."

"Sounds perfect. I'll be there," Joey said. The quiver was gone. Decision made. Action plan in motion. An appointment with human resources and a Monday start date. It was done.

"Now, let's get your picture taken."

Joey had completed her new-hire paperwork with the Director of Human Resources and had been ushered to a small office where she'd been fingerprinted by a kindly technical support employee whose name badge read "Tyrone Adams."

"My picture?" Joey was confused.

"Yes, for your ID badge," he said. "Stand over

there against the wall."

It was something she hadn't thought about, and immediately she wished she'd spent more time on wardrobe selection that morning. Turns out, it wouldn't have mattered. The picture was fuzzy and only her shoulders were visible. But something important happened in her heart when she held the plastic ID badge. JoAnn Russo. Black Bear Creek School District. The bar code and her employee number made her officially part of the education system. *Don't you dare cry here*, she scolded herself.

"Head over to payroll, and they'll have you fill out the direct deposit forms for your paychecks," Tyrone said. "Then come on back and I should have your technology ready."

"My technology?" More confusion.

"Yes. We will outfit you with a bionic arm, perfect for speedily grading papers, and a pair of high-powered binoculars, which allow you see through the minds of your students, so you know if they understood your lesson."

Joey blinked.

"I'm kidding. All of our teachers get a laptop computer and an iPad. I just need to finish installing the updates, and then you'll be all set."

"Really? Wow. Cool," Joey said. She'd not even considered the need for a laptop or iPad in the classroom—but of course! Her online teaching courses often referred to various interactive applications to make lessons more engaging for students. COVID-19 made technology not a luxury, but a necessity. In the busy-ness of it all, she'd never thought about how teachers actually accomplished these goals.

That night, she was like a kid with a new toy as she checked out the features of her iPad. The school had automatically loaded several educational apps for reading, math, and science. She'd been playing with it for hours.

"Look at this!" she showed Craig. "Mad Libs! Electronic Mad Libs! Remember those from when we were young? Here—I'm going to do one with you. Give me a noun."

"Tacos," Craig said.

"Okay. Now an adjective," she instructed.

"What's an adjective?" Craig asked.

"A description word," Joey replied.

"Fuzzy," Craig answered.

"Now a verb."

"Eat," Craig said. "Are you sensing a pattern here?"

"Eat Fuzzy Tacos?" Joey asked. "Yeah, OK. I get it. We can go to Fuzzy's for dinner. I'm just really excited."

Craig gently took the iPad from her hands and pulled her to her feet. He loved his wife's passion and was more thankful than he could express for this job. He'd known for a while it was what she needed. He prayed. He was patient. And eventually she, too, came to see the need to begin a new chapter for herself. "I know." He kissed her cheek. "I'm excited for you, too. This is a big step. We've both been through so much."

Unspoken between them were the words, *Since Emily died.*

DODIE

He went home with her!" Anne, the marketing assistant, lowered her voice as Dodie walked into the break room.

"Too late! I heard you. You know, gossip is bad for your complexion," Dodie jibed.

Sherry, the marketing manager, handed Dodie the coffee pot. "Happy Monday. Here ya go."

"So, what'd I miss?" Dodie asked. "Was Dave and Buster's everything you hoped for?"

"All that and more!" Anne said. "You really should have come."

"Aaron was working late on Friday. Again. I had to get home to the dogs," Dodie explained. Secretly she wasn't the least bit sorry to have missed the quarterly office outing. Without fail, someone always drank too much, acted the fool, and did something regrettable. Last quarter, one of the engineers got a DUI on his way home and lost his driver's license for twelve months.

"Who was it this time?" Dodie asked, clearly not worried about her own complexion.

"Lips," Anne explained, using the moniker they'd dubbed for the new sales rep. They guesstimated that a good portion of her monthly paycheck went to a plastic surgeon to pay for various body enhancements, including botox.

"What did she do?" Dodie dumped a mound of sugar in her coffee.

"Not what. Who!" Sherry offered.

"Who?"

"Brent," Anne whispered. "Someone saw them making out in Luigi's Mansion, and they left within minutes of each other."

"Dang," Dodie said. "Bad move." Brent was the Regional Sales Manager. A married regional sales manager.

"She'll be gone by the end of the week," Sherry predicted. Sherry's predictions were rarely wrong. She'd worked for Evertor Technologies longer than any of them.

"I say she'll be out by Wednesday," Dodie offered. "Want to bet lunch on it?"

"I'm in. I say he'll keep her for the rest of the month. He's a dog. He'll try and squeeze some more action out of her before he dumps her," Anne stated. She herself almost fell prey to Brent's wiles when she started out and loathed him vehemently ever since. Sherry and Dodie had saved her.

As it turned out, Dodie's guess was the closest. Lips didn't even come into the office that day, and Brent stopped by Dodie's desk just before noon to tell her to call the recruiter to open an ad for a new sales representative.

"Are we expanding?" Dodie asked innocently.

Brent shook his head. "No, Felicia quit," he stated.

"Oh! How come?" Dodie suppressed her smile. She hardly ever won a bet.

Brent shrugged. "Don't know. She called in and said she wouldn't be back. It's just as well. She wasn't really picking up on the product line." He knocked his knuckles twice on the desk. "Let's get someone good."

"Douchebag," Dodie mumbled under her breath as he walked away. As the Office Manager and lead Administrative Assistant, Dodie navigated the delicate relationship between the sales staff and the engineering staff. She reported to the Regional Controller, who traveled so much she was often the number one office go-to and responsible for keeping operations running smoothly.

She loved her job. Her boss, Chris, gave her a lot of rope and opportunity to stretch her skills. Her goal was to be a CFO one day, and this job was the perfect steppingstone.

"Dodie, how long have you been here?" Walt Grubman, Engineering Manager, asked, slapping a stack of papers onto her desk.

"Here at work today or are you talking big picture?" Dodie smiled at Walt.

"How long have you worked for this company?"

"About three years now, Walt. Why?" Dodie liked Walt. He was no-nonsense, followed the rules, and had as much disdain for Brent as she did.

"In your experience with this company, have we ever, ever, *ever* performed an equipment installation before the customer actually ordered the products?"

"Excuse me?"

"On Friday, Stupid Eric wrote up a sales order to install two full HP Z8 systems at Raymer. I was thrilled because we have two systems sitting in the back that were returned last month. Only this morning, as I began packing them up and checking the specs, I read the paperwork more closely, and Raymer hasn't even issued their internal purchase order to buy these systems yet. The little shit was trying to get me to install these without having a purchase order from the company."

"Yeah, that's a no-go."

"I already let him have it. I just wanted you to know. How'd he even get this order through the system without a customer P.O.?"

Dodie took the stack of papers from him and examined them. "Looks like he hand-wrote the words Purchase Order across the top of his quote. This order was put in by Amy. She used the quote number as the P.O. number. I'll have a talk with her." She laid the papers on her desk. "Sorry, Walt."

"If those idiot sales reps would follow protocol, we wouldn't have these problems," he said. "I'm out of here—I've got a training class at Lockheed."

"Later." Dodie sighed. This wasn't the first time Amy put an order through the system without the proper back-up. She was young—even younger than Dodie's twenty-six years—and frequently allowed the male reps to sweet-talk her into bending the rules. Dodie had sworn that after the last time, if Amy did anything like this again, she'd be gone. She knew Chris would support her decision. The company can't risk ordering thousands of dollars of equipment without a firm customer purchase order. They'd been burned before; two months ago Amy put a fifty-thousand-dollar order through at the end-of-month which had to be reversed. It makes them all look bad. She sent Chris a quick text, and after receiving his affirmative reply, she called Amy into the conference room.

She handed Amy the papers from the order. Amy didn't even take them.

"I know, Dodie. The P.O. wasn't in yet. But Eric said it would be here first thing this morning, and the customer really needs these systems."

"Amy, what's the date?" Dodie asked impatiently.

"The thirtieth."

"What always happens at the end of the month?"

Amy sighed. "Reps try and push orders through to boost their monthly numbers."

"What do you think would happen if Walt had installed these and the P.O. never comes through?"

"Shitstorm."

"Right. Shitstorm. We are the gatekeepers. We have to protect the company, not cater to desperate sales reps trying to meet quota. You have had two warnings and a write up over this. We've got to let you go."

"Are you freaking serious?" Amy stood, knocking her chair over.

Dodie remained calm. "You knew the order wasn't right. I'm sorry."

Amy yanked open the conference room door, slamming it into the wall. Dodie followed her back to her desk and watched as she slung her personal things into an empty copy paper box and looking very much like a cliché, marched from the office while her ex-coworkers looked on, mouths agape.

"This is your fault," Dodie poked an angry finger at Stupid Eric and returned to her desk. Now she had two ads to place.

The driveway was empty when Dodie pulled into it after work. "Of course," she sighed. Even though Aaron started work a full hour before she did, he was rarely home when she got there. They'd only been married for six months, and she saw more of him before they lived together than she did now.

"At least you guys are happy I'm home," she said to the dogs as they greeted her at the door with wiggles and kisses. It wasn't until they were walked, fed, and snuggled next to her on the couch that the headlights from Aaron's truck finally reflected through the front window. It was a full ten minutes until he came through the front door.

"What were you doing out there?" Dodie

asked, trying to keep accusation from her tone.

"What are you, my mother?" Aaron retorted, not even stopping for a kiss hello. He went right to the kitchen. "What's for dinner?"

"I made a ham sandwich. I can make one for you if you want," she offered.

She heard the refrigerator door bang shut. "I'll have cereal."

The tension that began when she saw his headlights traveled like lava through Dodie's shoulders and trickled down her spine. The last three weeks had been like this. Aaron comes home late, grumpy, and then isolates himself in their second bedroom-turned-study. She decided to head him off before he holed himself up. She followed him into the kitchen.

"How was your day?" she tried to sound bright. She studied his face as he leaned against the counter, eating his cereal with more intensity than a man's ever eaten cereal.

He gave a one-shoulder shrug. "Caught a fifteen-year-old shoplifter. She'd stashed some high-end perfume sample bottles in her purse. Moron." He shook his head.

"Aaron, is something wrong?" Dodie asked. She'd been mustering up the courage to put those words out there for a few days. She braced herself for the blast of sarcasm he'd become expert at detonating.

He considered his Cheerios for a solid minute

before answering. "I'm sorry, Dodes," he finally said, his tone flat. "Work's just stressful."

Dodie was shocked at the non-confrontational answer. "Oh. Okay. I thought you were mad at me or something. You've been—closed off."

He put down the spoon and looked at her. He forced his facial features into a semblance of his former self. It appeared to be a great effort. "I'm not mad. Just overworked. Hey, why don't we go rock climbing this weekend?"

"We haven't done that in months," she replied cautiously. "Not since our honeymoon."

"I'll see if Jason and Lucy want to come too," he suggested.

Before she could answer, he grabbed his cereal and brushed past her. The scent of liquor trailed behind him like a veil. She heard the study door slam shut a moment later.

"Just tell him you don't want them to go with you guys," Sherry instructed after Dodie shared her thoughts about Jason and Lucy at lunch the next day.

"I hate to do that when he finally wants to do something together," Dodie said. "I mean, he's been a hermit for weeks. He's either at work or locked in the study."

"What does he do in there?" Anne asked, taking a big bite from her burger.

Dodie pursed her lips. "I dunno. He says he's

working. Investigating cases, crap like that. His laptop never leaves his side."

"You don't buy it?" Sherry asked.

"He's in there an awful lot. Late into the night," Dodie's voice quivered. "He comes home smelling of either whisky or pot. Sometimes both. I guess they go out after work. Or at least he does."

"Why don't you go out for Happy Hour with him?" Anne suggested.

"Annie! That's the last thing I want to do after working all day. I'll go out once in a while, but every night? Ain't nobody got time for that. He's become a completely different person since we got married."

"Do you think he's stepping out on you?" Anne asked gingerly.

Sherry punched her in the arm. "Anne!"

Anne shrugged. "He's got to be up to something."

Dodie teared up. She leaned her forehead onto balled fists. "He's looking at porn."

"What?" Sherry asked, wondering if she heard her friend correctly. "Porn?"

"Yeah. Porn. I saw him. I walked into the study without knocking last week—to bring him a coffee. The computer screen was facing away from the door, but I saw the reflection of it in the window behind him. Naked women."

"What did he say?" Sherry asked.

"Nothing. He doesn't know I saw. I just put the coffee down and smiled. He didn't even say thank you. I went to bed. I laid there awake for two hours. When I fell asleep, he still hadn't come to bed."

"Oh, sweetie," Anne said. "I'm so sorry. Want me to bash him in the kneecaps?" She would do it, too. Anne believed that women should always be ready to defend themselves. She'd even tried to convince Dodie and Sherry to get their concealed carry weapons permit when she got hers the previous summer.

"Maybe later," Dodie smiled. "Perhaps rock climbing together will remind him of what he's got live and in the flesh." Dodie wasn't convincing herself. "And if I have to share the time with a couple of other people, well, at least it's something. Right?"

"Absolutely," Sherry said, coming around the table and putting her arm around her friend's shoulder. "You'll get through this. He'll come to his senses."

They were quiet.

"On a completely unrelated note, I didn't know you rock climbed!" Anne said. "You're a badass!"

"I've been doing it for years. I started in high school. It's actually how Aaron and I met," Dodie shared. "It's such a thrill."

"I can't imagine pulling my fat butt up the side of a mountain," Anne said.

"You use ropes and those safety clasps and everything, right?" Sherry asked with worry. As the oldest in the group—she was thirty-one—she felt protective of her friends.

"Of course! We always belay for each other." She added, "That means we secure each other to a safety rope. We're very careful. I promise."

"You're my hero. I could never do it," Anne reiterated.

"Sure, you could. We should go to the climbing gym sometime; I bet you'd love it." Dodie brightened.

"Yes, let's!" Sherry said. "I've always wanted to try."

"Only if we can eat Mexican food and drink margaritas afterward," Anne said. "And if I don't actually have to go more than three feet off of the ground."

"Deal," Dodie smiled. Her friends always could cheer her up.

Saturday morning finally arrived. Dodie was hopeful for a positive day with her aloof husband. She loaded the cooler while Aaron inspected their climbing gear. "Sandwiches, chips, lots of water. What else?" Dodie asked.

"Pack beer for afterward," he said. His phone buzzed with a text message.

"We only have three in the fridge," she noted.

He looked up from his phone. "Lucy just texted me. They're going to be here soon. You ready?" he asked.

"I'll let the dogs out one more time, then we're

all set."

Dodie's two chocolate Labradors, Benny and Joon, followed her out to their small yard. Dodie had purchased the townhouse with an inheritance left to her by her maternal grandmother. It was a cute two-bedroom that was a perfectly sized (and priced) starter home. Life in Boulder wasn't cheap, and Aaron had been renting an apartment when they'd met, so the townhouse was truly a blessing. Pricewise, Boulder was the Tiffany's of Colorado. But it made up for it with its glorious scenery, so Dodie always felt the trade-off for the high cost of living was worth it. The pooches sensed that they were going to be left alone for the day, so they ran a couple of laps around the yard, did their business, and came right back to Dodie. She rubbed behind their ears as she gave them a treat.

"I love you guys," she said. "Be good while we're out. I'll see you later tonight." She kissed the tops of their coffee-colored heads.

Piled in the back of Jason's SUV, Dodie's stomach was uneasy. She'd never felt apprehensive before a climb before, and she attributed it to the recent distance between her and Aaron. If any of the others noticed that she was quiet, they didn't show it. They chatted about work, the Broncos, and the upcoming Twenty One Pilots concert—which Jason and Lucy had tickets for.

"You guys should come with us!" Lucy spun around in her seat. "It's going to be epic."

Dodie loved the band, but she looked to Aaron, expecting a snide remark. He hated Twenty One Pilots and had actually forbidden her to play their music if he was in earshot.

Instead, he grinned back at Lucy. "Sure! That would be great! I'll look into it."

Dodie's momentary shock was about to result in her own snide comment, but the sudden view of the canyon took her breath away. They'd arrived.

The entrance to Eldorado Canyon State Park was only eighteen short miles from Boulder. Its golden rock walls screamed to be conquered, and it made Dodie's heart full to oblige them. The sun glistened like fairy twinkles off the surface of South Boulder Creek as they hiked to her favorite climb—The Bastille Crack. Of the nearly five hundred places to climb in Eldo Canyon, The Bastille Crack was the hot spot. The line for climbing wasn't too long, so they took up their place in the queue, and Dodie's apprehension turned to anticipation of reconnecting with the sandstone.

Lucy climbed first, with Jason as her belay. Her skill was solid, and Dodie watched her for a bit before getting to work readying herself. Aaron had taken a special interest in watching Lucy climb, and more than once Dodie had to repeat her request for Aaron to assist in securing her equipment and ensuring it all was true.

"Aaron! Is your belay brake secure?" she asked again with impatience.

"I told you it was!" he snapped back, not even looking at it.

"You did not tell me anything," Dodie shot back. "Do you even know I'm here?"

"Can it, Dodes," he said. "Get off my case."

Dodie briefly considered taking off her belt and throwing it at him. But as Lucy finished her climb and Jason waved Dodie over, the call of the cliff suppressed her increasing annoyance with her husband.

She walked to the foot of the wall and asked Jason to double check her line. After making sure her cams and carabiners were clipped to her belt, she looked over at Aaron, who stood ready.

"Belay on," he said, with more than a little bit of sarcasm.

"Climbing," she answered.

Dodie pinched her fingers into her chalk bag and smoothed the granules across her fingertips. *This is what life is all about*, she thought, as her hands grabbed hold of the rough surface and she became one with the mountain.

The Bastille Crack was a climb she'd done countless times, and as she reacquainted with her old friend, her spirit calmed. Except for the mandatory call outs for more rope or more tension, tranquility enveloped her as she ascended.

Lost in motion for what seemed an hour, it surprised her when Aaron shouted out, "Halfway!"

I've only gone forty feet? she wondered,

thinking that didn't seem right in relation to her place on the rock face. She glanced under her arm momentarily, to gauge Aaron's location in relation to her vertical. She knew she was a lot higher up than forty feet. She judged it to be more like sixty, which meant she only had about twenty feet of rope left. Aaron's attention wasn't on her, however. He held onto the rope with his hands, but his eyes were fixed on Lucy, who stood next to him, chatting. He clearly missed the halfway call that he was supposed to have made. She envisioned climbing down, walking out of that park, and not looking back. *Screw you,* Aaron, she thought, *and screw you, Lucy,* who should have known better than to distract the belayer.

"Climbing down!" she called out. Her enjoyment was gone.

Aaron yelled something in response, which Dodie took to be his signal that she could begin her descent.

Dodie unclipped the carabiner from the highest cam and hooked both onto her belt. Her fingers found a strong grip at waist level, and she lowered herself as her feet found a new ledge to rest upon. But the next cam gave her trouble. It would not release from its place in the rock. She struggled with it momentarily, then decided she'd have to unclip from it and leave it wedged there. As she went to open the carabiner, however, the cam suddenly dropped loose from its spot, surprising

Dodie so that her weight became off-balance. Without a secure hand grip, Dodie fell backward from the mountainside.

Expecting to only fall as far as the next cam, a precipitous realization hit her that the rope had more slack than it should have. The crack of her head against the rock ended any other thoughts.

JOEY

Six o'clock came early on Monday morning. The night before, Joey labored over selecting her first-day outfit. She woke up three times during the night to check her alarm, and in the brief intervals that she did sleep, she had her go-to panic dream—the one where she is running across her college campus looking for her class but can't find it. Good night's rest? No way.

"I'm so nervous," she confessed to Craig, as he packed a sandwich into her new nylon lunch bag.

"Honey, you'll be fine. Stop worrying." Had he said those words fifty times over the last several days? Probably. So why was she still worried?

"It's the unknown," she tried to explain. "They made it seem like the kids in the class were so difficult. What if I can't handle them?"

"They're kids. It's a middle school. How bad can they be? Aren't there four of you in the room?"

"Yes, I think that's what they said."

"If four adults can't handle nine or ten kids, then there's a bigger problem going on," Craig noted.

"I suppose. But these are special needs kids. What if I can't give them what they need?"

Craig just smiled at Joey. There really was nothing more to say about it. He zipped her lunch bag and held it out to her.

"I love you." He pointed to the door.

"Thanks. I love you, too." She took her lunch, grabbed her purse and backpack that held her iPad and laptop, and she was off.

Teachers were to report for eight a.m., and she arrived almost thirty minutes prior. The staff lot was sparse with cars. She sat in the office for fifteen minutes before the school secretary arrived, and after receiving a key to her classroom, she had plenty of time to wander the halls to find it.

"Can I help you?" a teacher carrying an armload of photocopies paused to ask.

"I'm looking for Room 618," Joey explained. "This is my first day."

"Welcome! I'm Rick Lee," he said. "I'd shake your hand, but—" he indicated his full armload. "618? What do you teach?"

"Joey Russo," Joey said. "Nice to meet you. I'm in the special education class."

"Ah! The fish-room," Rick said with recognition. "Yes, that's at the end of the next hallway."

"Fish room?" Joey inquired.

"It's what we call it. I forget what it even stands for—full inclusion, something, something."

"Oh. Okay," Joey said. "Yes, I guess that's me."

"If you need anything, I'm in 412. Just come find me."

Joey walked away feeling accomplished. She'd made a friend. Craig will be proud. Her heels clacked on the linoleum as she walked the long hallway that Mr. Lee instructed her to follow. Classroom 618 was indeed at the very end, just before a door that led to the outside. "NO STUDENT EXIT" was printed in white nylon lettering on the glass doors. A small placard that read:

FULLY INDIVIDUALIZED SUPPORT CLASS

was affixed to the concrete block wall next to the door.

"FISC. I guess that's what fish means?" she wondered aloud with a shrug.

Black paper covered the door's rectangular window from the inside, preventing a peek into the interior of her new classroom. With a shaky hand, Joey unlocked the heavy wooden door and pushed it open, only vaguely aware that she was holding her breath.

The light came on automatically as she stepped into the room, nearly scaring her to death, but what almost knocked her off her feet was the smell. It was a cross between milk that'd been spilled but never cleaned up, feet, and—was that urine? The repugnance stung her eyes so that she blinked several times to clear them.

"Dear Lord," she said aloud. She quickly

opened the door and pushed a rubber doorstop under the crack to hold it open. She stood in the open doorway and took in the surroundings. Mustard-colored cinderblock surrounded her on all sides. A low bookshelf lined one of the walls from which books of all colors and sizes screamed out to her, begging for organization—or at the very least for someone to line them up. She made a mental note to do that later. A large teacher's desk sat authoritatively near the back of the room.

"You must be the new teacher."

Joey jumped and spun around. The woman's employee badge read Sharon Johnson. She was younger than Joey—probably in her early 30s—with dark skin and an unruly afro that she attempted to tame with a thick blue headband. She wore black sweatpants and a neon pink sweatshirt. Tired Nikes completed her casual look, which was a noticeable contrast to Joey's crisp navy dress pants and cream-colored blouse.

"Sorry, didn't mean to scare you," the woman said.

"I'm Joey," Joey said, offering her hand for the woman to shake.

"Sharon Johnson," came the reply. "What's your last name?"

"Russo."

"I'm glad they hired someone—you are full time, right?" Mrs. Johnson looked momentarily wary.

"Yes, of course," Joey answered.

"Good. The sub they put in here couldn't do anything. She just sat in the corner," Mrs. Johnson indicated an empty red plastic chair near the bookcase. "When we needed the chair for a kid, she got all annoyed that she had to move." She shook her head in disgust at the thought. "You're going to want to wear something more comfortable," she continued, eyeballing Joey's shoes. "Those are going to kill your feet."

Joey looked down at her black pumps. "Oh. I wasn't sure what to wear. The dress code I got from human resources said–"

"Let me stop you right there," Sharon Johnson interrupted. "Our rules are a bit more flexible. First off, ain't no one from district office ever gonna come down here, and if they do, when they see what we deal with, they won't have nothin' to say about no dress code."

Joey nodded. A pang of fear rolled around her stomach. *What we deal with?* Another woman came into the room. She was a petite Asian woman who introduced herself as Tam. Tam's name badge was flipped backward, so Joey wasn't sure if this was her first or last name, but when Mrs. Johnson introduced Joey to her as simply, "Russo," Joey figured that last names were the way they rolled.

"Nice to meet you," Tam said. "You gonna stay, right?"

Another pang. "Yes," Joey said, less confidently

this time. "Why does everyone keep asking me that?"

Tam took both of Joey's hands in hers and looked her in the eye. "Listen. These kids are our highest needs kids in the district. They're very low. They don't understand much. We have a structure and routine we follow. Every day. If they do work, that's fine, but we just want them to follow the routine. It's like a wrestling match to get them from one thing to the next."

Joey just stared at her. She had no idea what to say.

"Don't be scared," Tam let go of Joey's hands. "Johnson and I will help you. Just do what we do. The more hands, the easier it is. We help each other."

At 8:35 Tam indicated that Joey should follow her and Johnson. "Let's go get 'em."

At the doors to the outside, Johnson explained, "The SpEd bus arrives right at 8:40. We meet them outside this door and walk them to the classroom. Three of the kids are brought by their parents."

At 8:40 on the button, a yellow school bus pulled up to the curb to the right of the doors. Tam wedged another rubber doorstop under the outside door, and they walked to the bus. Through the bus windows, Joey could see the kids standing, gathering belongings, and moving to the front. Her stomach was doing flip flops.

Will they like me? she wondered.

The bus doors opened with a hiss.

"Okay, Lucas, let's go," Tam encouraged, and a thin boy with red hair held the handrail down the three steps and exited the bus. Tam took him by the arm and guided him toward Joey.

"Hang onto him," she instructed. "I'll guide the others over to you."

Lucas walked to where Joey stood. She wasn't sure if "hang onto him" was a literal directive, but he reached out and took her arm.

"Hi," he said with a child-like voice that didn't match his height. "I'm Lucas."

"Hello, Lucas," Joey said. "I'm Mrs. Russo."

"Hi Russo," he said. He let go of her arm and stood closely behind her. Tam guided two more students her direction: an extremely large boy and a sweet-faced, smiling girl with Down syndrome. The boy was Ivan, and the girl was Leah. Joey's trio stood in a small huddle. Next off the bus in quick succession came three gangly white boys, all with dark brown hair, glasses, and dressed in tan corduroy pants and grey hoodies. They bounded with energy.

"Stand still, find your buddy," Johnson said sharply. Each reached out and took the hand of another. "Triplets," she explained in response to Joey's stare. "I got these three. Let's go, Russo."

Joey felt Lucas reaching out for her hand. She took it, and the other boy took the hand of the girl. They followed Mrs. Johnson's lively train back into the building and into the classroom.

"I'll wait here with them," Johnson explained. "You go help Tam with the others."

When Joey arrived back outside, a white Mercedes was pulling away from the curb, and another student stood with Tam.

"This is Katie," Tam said to Joey. Katie wore a pink headband that sprouted two fuzzy pink cat's ears. She also wore a pink My Little Pony backpack which had straps so small, Joey was sure they must be cutting off circulation in Katie's armpits.

"Hello, Katie," Joey said.

Katie looked up at Joey.

"I like your headband," Joey said, smiling.

"Oh, yes, she wears that headband every single day. Don't you, Katie?" Tam rolled her eyes, having made her comment in a sarcastic tone that made Joey feel embarrassed for Katie.

"Yes," Katie answered timidly.

"It's very pretty," Joey said sweetly, trying to overcompensate Tam's mean tone with kindness.

An old minivan with as much rust as it had paint rolled up to the curb, brakes squeaking so loudly Katie covered her ears. The woman driving nodded to Tam, who opened the passenger-side sliding door, which creaked in protest.

"Come on, Thomas," Tam said.

A boy sat in the center bench seat, shaking his head wildly.

"Time for school, Thomas," Tam said again.

Thomas continued to shake his head and began slamming himself into the seat back.

"Stop it, Thomas," the woman driving ordered. "Get out of the car right now!"

Thomas stopped slamming but didn't budge.

"Don't make me come up there and get you," Tam warned. "If I do, you have to sit out at recess."

Thomas looked sharply at Tam. "Recess?" he said. "I want recess!"

"Then you have to get out of the van," she replied.

"Go on, Thomas," the woman ordered again. "I have to get to work."

Joey realized Thomas wasn't even wearing a seatbelt. He scrambled out of the van, nearly knocking Tam over.

"Recess!" he yelled, as he ran for the doors to the school.

Tam slammed the van door, and Joey was sure the mother was speeding away before the door was even fully latched.

Tam shouted, "Wait here for Travis!" to Joey and ran after the boy.

"Thomas naughty," Katie said.

Joey had no idea how to answer. Thomas beat Tam to the school building, letting himself inside. Tam followed, then returned a few moments later, alone.

"Every eff-ing day we go through that. Today wasn't too bad, though. Sometimes I have to climb in and get him."

"Get him?" Joey repeated. "How do you—"

Before she could finish the question, another car pulled to the curb. This one was a shiny maroon sedan, and Tam opened the back-passenger door. A thin boy quietly emerged.

"Bye, Travis," the male driver called after him. "Love you."

Travis waved a hand in reply. *His backpack is huge*, Joey thought, as he struggled to put it to his back. On second look she realized the backpack was a regular size; the boy was really small.

"Good morning, Travis," Tam said. The boy waved a hand again. He held onto the straps of his backpack with both hands, seemingly to steady himself, for looked as if the pack would topple him backward if he let go.

Tam led the way, followed by Travis and Katie. Joey brought up the rear and they returned to the classroom.

Joey heard the garage door when Craig arrived home. She willed her body to get up from the couch, but it didn't listen. Craig found her face down, nose pushed between the cushions, one shoe dangling from a limp foot while the other lay upside down on the floor. Her cream-colored blouse was now wrinkled and untucked, and one flaccid arm hung from the couch as her fingers rested on the wood floor.

Craig's laugh did nothing to budge her. "Rough day, sweetheart?"

He sat on the footstool. Joey couldn't even lift her head as she answered. "I can't move."

"That bad? Or was it that good?"

"Ugh," Joey replied. She turned her head to the side and looked up at her husband. "I haven't been this tired in," she paused, "ever."

"In ever?" Craig laughed again. He leaned over and rubbed her back. "You poor thing."

She used what little energy she had left to push herself up to a sitting position. She looked at Craig. "I don't even know where to begin."

He smiled at his wife. "You made it home. That's a start."

"Barely," she clarified.

"How were the kids?" he asked.

Her eyes pooled up with tears. "They're so—" she stopped, searching for the right word. But there was no one right word. A hundred adjectives spun through her brain. Their faces flashed through her mind. The harsh words laced with frustration from her coworkers echoed through her ears. The stares from the other teachers and students in the cafeteria when they brought the students to the lunchroom reflected in her eyes. How were the kids? She shrugged. She wiped her cheeks.

Joey knew by the way her husband looked at her that he understood. There was no one place to start to describe her day.

"Why don't you take a bath?" he suggested. She nodded and found the strength to get up from the couch.

The glorious hot water soothed her aching muscles and helped her feet forgive her for trapping them in the evil black pumps. "I'm sorry, toes," she apologized to the bright red digits poking up from the bubbles at the end of the tub, "I won't do that to you again."

"Would you like a tea?" Craig came in, bearing a steaming mug. "Sugar and milk, just how you like it."

She gratefully took the mug and sipped. "Oh, that's nice," she cooed. "Thank you."

"Were you talking to your feet?" Craig asked with a raised eyebrow.

"Perhaps," she answered. "I need them to forgive me so we can do it all over again tomorrow."

Craig moved to the end of the tub and perched on the side. He took the foot closest to him in his hands and dug his knuckle into the arch.

"Yow," she said. "Don't stop. But yow."

"It's been a while since you've been this sore," he noted.

"It was non-stop. All day long," she said. "From the moment the bus arrived until we took them back out to meet the bus at 3:30. I'm not kidding—we didn't stop."

"Did you eat lunch?" he asked with concern.

"Yes," she said. "By the time I found the

teacher's lounge I had about eighteen minutes to rest. It felt so good to sit down, though, I forgot to go to the bathroom."

"What are the other teachers like?" he asked.

"A nice guy named Rick helped me find my classroom. He teaches English, I think. The other teachers in my room are—how can I put it—tired? I want to like them, but everything they do is laced with negativity. Even the way they talk to the kids makes me feel sad inside. Like they see them as a task to be completed—not kids who need to be taught."

"What did you teach them today?" he asked.

"That's just it," she replied. "I didn't teach them anything. All I did was shoo them from one activity to the next, keeping to a schedule that no one except for Mrs. Dunne cared about. Twenty minutes here, twenty minutes there. We'd just get settled into doing one thing and her timer would go off and we had to switch to something else. It was exhausting."

Craig continued to rub her foot.

"There is this one sweet boy named Ivan. He's a big boy; he's at least a foot taller than I am and he is so big around. His poor pants were bursting at the seams, and everything was such an effort. I'm not sure what his disability is, but his world revolves ever so slowly. I asked if he wanted to read a book. He nodded but didn't move. So, I went over and took something off the shelf for him. Honestly

Craig, those books are in such disgusting shape. The pages are ripped; the covers are ratty. I picked one that had Arthur on the cover—you know that kid's cartoon that Emily used to watch? Well, I took it over to him, and his smile just lit up the room. He held that book and looked at the cover. That's all he did. He traced his pudgy fingers over the picture. It was like he didn't know what to do with it. I took it from him and opened it to the first page of the story. I literally read two sentences and Dunne's stupid timer went off.

"'Switch activities,' she barked from her desk. Well, I didn't move. I stayed there, reading to Ivan. 'Ivan needs to go to the blocks station,' she tells me. I looked over at her and said, 'We'll go when we're finished with this book. We just got started.' You would have thought I suggested something ludicrous. She said, 'Fine. But try and get started more quickly next time.'

"Can you believe that? I was reading to him. Reading! And she wanted me to stop so we could stick to her stupid schedule."

"I am sure they have the schedule for a reason," Craig offered.

"I know. I heard the lecture." She mocked Mrs. Dunne's arrogant tone. "'Kids need consistency. Especially these kids.' But the schedule can't be more important than anything else. Where does spontaneity come into play?"

"Give it time," Craig said, standing. "This was

only day one. You've got a long way to go."

He left her to stew in her thoughts. Recalling what had happened with Ivan made her angry, but Craig was right. She's the new kid on the block. She's got to learn the ropes. The feeling in her gut, though, was that the ropes were frayed and tattered and in desperate need of upgrading. It wasn't until she was in bed drifting off to sleep that night that she realized she'd mentioned Emily's name during her rant to Craig and it didn't hurt her heart.

Each morning's classroom routine began with circle time on the carpet. Tam sat on a chair, and the kids made a weirdly shaped oval around her. Joey and Mrs. Johnson each took up a spot at the back of the carpet, so the three teachers made a triangle of sorts around the kids. One of the triplets—Gary—did not like the carpet, so he sat just off the edge on the linoleum. If any part of his body accidently brushed the carpet's edge, he let out a squeal that made Katie grab her ears and respond with her own yelp. This see-saw interaction of theirs happened every day, and by Thursday, Joey was pretty sure that Gary intentionally rubbed his leg on the carpet, just to instigate Katie's scream.

Carpet time began with the saddest rendition of a "Days of the Week" song that Joey ever heard. No one except for the three teachers sang, except every so often one of the other triplets—Matt—would call out the word "daaaaayyyyy!" The awful song was followed with a one-sided discussion where Tam told the kids the current month and date, discussed the weather, and counted how many days were left until Christmas break. Each day she chose a new helper to stick the date onto the laminated calendar on the bulletin board. Thursday's helper was Thomas. When Tam handed him the number twenty and instructed him to put it on the calendar, he raced into the bathroom and slammed the door. A moment later they heard the toilet flush.

"He better not have flushed that number again," Johnson said. She stormed off to the bathroom door and yanked it open. Thomas sat on the toilet, with his pants in a pile around his ankle. Fortunately, he was still holding the number. Johnson snatched it from him and handed it to Joey.

"Put this on the calendar," she said. Joey felt her stomach flip. She took a Lysol wipe and gave the number a quick cleaning, then stuck it on the calendar before washing her own hands.

"And then, once Thomas was finished with his 'bathroom poops,' as he came out and announced, I had to take Kyle—one of the triplets—to the nurse because he threw up. On the rug!" Joey lamented the remainder of her day to Craig that night over dinner.

"That explains the shower when you came

home," Craig grinned.

"It's not funny. There are so many body fluids passed around that room. Lucas likes to lick things. I have to keep a constant watch over what he's doing so I can chase after him with the Lysol. It's horrifying. No one tries to help him stop licking. It's like that is the least of the worries."

"Didn't think it would stretch you this far out of your comfort zone, did ya?"

"Lord, you have no idea," Joey said. "It's germ-a-palooza in there. We had to go down to the gym so the janitorial staff could clean the carpet. I am so glad tomorrow is Friday."

Fridays were a pleasant contrast to the rest of the week. Students had two whole hours of free play, during which they could explore any of the activity stations for as long as they wanted. Mrs. Dunne didn't even stay in the room once she took roll, and Tam and Johnson plopped themselves into chairs and chatted with each other the entire time. Joey, however, saw her opportunity to make deeper connections with the kids. She found the Arthur book that Ivan liked so much and sat herself into one of the beanbag chairs. Curious, Ivan came over and sat down next to her, leaning his weight against her, his eyes cautious.

Joey patted his thick leg. "It's alright. You can read with me." She opened the book and began. "Arthur's New Puppy." She pointed to the words on the title page. Upon hearing the word puppy, Katie dropped the blocks she held and scrambled over. She plunked down on the other side of Joey, half-on, half-off the beanbag chair, no qualms about invading Joey's personal space.

"Arthur loved his new puppy," Joey said. "And Pal loved Arthur. 'He's a very active puppy,' said Arthur."

"Naughty puppy," Katie said.

"That's right, Katie!" Joey said, pointing to the words. "The next words say, 'He's a very naughty puppy.' Do you know this book?"

Katie nodded. "Momma reads."

"Do you want to read it to me?" Joey asked.

Katie shook her head. Joey continued to read and every so often Katie would join in and finish a sentence or start the next. Ivan listened, wide-eyed. When the last page was read and the cover closed, Ivan said the first word Joey had heard him say. "Again."

Joey was shocked. "Ivan! Would you like me to read this again?"

Ivan nodded. "Again."

Joey beamed. He spoke to her! Katie snatched the book and threw it across the room. "No book!" she yelled. "No more puppy!"

Ivan put his head down. Joey looked crossly at Katie. "Katie! That wasn't nice. Go get the book."

Katie folded her arms and turned her back to Joey.

"Katie," Joey directed, "stand up, walk over there, and pick up the book."

Joey wasn't entirely sure what she'd do next if Katie didn't mind the instruction, but to her shock and surprise, Katie retrieved the book. She handed it back, not to Joey, but to Ivan.

"Sorry, Ivan," she said.

"Sorry, Katie," Ivan repeated.

"Ivan, you don't have to say, 'Sorry,' you should say, 'I forgive you,'" Joey coached.

"I forgive you," Ivan said.

Joey was so happy she hugged Ivan as best as she could around his thick shoulders. "Good job, Ivan! And good job, Katie!"

"Katie good girl," Katie said.

"Yes, Katie is a good girl," Joey agreed.

It was the best day Joey had in a long time.

DODIE

Luminescent purple wings glittered in the summer sunshine. Dodie ran through the field, arms flung wide, fingers gently brushing the thin wings, giving each butterfly a gentle send-off into the blueberry sky. There was no pattern to her trail. She swirled in a large figure eight, she zig-zagged up and down the rows of yellow petals, she made large circles. Liberation flowed like a cape behind her. Butterflies took flight and landed again. The breeze tickled her cheeks.

As she ran, however, the tickle turned annoying. The tickle became constricting, like the breeze was suffocating her. Her hands went from feeling the silkiness of the flowers to clutching her cheeks, trying desperately to stop the pressure on her face.

"Doctor! She's waking up!" Dodie heard a voice call. Hands pulled her arms from her face and held them to her sides. "Dorothy, it's okay, sweetie. Don't pull the mask. You need the oxygen."

Dodie opened her eyes. The summer meadow was gone. The butterflies and sunflowers faded away, replaced by a face she did not know. It was a woman. She was surrounded by shadows.

The pressure on her mouth and nose was maddening. She tried again to pull her hands to her face to remove whatever horrid contraption was there.

"Dorothy. No. Leave the mask alone," the woman instructed firmly. *Dorothy? Who was this woman? Who's Dorothy?* Dodie relaxed her arms and blinked. *I'm Dorothy.* She closed her eyes. It was nicer this way. The darkness faded to purple, and she dreamed again. This time of the open seas.

"Will she wake up?" a male voice pierced her peaceful world.

"We believe so," another male voice said. "We just don't know when."

Dodie knew the voices were talking about her, but she had no desire to respond to them. There was no need to let them know she could hear their words. She'd keep it a secret that she was awake. *Was she awake?* She wasn't entirely certain. She shut the voices off and went back to her own place.

There was something heavy on her legs. She'd been flying on a winged horse, high above pink mountains, chatting with the green-eyed dragon that kept pace with her. He was her friend here. They'd traveled all across the countryside together. He asked if she'd seen the ruby peacock. *Not yet*, she said. She hoped to be granted audience with him soon. The ruby peacock ruled the country. He decided who could live in the magical land and who had to leave.

Then the pressure started in her legs. It was pulling her down, down, down. She was losing her balance, about to fall from the horse.

"Excuse me," she said to the dragon, "I have to see what is going on."

She tried to move her legs away from the source of the pressure. As she did so, she heard someone call out excitedly, "She's moving! Her legs are moving!"

Oh bother, she thought. *It's them again.* She was going to have to open her eyes and see what was happening. She entered their world. The face looking back at her was one she recognized. It was smiling. It was a face that made her happy.

"Dodie. It's me, Annie," the smiling face said.

Annie? I know this person, Dodie thought. She tried to smile back. But the contraption stopped her smile.

"It's alright, Dodie, I'm right here," she said. "Did you like having your legs massaged? I can keep going."

Dodie did like having her legs massaged. She tried to nod. Anne got the message and went back to Dodie's calf muscle, gently kneading it between her hands. "I'm so happy to see your eyes, Dodie," she said kindly.

Maybe I'll stay in this place for a while, Dodie thought. *I can always go back to the dragon if I need to.*

A man came into the room. He looked at Dodie. Dodie blinked back at him. He smiled.

"Welcome back," he said. *Did he know about the magic place?* Dodie wondered. "We are glad to see you."

Dodie didn't try to remove the contraption. Instead, he continued talking as if she could respond. "My name is Doctor Jones. You are in Boulder Mercy Hospital. You had a bit of an accident, and we are taking care of you."

Dodie's mind was suddenly awash with revelation. She'd been climbing. There was the mountain. Aaron. Lucy. The rope. The carabiner wouldn't come loose. But then it did. She fell.

Her eyes widened, fear increasing with each remembrance. She tried to move. She couldn't. Panic coursed through her inner self.

"It's okay, Dorothy," Doctor Jones reassured. He put a hand on her arm. "Nurse!"

A woman appeared from her right and made an adjustment to the plastic bag that hung next to her bed. A moment later she felt coolness enter through her arm. Liquid flowed through her body, until it reached her center. The panic subsided. But she remembered.

"There you go," the doctor said. He kept his hand on her other arm. Anne had stopped rubbing Dodie's calf, but Dodie could see her at the foot of the bed. Dodie looked into Anne's eyes, pleading with her for comfort.

"You're alright, Dodie," Anne said. "You're going to be fine."

Dodie tried to nod again. She closed her eyes, but this time, she didn't visit the dragon or the pink mountains. She just slept.

"Dodie, wake up," another voice intruded the blackness. "Wake up, Dodie. Come on, Dodie."

She could not choose to make it go away this time. Her body betrayed her. She had to awaken. She opened her eyes. It was Aaron. She knew his face instantly. It made her angry.

"Hey! She's awake," he said. "Hey, nurse! She's up!"

Why won't he shut up? Dodie wondered.

A woman appeared at her side, thankfully replacing Aaron's presence. Her turquoise scrubs had little unicorns all over them.

"Hey there, champ," the woman said. "I'm Kelly."

Dodie nodded. The movement was easier than the last time she'd tried. Kelly took Dodie's hand. "Can you squeeze my fingers?" she asked.

Dodie willed it to happen.

"Good!" Kelly said. She took her other hand. "Same thing." Dodie squeezed. "Excellent, Dorothy." Kelly went to the foot of the bed and uncovered Dodie's feet. She traced her finger along the bottom of Dodie's foot. Dodie flinched with the tickle. "Great. How about this one?" She touched her foot and Dodie again reacted. "Nice job. I'm going to go talk to the doctor and we'll right back."

Kelly's calming figure was replaced with Aaron. Dodie wished she could tell him to go away, but the words wouldn't come. She didn't know how to navigate the contraption covering her mouth.

The doctor appeared from the other side of the bed. "Well, howdy! It's nice to see you." It wasn't the doctor she remembered. This was someone else. "I'm Doctor Chen," he explained. "I'd like to take the oxygen mask from your face. But don't try and talk just yet. Give me a minute."

He gently reached behind her head and loosened the elastic that held the mask over her nose and mouth. It felt like a scab peeling away. She pressed her lips together.

"I'm going to have the nurse put some Vaseline on your lips. They probably feel really dry," Doctor Chen stated. "And I want to give you a little bit of water to drink before you try and speak."

Kelly held a tiny water cup to Dodie's mouth and allowed a little bit to trickle in. It evaporated before making it anywhere near her throat. The nurse waited a moment, then did it again. This time a couple of drops made it to the back of Dodie's mouth. Her tongue was thick.

"Can you talk?" Kelly asked.

"Eh," Dodie heard her voice. "Ah. I. Moe." What were those sounds? Her throat felt as big around as a tree trunk. She looked at the water cup. "Wah."

Kelly held it to her lips for one more drink. "I don't want you to have too much at first," she said. "I don't want you to throw up. You haven't had solid food in a couple of weeks."

Dodie frowned her eyes. *A couple of weeks? What the hell happened to her?*

"Am I hurt?" she asked. It came out sounding like, "eh eye hur?" and she felt like an idiot. Of course, she was hurt. She was in the freaking hospital.

"You had a bad fall," Kelly said as gently as possible. "You hit your head on the rocks. You also dislocated your hip and cracked your pelvis. You've had two surgeries and have been in and out of a coma for the last ten days."

Dodie's eyes decided to cry. She couldn't stop them. She remembered none of these awful things, but she knew what the words meant. Her pelvis. Her hip. Her head. A coma.

"Out," she said, looking at Aaron. *Well, that came out clearly.*

"Dodie, I—," he stammered.

"Out," she said in a pitiful voice that didn't even sound like it belonged to her. She closed her eyes again.

"Maybe it would be better if you give her some space," Kelly suggested to Aaron in a kind voice.

"Yeah, okay," he agreed. Dodie heard him leave. She waited until she heard the door close before opening her eyes again. She looked at Kelly with tears flowing freely.

"Don't worry, Dorothy," Kelly said. "We'll take care of you. You'll get through this."

"Dodie," Dodie corrected her in a pathetic whimper.

"Okay. Dodie." Kelly patted her hand and left. It must have been close to nighttime. She could see the sky growing dim through the curtained window. It took effort for Dodie to think about this fact. When Kelly came back, Dodie asked for more water.

"Just a bit," Kelly cautioned. "We're still going to feed you through the I.V. until the doctor can see you tomorrow. If he okays it, maybe we'll try something soft to eat in the morning."

Dodie nodded. She sipped the water, hoping it wouldn't make her have to pee. Then she wondered—what if she needs to pee?

"Bathroom?" she asked. It came out more like "bafoom."

"You have a catheter in," Kelly said. "It takes care of it for you."

Dodie took a deep breath. Everything ached.

Doctor Jones came to Dodie's room bright and early the next morning, as a male nurse was busy taking her vital signs. Dodie had slept soundly and was terribly thirsty. The nurse brought her a cup of water.

"Not too much," he said, sounding just like

Kelly as he held it to her lips.

Doctor Jones was checking her chart. "Dorothy, this looks really good," he said with a smile. "I think we can try you with a little breakfast today. Green Jell-O sound good?"

"Is it avocado flavored?" she asked, surprised at the strength in her voice. A huge contrast from last night.

"Hey! You sound good," the doctor replied.

"Throat is sore," she said.

"Makes sense. You haven't talked in a bunch of days, and you had a breathing tube down your throat for a while. A little later today, we'll do a scan on your pelvis. I need to see how it is healing from the surgery. I know the doctor explained to you last night some of what happened. We can talk more about it later. We'll go over everything after you've been awake for a while. Is that alright with you?"

Dodie was full of questions. *How could this have happened? Why wasn't her rope secured? Did Aaron have her off belay?* But nothing she felt like formulating right now. She didn't want to think beyond the present moment. She closed her eyes to trap the hot tears inside.

"It's a lot to take in, I know," the doctor said. "One day at a time. You'll heal. I am going to send another doctor—a psychologist—in to talk with you today."

"Psychologist? Why?"

"Sometimes it helps to talk to someone who can

help you work through your questions."

Made sense. Dodie nodded.

"I'll go see about that avocado Jell-O," Doctor Jones promised with a wink as he left.

The morning passed slowly. Dodie looked around the room at the vases of flowers and balloons that lined the table near her window. She'd asked the nurse to hand her the cards. A vase of flowers from Anne and Sherry. Another from Chris, her boss. Walt and the engineering team sent a bouquet of balloons that burst from a small green plant. There was another small plant, and the card attached read "We ruff you. From Benny and Joon." It surprised her that Aaron would be so considerate.

She tried the television, thinking it would take her mind off her questions, but turned it off almost immediately. Whoopi Goldberg's drivel only infuriated her more. She ruminated for what seemed like hours how such a fall could have happened. She couldn't get her mind around why her rope had so much slack. Dodie watched the clock. Anne and Sherry would be heading to lunch soon, and she wished she were there with them. Anne texted that they'd be by after work to see her.

At eleven-thirty there was a knock at the door. Chris poked his head into the room.

"Hey there, slugger. Can I come in?"

"Yes! Please do," Dodie begged.

Chris pulled a chair up next to her bed. He placed a hand tentatively on the rail of the bed. "You gave us quite a scare."

"Sorry about that," Dodie said. If she spoke slowly, her words were clearer and her throat scratched less.

"How are you feeling?" he asked.

"Everything hurts. My midsection feels like it's trapped in some sort of medieval torture device. There's a plastic brace squeezing me together down there."

"I came by a few times while you were—um—out," Chris said. "I talked to your husband. He seemed so worried about you."

"Did he?" Dodie heard the sarcasm drip from her voice. Chris raised an eyebrow. "Sorry. Not sure where that came from."

"You've been through a lot," Chris said. "Have they said anything about recovery time?"

Dodie shook her head. "They haven't said much of anything." She felt awkward in the pause, like she should know more about her own body and what was going on with it. "So, what's new at the office?" she asked.

"Brent hired a new sales rep, a guy from Michigan. He seems alright. I hired someone to replace Amy."

"Sorry about that," Dodie said again.

"Stop apologizing. You did right by firing her. She was a liability," Chris said. "I hired a woman who is a bit older. She's a rule-follower. She definitely won't put up with the sales reps' crap."

Dodie smiled. "That's good. Walt will like that." Unsure of why, she started to cry.

"Hey, now, it's okay, Dodes," Chris reassured. "You're going to be fine."

"I've lost two weeks of my life," she said. "You have done so much. You've hired people! I was just—here. What the hell has happened to me?"

He handed her a tissue, which she held to her face. The door opened and a woman in a white lab coat entered.

"Hello?" she greeted them cautiously. "Can I come in?" Dodie nodded. "I'm Doctor Veal."

"I guess I should go," Chris said, standing.

"I'm glad you came by," Dodie said. "Really."

"I don't want you to worry about work. We've got it covered until you get back. And we need you, so don't get any ideas that this cushy hospital bed is the place to stay."

Dodie smiled. "I won't. I promise. Tell everyone I said hi."

"Oh, hey, I nearly forgot." He pulled a Snickers out of his pocket and offered it to Dodie. "For you."

She hugged it to her chest.

The new doctor replaced Chris in the guest chair and introduced herself as the psychologist Doctor Jones had requested. Her name was Doctor Veal.

"But you can call me Kathy. Okay, Dorothy?"

"I go by Dodie," Dodie corrected.

"How are you feeling, Dodie?" the doctor asked.

"Terrible. My entire lower body feels trapped. My arms and neck ache like crazy. And I had Jell-O for breakfast. Do you know if I can eat this Snickers?"

"We can ask the nurse," Doctor Veal smiled. She pushed the call button and Kelly appeared, promising to find out if Dodie could eat her Snickers. "Dodie, has anyone talked to you about the extent of your injuries?"

More than a little trepidation filled her stomach. What weren't they telling her? "No. Not really. Why? What don't I know?" she asked the doctor.

The doctor took a deep breath. "There really isn't a delicate way to say this, so I am going to lay out for you what happened. As you fell, you hit your head against the side of the mountain, which as best as we can tell rendered you instantly unconscious. You continued to drop another fifteen to twenty feet and your pelvis was smashed into a jagged outlaying of rock. This stopped your fall."

"Okay," Dodie said. "That kind of matches what the doctor said."

"The injury to your pelvis caused a grade IV laceration in your cervix, right where the cervix and uterus come together. This brought on some internal bleeding. By the time you arrived at the hospital, there was quite a lot of blood internally. You were rushed into surgery to find and repair the bleed. The doctors worked quickly and got it stopped. They decided to keep you in an unconscious state—a medically-induced coma—to allow time for the swelling in your brain to reduce. Sometime over the next 48 hours, however, your vital signs crashed, and you were taken back into surgery. The initial surgery had complications and another repair was needed. This time, however, the doctors deemed it necessary to remove your uterus." She paused here, for the information to sink in.

Dodie blinked at her, processing the words. Remove her uterus? "My uterus?"

Doctor Veal leaned forward. "I'm so sorry, Dodie. This means—"

"I won't be able to have kids," Dodie finished the sentence for her.

"I'm so sorry," she said again. "There are other ways for women—"

Her chest crushed her heart as the weight of this news settled there. She stopped the doctor from talking. "Could you leave please?" she asked Doctor Veal.

"I can, but I would like to stay and sit with you."

"Whatever," Dodie replied. *I can't have children. I'll never be pregnant.* The thoughts layered upon themselves, morphing into one giant orb of despair.

When Nurse Kelly returned, Doctor Veal gave a nod. Dodie knew what it meant. *She knows.* Kelly adjusted Dodie's I.V. drip.

"I'm giving you some pain reliever," she explained, "and something to help you rest for a bit. You've been up all morning, and it might do you well to get some sleep. Your pelvic scan won't be until 3:30."

Dodie nodded weakly and turned her head to look out the window. "Would you open the curtains?" she asked. Doctor Veal obliged. Dodie was asleep before Doctor Veal even returned to her seat.

She woke to the orderlies preparing to wheel her to get her pelvic scan. They'd already lifted her onto the gurney and had the portable I.V. bag ready to travel along. In her sleep, the green dragon had visited her, but she had nothing to say to him. Like a child, she'd folded her arms and turned her back to him. Now that she was awake, she had nothing to say to the orderlies either. Or to the technicians who completed her scan. When they deposited her back in her room, she closed her eyes and prepared to shut the world off once again. She had nothing to say to anyone.

"Dodie?" Sherry's voice intruded on her silence. She opened her eyes. "Can we come in?"

She wouldn't shut out Anne and Sherry. Never

them. But everyone else? Perhaps. Anne came in carrying a huge stuffed panda. She placed it on the bed next to Dodie, then kissed the top of Dodie's head.

"Sorry it took us so long to get here. We had to spend the day at the office," Anne said sarcastically with an eye roll, which made Dodie smile.

Sherry took Dodie's hand. "I'm so glad to see you awake. We came by every day while you were—sleeping."

Anne added, "This one here even read to you." She tilted her head toward Sherry. Dodie noticed the book on the side table for the first time.

"Dragonflight?" she questioned. "Is that what you read to me?"

Sherry nodded. "It was the most interesting thing in the hospital gift shop."

Dodie reached her hand out to her friends. "Thank you." The three held hands for a moment, and Dodie began again to cry.

"What's wrong, Dodes?" Anne said. She handed her a tissue.

Dodie told them what the psychologist shared with her. Anne and Sherry cried with her until their eyes ran dry and there was nothing left but to quietly contemplate the ramifications of this big news.

"I wonder what kind of complications there were?" Anne said. "Did they not tell you?"

Dodie shook her head. "The doctor who told me

didn't elaborate. And I didn't think to ask questions. I don't even know what to ask."

"Has Aaron said anything?" Sherry asked.

"He hasn't been back since yesterday. I kind of threw him out," she admitted.

"You what?" Anne said, surprised. "You threw him out?"

Dodie exhaled a deep breath. "That morning—the day I fell—we had been arguing. He was acting like such a jerk. He was paying much more attention to Lucy than he was to me or to my climb. When I woke up, I remembered it all. How he missed my halfway call out. When I stood on the ledge preparing to come back down, he wasn't even looking at me. He was enthralled in whatever Lucy was saying. I wanted to climb down and punch him in the face. But that never happened. I couldn't bear to look at him standing next to my bed."

"Oh, wow, Dodie." Sherry squeezed Dodie's hand.

Changing the subject, Anne walked over to the display of flowers. "Do you like the plant from your pooches? We got you a little dogwood sprout. Get it?"

"That was from you guys? Thank you." Dodie felt like an idiot. Of course, it wasn't from Aaron.

Nurse Kelly came into Dodie's room with a tray of food. "Hey there," she said. "Anybody hungry? Since you did such a stellar job with the Jell-O, you've been promoted to broth and unsweet applesauce. Oh, and more Jell-O. But sorry, you have to save the Snickers. At least for one more day."

Anne inspected the tray. "Looks grand!"

Sherry and Anne stayed with her through her dinner. A few more tears were shed, and they promised to be back tomorrow. Dodie assured them that they didn't have to be there so much—that they should be with their own families—but secretly she was thankful. She had no one else.

JOEY

What on earth are you doing with those?" Craig asked, staring at the armload of books Joey dumped onto the store counter. "Do you have some new addiction I should be aware of?"

"These are for Ivan," Joey stated plainly. "Well, they're for all the kids. But I really think Ivan will like them. I got every Arthur book they had."

"Shouldn't the school buy books for the kids?"

Joey snorted. "Ha. You'd think so. Apparently buying books is a weeks-long process. But our bookshelf looks like something out of the Addams Family library. I even found a giant spider living cozily on the bottom shelf. I asked Mrs. Dunne if we could get new books. She just laughed. She didn't even answer me."

"Well, then. Thank goodness for used bookstores," Craig said, pulling out his debit card. If Joey wanted books, then books she would get!

Joey arrived at school before 7 a.m. She cranked her favorite playlist and set to work. Armed with a a roll of clear box tape and cleaning supplies, she pulled all the old books from the shelves. Singing her favorite songs distracted her from considering what the dried goo and sticky stuff was as she wiped the bookshelves. When every inch was as squeaky clean as possible, she began restocking. Any book that wasn't in readable shape got set to the side for some TLC. Joey had just finished tucking the edge of clear tape over the last torn cover when Tam and Johnson got there.

"It smells clean in here," Tam observed suspiciously. "What'd you do, Russo?"

"I made our bookshelf less scary. More kid-friendly," she said proudly.

Johnson shrugged. "Won't last. These kids don't know how to take care of anything."

The negativity was not about to deflate her.

"Well then, we need to show them how to take care of things. Don't we?" Joey challenged back. *Take that, Negative Nelly.* Johnson raised her eyebrows but held her retort.

Each morning, the teachers rotated through different activity stations with their students. Joey's group had to visit math and science before landing at the bookshelf. Joey couldn't wait to show Ivan the new books. So as not to overwhelm him, she picked just one of the new Arthur books and held it out.

"Arthur," Ivan said.

"Yes, Ivan! That's Arthur." Joey pointed to the word Arthur, then to the book title below. "This book is called *Teacher Trouble.*"

Ivan pointed at Joey. "Teacher," he said.

The first time Joey heard the word "Mama" directed to her was January 14, 2012. Emily was ten months old at the time. It was the most beautiful word Joey had ever heard. Ivan's spoken word "teacher" was the most beautiful thing Joey had heard since Emily died. She was taken back at how satisfying it was for him to acknowledge her in that way.

He sat heavily onto the floor with the book in his lap. "I read," he said, opening it to the first page. Lucas and Katie—the other students in Joey's group—sat next to him.

"The beh rain," he began. Joey looked over his shoulder. "The bell rang" was the correct first sentence.

"Great job, Ivan!" she said, surprised.

He looked at her. "Sit down. I read," he pointed to the carpet. She sat.

As she listened to him share the tale of Arthur and his super-strict teacher, she realized that he knew a lot more about reading than she thought he did. He knew the starting sounds of most of the words, and he read familiar sight words nearly perfectly.

She felt foolish. *"They can't read"* was one of the first things that Tam had told her about the kids. *"At book station, you can read to them if you want or just give them books and let them look at the pictures."* With shame, she understood that she'd taken what Tam and Johnson told her about the kids' abilities as truth and didn't bother checking out what her students were capable of for herself. In other areas of her life, she'd always checked facts before making decisions, and here, in one of the most important jobs she could imagine doing, she did exactly the opposite. *I wonder what else I misjudged?* she thought. When Ivan finished reading *Teacher Trouble*, Joey picked another from the shelf.

"Ivan, I really liked listening to you read," Joey said. "Do you want to read another one?"

Ivan shook his head and pointed at Joey. "Teacher's turn," he said, handing her the book.

"Let's do a different one! Lucas, would you pick out a book?" Joey suggested.

Cautiously, Lucas reached over to the new Arthur books. He pulled the first one he touched from the shelf and handed it to Joey.

"*Arthur's Underwear*," Joey read the title. Katie started giggling.

"Underwear?" she asked, grabbing the book from Joey's hands. "I want to see underwear." She pointed to the picture on the cover of an embarrassed Arthur. Her laugher was infectious. Students from the other stations came over to see what was so funny, and within a minute, all were taking turns pointing at the cover and laughing until they collapsed on the floor in exhaustion. Joey just smiled. In the few weeks she'd been there, not once did she see laughter like that take place in the classroom. It was wonderful, and she immediately started thinking about how she could create more opportunities for them to enjoy school.

The fun lasted only as long as it took for Mrs. Dunne to realize that the students were all at the bookshelf.

"Back to your stations," she barked from her desk. "Right now! Gary! Travis! Go to the math table."

Joey's face reflected her disgust at Mrs. Dunne. "They're having fun. Let them laugh for a change." She saw Tam's eyebrows raise at Johnson. Insubordination? Inconceivable!

Dunne glared at Joey. "Mrs. Russo. Please control your students and encourage the others to return to their stations." The condescending tone make Joey want to scream. She took the Arthur book gently from Gary's hands and put it out of sight.

"I'm glad you like the book," she said. "Maybe when you come to books station, you can read it. Everybody go back to their teachers now."

With the book no longer available, the students returned to their respective activities.

Joey picked a less funny Arthur book, gave her own glare back to Dunne, and read with as much passion as she could muster through her frustration.

Even though she promised herself she wouldn't, the next morning, she couldn't help venting to Tam and Johnson.

"Tell me. Why is it such a big deal? They were laughing for goodness' sake! She acted like they were starting a riot!"

Tam shrugged. "We do things the way we do things in here," she said. "It's her way or no way at all."

"That's not right," Joey stated with assurance. "Kids need flexibility. They need joy! They need to do things to stretch them out of their comfort zones."

"These kids like their comfort zones," Johnson said. "They don't want to be stretched."

Joey looked at her with shock. "Do you really believe that? Because I don't. I saw Ivan's face when he was reading. You both told me they couldn't read. He read that book. He read the words! I think they can do a lot more than they are given credit for."

Her words made Johnson angry. "You think you know so much, Miss Teacher. We just tryin' to survive in here. It's not all sunshine and rainbows."

Joey generally avoided confrontational situations. But her resolve that the attitude in this classroom was dismal was stronger than her fear of Johnson. "Believe me, Mrs. Johnson, I know the world is not all sunshine and rainbows. But I also have worked with children enough in my lifetime to know that children need adults who believe in them. They need adults to take them by the hand and say, 'I know you don't know how to do this. But

I do! And I can show you the way.'"

Joey walked out of the classroom with her chin up. She decided to grab a Diet Coke from the teacher's lounge. While there, she ran into Mr. Lee.

"Hello, Mrs. Russo!" he said brightly. "Nice to see you."

"Thanks, Mr. Lee," she answered, a little less brightly.

"You doin' okay?" He looked genuinely concerned.

"Honestly, I'm a little frustrated," she said.

"Pull up a seat. What's wrong?" He sat at one of the café-style tables in the teacher's break room. She took her Diet Coke and sat across from him.

"I don't want to sound like a complainer," she said.

He shook his head. "No judgement. After twenty-five years in teaching—all of them here at this school—I know the value of venting to a trusted source. Come on. What's up?"

She sighed. "I feel as if I am the only person in that classroom who thinks our students are capable of learning," she began.

He pursed his lips and nodded. "What makes you feel that way?"

"We do the same rote routine every single day. Even Fridays, which are supposed to be free days, have the same routine to them."

"You can make learning happen in the middle of a routine," he countered.

She thought about that. "Yes. But not if the teachers have become as mundane as the routine itself. The students scribble on worksheets with very little guidance. They are expected to look at books, with no expectation that they will read them. They are given blocks and crayons and other manipulatives with no direction or opportunity to explore what can be done with them. They do the exact same things. While the teachers sit in the exact same places, taking about the same things with each other, counting the minutes until it is time to order the students to stop what they're doing and go do the next thing. It is excruciating!"

Mr. Lee tilted his head to the side. "Sounds like you aren't fitting in with the routine."

Joey's eyes widened in shock. "I'm sorry. I shouldn't have questioned—"

He shook his head. "No! Don't apologize! I'm not saying that not fitting in with what they're doing is a bad thing. My question to you, Mrs. Russo, is what are you going to do about it?"

"What can I do?" she asked.

He stood and picked up his coffee mug. "Do what's best for the kids, and you'll never go wrong."

She thought about his advice all that day. In every decision she made, she first asked herself, "What is best for this kid?" And she did whatever her heart deemed the answer.

At the math station, "What's best for the kids" turned out to be counting the crayons and grouping them into color groups, instead of giving each kid a crayon to scribble on the paper with.

At the blocks station, "What's best for the kids" turned out to be creating a castle by taking turns adding blocks one at a time, instead of each student gathering his or her own little pile and stacking them in isolation.

At the bookshelf, "What's best for the kids" involved reading a book altogether, with Joey reading a sentence and the students repeating after her.

Her end-of-the-day exhaustion brought with it feelings of satisfaction. Something she realized had been lacking.

Wednesday of that week held a truckload of new surprises. When Joey got to school, Mrs. Dunne was already in the classroom, along with Mr. Matthews and three other people Joey had not seen before. They were in a heated discussion.

"I'm sorry for intruding," Joey said, and she turned to leave. No one stopped her. She waited in the hall. Tam arrived shortly.

"Why are you out here?" Tam asked.

"There is some kind of discussion going on in there," Joey said. "It didn't feel like I should stay."

Tam peeked in the door. "Shit," she said in a whisper. "Those are Adam's parents."

"Who is Adam?" Joey asked.

"Adam is Satan himself wrapped in the skin of

a very violent little boy," Tam said flatly. "He is the worst kid on the planet."

"That's pretty harsh," Joey said with a frown.

Tam pulled up her sweatshirt sleeve to reveal a light pink scar about three inches long on her forearm. "See this?" Joey nodded. "Adam did that with his fingernail because I asked him if he had to go to the bathroom."

Joey looked at the scar. It was permanently embedded on Tam's arm. "A kid did that?"

Tam nodded. "Adam. He's the reason the lady before you had a nervous breakdown."

"A what?"

"A nervous breakdown. Adam started off the year here. He was so angry and aggressive to the other kids, we had to put him in his own room. It's the room right next door here." She pointed to room 616. "He stayed in there all day, and we took turns having to sit with him. It's hell. If he gets really going, you push the button, and the SRO will come help you."

Now Joey's head was spinning. "What button? What's an SRO?"

"We haven't needed it since he left, but every classroom has a panic button. When you push it, the principal, assistant principals, and the SRO are notified. One or all of them will come running. If Adam's in the building, usually everyone shows up. The SRO is our on-campus security resource officer."

"Where's Adam been?"

"After what he did to the other teacher, he was suspended, pending a psychiatric evaluation. We were hoping he'd never come back. But the fact that his parents are here makes me think that isn't going to happen."

"Would they really expect us to take care of a kid who is violent?"

"Please, girl, no one cares how hard it is on us. We have to take care of all kids," she said the last bit in a mocking tone that obviously she'd used before.

"Of course we do!" Joey agreed whole-heartedly with the sentiment. *But violence?*

Joey suddenly realized the reason behind Mr. Matthews's concern as to whether Joey could *handle* this job.

At that moment the heavy door opened. Adam's parents and the other person with them left the room, not even pausing to acknowledge the teachers waiting in the hallway. Tam and Joey went inside.

The normally jovial Mr. Matthews had been replaced with an angry version.

"You'll have to figure it out," he was saying to Mrs. Dunne.

"I don't have enough staff in here to always have one teacher out. The other students are grouped in threes. When we've had to put more than that together it creates problems," Mrs. Dunne argued back.

"There are four of you," Mr. Matthews mathed out for her. "Three of you can be with the students and one of you with Adam. I don't see how you can say there aren't enough staff."

Joey knew that answer. Mrs. Dunne left out the fact that she never took a group of students. She sat at her desk all day, pontificating about what should be happening, but never actually doing anything.

Mr. Matthews continued. "According to my math, you have exactly the right number."

"What about teacher breaks and lunch?" she kept trying but was obviously defeated.

"At eleven, I'll send a para down to cover teacher lunches. The teachers cover during your lunch, correct?"

"Yes," Mrs. Dunne said.

And we cover for you throughout the rest of the day, Joey thought to herself.

"Well, then it's settled. I want to have a brief after-school meeting with all of you tomorrow. We need to be ready for Monday." He acknowledged Joey with a grim smile as he walked past her.

Tam waited until he was fully gone before saying anything. "That little monster is coming back?" she demanded to Dunne.

Mrs. Dunne stood and ran her hands through her hair. "I know, I know. The parents brought a litigation expert to the school this morning. They are demanding their son receive the public education he is entitled to. They finally put him on medication. They've already been to central office."

"What did the psychiatrist say?" Tam asked.

"According to their doctors, with meds Adam should be able to conduct himself appropriately to be in a controlled school setting."

"What about the scratching? The fact that he throws things? That he screams obscenities?"

"The new medication is supposed to control all of that," she said. "The parents say he has been on it for three full weeks now and has had none of the outbursts like he had before."

"So what are we going to do? Keep him in isolation again?" Tam asked.

"Matthews is going to tell us how they want it to look. He's meeting with the head of SpEd for the district today. We'll know more then. Plan to stay after school tomorrow."

Tam rolled her eyes and turned away in disgust. "I should have pressed charges," she said to no one in particular.

A disheveled Mrs. Dunne waddled her way from the room. As she adjusted her sweater, Joey noticed a tattoo on her shoulder. It was the face of a little boy.

"I am terrified of this kid, and I haven't even met him yet," she admitted to Craig. "I have no desire to be scratched up. You should have seen the scar on Tam's arm. It's permanent!"

Craig was slicing chicken to make fajitas. He stopped and pointed the knife at Joey. "If anyone touches you, I'll bring a hailstorm on that school."

His protectiveness made her smile. "Put the knife down, Rambo. They say he is on meds now. Meds which will stop the violent outbursts."

"I mean it, Joey. If that kid touches you, let me know right away. You're my wife and I won't have anyone hurting you. I don't care how old they are," he resumed dinner preparation.

"You should have seen Johnson's face when she came in this morning and Tam told her Adam would be back. She said words I've never heard before, turned, and walked out of the classroom. She didn't come back until the kids started arriving, and she shot the nastiest looks at Mrs. Dunne all day long. I don't think Dunne cared though. She has her own problems. If there is one good thing that's going to come of this, it's that Mrs. Dunne is going to have to get up off her butt and help us out in the classroom. Matthews ordered it."

A veil of dread hung over the classroom the next day, and the students felt it. They were less compliant than usual, argumentative, and not wanting to follow routine. Even during recess, their favorite time of day, they fought over whose turn it was on the swing or with the ball.

With an hour before dismissal, Dunne made a decision. "Let them free play. I want to talk to you all before our after-school meeting."

They sat around one of the student worktables, positioned in the center of the room so they could see the activity around them.

Mrs. Dunne sighed. "I'm as pissed as you are that he is coming back. It was a horrible start to the year. We had no idea what we were in for, and the parents did not reveal to us the extent of his needs. In our after-school meeting, I am going to insist that he have a new BIP in place." She turned to Joey. "That means a behavior intervention plan."

Joey nodded. "Yes, I am aware."

Dunne continued. "If there isn't an accurate and updated one, this could buy us more time. I want to know exactly what they expect us to do and what we are not to do, if and when this kid gets violent. Tam, I know you could have brought charges. You still can. You can even demand to be changed to a different position now if you want. Because he injured you, you don't have to work with him. Have you thought about that?"

Tam nodded. "I have. I talked about it with my husband last night. I'll continue for now and see what happens."

Dunne sighed again. "We can stock the classroom next door with things from the activity centers. I can buy more things if needed. We have a small budget, and on the heels of this kid coming back, I am pretty sure they'll give me what I ask for. At least for the next little while."

Together the four of them brainstormed activity center ideas, and Dunne wrote the suggestions down. In an odd way, it was the first time Joey felt like they were a team. It was kind of nice. They even walked together down to the library for their after-school meeting with Mr. Matthews, the Special Education Director, Carmen Rodriguez, and two of the district's school support staff. Mrs. Rodriguez took charge of the meeting.

"Next week, Adam Gonzalez will be returning to school. He was suspended following the incident with another teacher and the injury he gave Mrs. Tam. His return required a psychiatric evaluation and report. His parents completed the evaluation, and he is now on medication to control his violent outbursts. The parents' lawyer contacted the state education agency, and we are required to allow him back in school for a probationary period of ninety days. During that time, if he exhibits violent behavior that goes above and beyond that which is deemed as normal outbursts of anger for a thirteen-year-old, we can request his probation be revoked and he will resume suspension." She paused, anticipating that someone would have a comment. Mrs. Dunne certainly did.

"Can you please more clearly define 'violent behavior above and beyond that which is deemed as normal for a thirteen-year-old boy'?"

Mrs. Rodriguez smiled. "That is rather vague, isn't it?" Everyone nodded. "Unfortunately, it is vague. I am not sure what parameters we are to put around it. But I'd like to discuss some here."

"Is there a new BIP in place?" Mrs. Dunne asked.

Mrs. Rodriguez shook her head. "Over the first thirty days of the ninety-day probationary period, we are to put one together. We are going to rely heavily on you ladies who are with him in the classroom to make suggestions as to strategies that will help him be successful in the classroom."

Tam interjected. "We're flying blind, here. We have no idea what to do with this kid. We were in full-on survival mode the last time he was here. We couldn't even have a teacher supervision schedule with him. The teacher who went into the classroom with him was the teacher who could emotionally handle it in the moment. That's how we decided who had to be in the room with him. Do you even realize just how bad it was?" The emotion with which she said this surprised Joey.

Mrs. Rodriguez reached over and patted Tam's hand. "I can't imagine. I read your reports. You know we can have you relocated to a different school if you want."

Tam shook her head. "This is my job. I shouldn't have to move schools."

Mrs. Rodriguez nodded. "I know." To all of them she continued. "Please believe me, I know this is asking a lot from you. To have him in with the other students will be—"

"What?" Tam, Dunne, and Johnson all said at once.

Mrs. Rodriguez's face was puzzled. "He will be in the classroom with the other students."

"Absolutely not!" Mrs. Dunne roared. "There is no way I will endanger the other students with—" She stopped short of finishing her sentence. "With his presence."

"By law, we have to give him the opportunity to educated in the least restrictive environment," Mrs. Rodriguez explained.

"I know the law," Dunne said. "I also know the law is meant to protect all students."

"We must give him the chance to be with other students, on his new medication, to see if we can educate him in the least restrictive environment for his disability."

"This is unbelievable," Johnson muttered.

Mr. Matthews spoke up. "Let's make a plan. If he shows up to school and has clearly not taken his medication, you are to isolate him and alert me immediately. I will call his parents and demand they come get him. We will have the SRO sit with him until Mom or Dad arrive."

The teachers looked to one another. "That sounds reasonable," Mrs. Dunne said. "I can't have my teachers, nor my students, put in physical harm's way."

Tam and Johnson nodded.

Mr. Matthews continued. "We will have him in

the classroom, with one of you assigned to him at all times. The other three of you will have the kids grouped as you typically would.

You can take turns with him or do whatever you think best, Mrs. Dunne. But I want to be able to document that we have one-to-one supervision with him. In a perfect world, if the medication is working, we can assimilate him into a group with other students. Record everything."

"So, every single day we have to write up a report?" Mrs. Dunne clarified.

"It can read like a time sheet. For example, 'From 9:00-10:00, Russo worked with Adam on academics. From 10:00-11:00, Tam supervised Adam during recess. Etcetera," Mr. Matthews said.

"Good Lord," Mrs. Dunne said. "More paperwork. That's great."

"I catch the sarcasm, Mrs. Dunne," Mr. Matthews said. "We need to be able to show that we are doing all we can for this student. Especially if this is ever brought before a court of law."

Joey took it all in. It felt like a movie. Did these kinds of things really go on in the schools? She dreaded Monday like she hadn't dreaded anything in a long time.

DODIE

Aaron stayed away. He had texted her once to ask if he could come by, but he obliged her short response, "I'm not ready to talk to you yet." She'd also asked Anne and Sherry to give her a day to rest and think about what she wanted–needed–to do. At the end of the second day, Anne and Sherry brought a peach smoothie and came prepared to help her brainstorm her next move.

Dodie took a deep breath, then shared what was impressed on her heart. "I'm going to ask Aaron for a divorce."

The three girls looked one to the other. Dodie took a sip of her smoothie and raised her eyebrows.

"Are you sure?" Anne said.

"I know it hasn't even been a year, but he is not the man I married. He's an emotionless shell. I didn't sign up for that. Actually, no. He has emotion. It's all mean. And if I'm not able to carry children, the thought of living alone with him forever makes me feel nauseous."

"Does he know about the hysterectomy?" Sherry asked.

Dodie nodded. "Yup. I asked the doctor if he knew. He actually had to sign off on it since he is my next of kin and I was unconscious."

"Are you sure?" Anne asked again. "This is a

huge decision. I don't want to see you make it under tough conditions and then regret it later." She reached for Dodie's hand.

Dodie squeezed her fingers around Anne's. "You guys are my best friends. After all I've shared with you, do you think it's a mistake to leave him?"

Sherry shook her head. "Honestly? No. You deserve to be treated like a princess. What do you think he's going to say?"

Dodie shrugged. "I'd be surprised if he's even bothered by it at all. I feel like I'd become more of an inconvenience than anything. I don't want to be someone's inconvenience. I want to be someone's everything."

"I'm going to go down to the cafeteria and grab a coffee," Anne said. "Anyone want anything?"

Anne and Sherry had brought Sherry's iPad to the hospital, and the girls planned to binge watch some Gilmore Girls on Netflix. Dodie had at least another two weeks in the hospital to undergo intense physical therapy and ensure her pelvis healed well.

While Anne was gone, Sherry caught Dodie up on the office gossip. The new administrative assistant was a grizzly bear when it came to the sales reps, and Dodie liked hearing stories of the reps skulking around with their tails between their legs because of deals gone awry or paperwork not in ship-shape.

Suddenly, Anne rushed back into the room,

closed the door, and pulled a chair up close to Dodie's bed.

"Oh my gosh, you won't believe what I just heard," she said breathlessly.

"Where's your coffee?" Sherry asked.

"I don't know," Anne said, looking into her hands as if surprised the coffee wasn't there. "Doesn't matter—I heard something. It made me think of something."

She waved them in closely and looked around the room. "There's no one else in here, is there?" she asked in a whisper.

"What the heck, Anne?" Sherry said, annoyed. "It's just us."

"Sh!" Anne hushed her. "This is serious."

Sherry and Dodie looked at each other, then Anne leaned in toward Dodie.

"You know how the cafeteria has the coffee bar in the center of the room?" she began.

"No. I haven't been down there," Dodie said with a grin.

"Right. Sorry. Anyway, the cafeteria has a coffee bar in the center of the room."

"So, I've heard," Dodie said.

"So! I was the only one down there, getting my coffee, and the side I was on had no French vanilla creamer," she said, still in a quiet, conspiracy-theory voice. "I went around to the other side. I guess a couple of doctors came up on the front side of the coffee bar. They couldn't see me because of the coffee pots in the center."

"And because you are four-feet tall," Sherry added.

"Four-eleven. Whatever. They thought they were the only ones in there. One of the doctors said something about a hysterectomy, so my ears perked up. I don't know what he said, but the other one replied, 'No one has said anything about it.' Then the other one said, 'Did the patient ask for the specifics?' And the other guy said, 'I don't think so. The description is in the surgeon report, but patients never read the details. Lawyers would say the nick caused the infections which created the need for the hysterectomy.' Then the first guy said, 'It probably did.' And the other one said, 'Most likely. But I'd prefer not to have that conversation.'"

"Were they talking about Dodie?" Sherry interrupted.

Anne shrugged. "I think it's possible."

Dodie thought about what she just heard. "But I don't have a lawyer," she said.

"No, you don't. But if you knew that a nick or whatever that means caused them to do a hysterectomy, I bet you would want to get one," Anne said.

Dodie's peach smoothie suddenly didn't sit well. "Bucket," she said. But it was too late. She threw up smoothie all over the front of herself and on her bed covers.

Anne pushed the call button for the nurse.

Dodie threw up again, filling the creases of her soft white bedcovers with orange liquid.

"I'm—sorry—" she said between heaves. She hated vomiting.

"Oh, Dodes, it's okay," Sherry rubbed her back.

The nurse took stock of the situation and shooed Anne and Sherry aside.

"It's alright, darlin'," she assured. "We'll clean you up."

Dodie had lost her modesty through this whole experience and allowed Nurse Kelly to help her undress. Sherry passed her a clean night gown, and once Dodie was in fresh clothes, the nurse expertly changed the bedding with Dodie still in it.

"Thank you," Dodie said with a weak voice. "I don't know what happened."

"Peach smoothie?" the nurse questioned, raising an eyebrow at Sherry and Anne.

"The doctor said I could try some regular foods," Dodie argued.

The nurse tilted her head. "You probably just had too much. Feel better?"

Dodie nodded. "Yes."

"Just water for the rest of the night," she ordered. "I'll bring a full pitcher." She left the room with an armload of rank linens.

"Did I make you barf?" Anne asked. "I'm sorry. What should we do?"

"For now—nothing." Sherry advised. "I think Dodie should talk to a lawyer and see what's what."

"We don't even know if they were talking about me," Dodie objected.

"But what if they were?" Anne asked.

"Did they see you?" Dodie asked.

Anne shook her head. "I don't know who they were. I stayed low." Then she pulled out her phone. "But I have the conversation recorded."

Sherry shook her head incredulously. "What? In what world do you have a recording of that conversation?"

"Y'all know I've been writing a book," Anne said defensively. "I record myself when I get ideas. The guy who took my money at the cash register was gorgeous. And his nametag read, 'Zeke Bulwark.' Isn't that a great name? I started to envision a romance between a hospital orderly named Zeke and a gift-shop volunteer. Or maybe between the orderly and a girl who is coming to the hospital to visit her grandpa who is dying from—"

"Annie! Focus!" Sherry cut in. "The recording?"

"So, I pulled out my phone and started recording my idea for the story. I never hit stop when the guys started talking."

She pushed play. Anne's voice began excitedly describing her Hallmark-movie plot. Dodie didn't think it sounded half-bad. The sound of her footsteps as she talked were heard, then her voice stopped abruptly, and two muffled male voices began. She upped the volume, and they could be heard a bit more clearly, their conversation mirroring what Anne had described so far. Then the voices continued.

"I wrote it all in the report."

"Damn, you got lucky."

"Yeah. I gotta get back. See you later. Hey—and don't say shit about anything."

"You know I won't."

The voices stopped. "That's the end of it," Anne said. I was terrified they were going to see me. I didn't breathe until I was sure they were gone. Then I booked it out of there."

"Could they really be talking about Dodie?" Sherry wondered. "Can you air drop that recording? Send it to me and to Dodie so we all have a copy."

Anne did so. "Now what?" she asked. "You need a lawyer?"

"I can't find a lawyer from in here," Dodie was shaking. Surely this conspiracy theory of Anne's wasn't about her. Was it?

"We'll help you," Anne declared. "If it isn't about you, it's got to be about someone? What a story that would be." She spread her hands as if reading a marquee. "Brilliant women solve hospital cover-up."

Sherry shook her head at Anne. "You're too much. I'll ask Chris if he knows anyone we can talk to," Sherry offered. "He's got a guy for everything. I'm sure he'll know someone."

Long after the girls left, Dodie lay awake. She stared at the ceiling tiles, which were as familiar to her now as the tile patterns on the floor in her grandma's kitchen. For some reason, the hospital reminded her of her grandma, and it was just then that she realized why. She hadn't been back in this hospital since Grandma died. Almost three years ago, as a matter of fact. Both of Dodie's parents died in a car accident when Dodie was just one year old. They'd left her at Grandma's for the weekend, so they could go skiing. A late night, an icy road, a tight mountain curve, and a tractor trailer made it so they never came to pick her up. She'd been raised by her grandma; no cousins or other relatives to intrude on the bond they shared. Grandma's death had left a hole in Dodie's heart.

As she reflected on this now, she realized she'd met Aaron shortly after the passing of her beloved grandma. She wondered—had she tried to replace Grandma's love with Aaron's? Perhaps. Perhaps she saw him as more than he really was because she needed him to be more. By morning, her conviction was solid that Aaron was a mistake of her own doing. And she would undo it.

She texted him in the morning, asking if he could stop by after work. "Sure," came the one-word reply.

At nine a.m. the doctor removed the pelvic

brace and checked her over. "You're healing really well," he said. Dodie had a sharp intake of breath. It was the same voice she'd heard on the recording. "Is something wrong?" he asked.

"No," she replied. "I just felt a twinge of pain right here." She pointed to her hip flexor. It wasn't a lie.

"We're going to get you down to physical therapy this morning and start you walking again," the doctor said. "My goal is for you to be released in the next two weeks. It's totally doable."

Dodie smiled. "Sounds great."

Physical therapy was anything but "great." She recalled every movie in which she'd seen the accident patient frustrated by his or her lack of progress. Watching the screen, she'd always found those scenes frustrating—like, why can't that person just accept the fact that he can't walk, and he needs to work at it? But now, she understood. She wanted her body to do things that it simply wasn't cooperating to do. By the end of the thirty minutes, she was back in the wheelchair, with hot tears of frustration to show for the effort.

"Don't worry," the therapist said, sounding just like the therapists in the movies. "It takes time. You'll get there."

Once wheeled back to her room and settled with her lunch, she let her mind return to the matter of her hysterectomy. This was a big deal. A very big deal. She wasn't sure she was up for any of it.

Her phone rang. It was Anne.

"Hey Annie," she answered.

"Is anyone else in the room?" Anne asked.

"Nope. Just me."

"Chris's brother-in-law is an attorney," Anne began.

Dodie suppressed a smile. "Of course he is." They jibed Chris all the time that he "had a guy for everything." No matter what you needed, Chris knew someone in that line of work.

Anne continued. "His firm has a division that works with personal injury and medical malpractice suits. Would you like someone to come to the hospital and speak to you? They will come right out."

That was fast. "Wow. Okay. Sure. Can you guys be here too?" She needed support.

"My morning is open. I'll check with Sherry. Let me go talk to Chris and I'll text you the time." Anne hung up.

At one o'clock, Anne, Sherry, and Chris arrived. Five minutes behind them came Chris's brother-in-law, Jerry, and the firm's lead malpractice attorney, Rene DeFausto. Mrs. DeFausto fit the archetype of a strong female, take-no-crap-from-anyone attorney. Her grey power suit was tailored impeccably, and she stood a good two inches above both Chris and Jerry in her pencil back Jimmy Choos.

They filled the tiny hospital room. A passing nurse poked her head in. "Everything okay in here?"

"Yes ma'am," Dodie replied. "Some friends from work coming to visit."

The nurse smiled and closed the door.

"Sorry for the ultra-formal look," Rene said. "I normally would not come marching into a hospital looking all lawyery for a first meeting like this. I was in court and didn't have time to go back to the office."

"I appreciate your coming on such short notice," Dodie said. "Actually, I'm surprised how fast this is happening. I don't even know if we're wasting your time. If we are, I don't know what I can pay you."

Jerry cut in. "Stop. Let's see what's what first. It's better to act as closely to the incident as possible, so don't worry about us. We are used to acting fast."

"Take us through what happened and what you know," Rene prompted. She opened the voice record app on her phone. "May I record?"

Dodie nodded. "Where should I start?"

"In the words of Glenda, the good witch from the Land of Oz, it is always best to start at the beginning," Rene said.

Dodie smiled at the reference to one of her

favorite classics. She liked this woman.

Walking them through the morning of the rock climb was painful. She left nothing out— Aaron's fascination with Lucy, her initial uneasiness with letting him belay her, her call out that she was climbing down, and the last thing she remembered from that morning, the carabiner pulling loose from the rock and the sensation of falling.

She explained that when she finally was fully conscious, she threw Aaron out of the room and has since decided to divorce him. That raised some eyebrows, but no one commented. Then she told of the psychologist's visit and how they informed her that she would not be able to carry children. She recounted Anne's version of what happened in the cafeteria and what Anne overheard at the coffee bar. She told it all with surprising detachment from the emotions. It felt like it happened to someone else.

"This morning, when the doctor came to remove my brace before physical therapy, I know it was the same voice I'd heard on Anne's recording." Her story was complete.

The lawyers were quiet while she spoke. Now they had all the questions.

"First of all, I am so sorry you are going through this. You are a brave, strong woman," Jerry said respectfully. "Chris said you are like family, and that is how we will treat you. Okay?"

Dodie looked at Chris and smiled. "Thank you."

"Are you sure you want to divorce your husband?" Jerry asked.

"Extremely sure. I can't imagine living with him for the rest of my life—especially now." Her tears broke free. It wasn't happening to someone else. This was her life. Her uncertain, fuzzy-futured life. Sherry gave her a tissue and took Dodie's hand.

"We love you, Dodes," she said.

Dodie smiled at her friends, then looked at Jerry. "I am sure."

"Does Aaron know about what Anne overheard?" Rene asked.

"No. He hasn't been back here for me to tell him," Dodie said. "He is supposed to come by tonight. I'd planned to talk to him, maybe see if he knows anything? And also, I am going to tell him I want a divorce."

"Do not tell him anything about what Anne overheard," Jerry instructed firmly. "Not a word. If he even suspects there will be financial gain in your future, he could jam you up."

Dodie was confused. "Financial gain?"

"If they are truly at fault and caused the hysterectomy by negligence, you are looking at a lawsuit. It could be worth a lot of money," Rene said quietly.

Dodie blinked at Rene. A *lot* of money?

Rene didn't want them to play the recording aloud in the hospital room in case someone walked in to overhear. Instead, Anne airdropped the file to both Rene and Jerry, who listened through their own headphones.

"I'll get investigations on this," Jerry said to Rene once they heard the file. Then he looked at Dodie. "I am also going to launch an investigation as to how this accident could have happened. I want to know why your equipment wasn't how it should have been. For now, you need tell Aaron that you have spoken to an attorney regarding filing for divorce. That's it. Give him no other details. Okay?"

Dodie nodded. "Should I have someone else here with me when I talk to him?" Their faces appeared blurry through her salty eyes.

"That's up to you. It might not be a bad idea," Jerry said.

Rene reached over and placed a kind hand on Dodie's blanket. "This is a lot. Your whole world has been turned upside down. Take it one small step at a time. You might start to feel overwhelmed or panicked. If that happens, take a deep breath. Get a drink of water, or orange juice. Get healthy. Your physical therapy is extremely important. Regardless of how this all came to be, you have a future that is full of good things, Dodie. You take care of getting healthy, and we'll handle the rest. I'm going to suggest that after you talk to Aaron this evening, you give him Jerry's card. Tell him Jerry is your divorce attorney and all future communications will need to be through him. That is, if you want to hire us. No pressure, we will take your lead."

"What about my dogs?" she asked. "And my townhouse? Those are all my things from before we were married. I bought the townhouse outright with the money I inherited following my grandma's death."

"One thing at a time," Jerry said. "Do you think he will stop taking care of the dogs if you tell him you want a divorce?"

"I think it's highly likely," Dodie said with sad realization. He never had really embraced them as "his" dogs too. He always referred to them as hers.

"Dodie, I can take care of the dogs for you," Chris offered. "You know that Suzy and I have a lot of land and Georgie would love a couple of playmates for a while."

Dodie nodded. "Thanks, Chris." Deep breath. "Okay. I can do this."

Chris promised to come back after work to be present for her conversation with Aaron. Dodie knew Aaron would be rattled at Chris's presence. In fact, now she was counting on it. She napped the afternoon away until Chris returned at six o'clock.

"He's not here yet?" Chris said, taking a seat.

"Nope. I expect him soon. He texted me five minutes ago that he was just leaving work."

Twenty minutes later, Aaron entered Dodie's

hospital room. He glanced at Chris, then turned his eyes back to Dodie.

"Didn't know you had company," Aaron said. "Want me to come back?"

"No, it's fine. Chris came by to see how I was doing," Dodie said.

Aaron gave an awkward nod of hello to Chris and sat in the other guest chair. "How are you feeling?"

"Pretty sore. Physical therapy was rough today," she said.

Aaron shifted in his chair. "Dodie, I need to talk to you." Right to business. He glanced at Chris. "It's kind of personal."

"I don't mind having Chris here if you don't mind," she said cautiously. He wanted to talk? She glanced at Chris who raised his eyebrows and nodded encouragingly.

Aaron shrugged. "Fine by me." He pulled a business card out of his pocket and dropped in on the blanket that covered her lap. "I spoke with an attorney. Did the doctors tell you—"

"About the hysterectomy?" Dodie offered. Aaron nodded. "Yes. They told me."

Aaron nodded again. He searched for the words to come next. "Listen. Lately things haven't been good for us. Even before your—" He stopped again. "Even before. I talked to an attorney. I think maybe it would be best if you and I took this opportunity to go our separate ways."

Dodie squinted her eyes at him. "You want to divorce me?" she clarified. She reached over and picked up the card. "Is this a divorce attorney?"

"I know the timing is terrible," he said. "And things are up in the air for you right now. But I didn't want to string you along because I know you'll be needing to make plans for when you get out of the hospital."

"Oh, when I get out of the hospital, I plan to return to my townhouse," Dodie stated clearly, anger rising in her voice. "My townhouse."

"Actually, Dodie, I already moved out of it," Aaron said sheepishly. "I don't want it."

"Where are the dogs?" she demanded.

"I've been going by in the morning and afternoon to let them out and feed them," he said. "And I've been paying a dogwalker to come by when I can't make it there."

Dodie looked to Chris to gauge how she should react. He cleared his throat. "Hey, why don't I come by and get the dogs and take them to my house until Dodie is released from the hospital? I'll keep them until she can take care of them herself," he offered. "That'll be one less thing for you to worry about, Aaron."

Aaron looked relieved. "Hey man, I'd appreciate that." He held out a hand for Chris to shake.

Dodie shook her head in disbelief. He was looking for the easy way out. "Where are you staying?" she asked.

Aaron was ready for this question. "I got a place in Boulder."

"Alone?" Dodie asked.

Aaron didn't reply.

"With a female friend?" Dodie clarified. When Aaron still didn't answer, Dodie continued. "It's going to come out anyway, Aaron. Just shoot straight with me."

"Yes, Dodie. I got a place with a female friend," Aaron said with aggravation in his tone. "But that's not why—" he stammered. "I just don't think you and I—"

"Stop. It's fine. This is just perfect," Dodie said with her own aggravation.

The room was quiet. Chris cut the silence. "So, um, Aaron. How do you want to handle the divorce?"

Aaron seemed grateful for the prompting. "My attorney said he will send over a draft of a divorce agreement. But Dodie, all I want is a clean break. I took only my things from the townhouse. Anything that was yours before we were married you can have. I'll take my car. You keep yours. We both make about the same amount of money, so there's no need for alimony or anything. Don't you agree?"

Dodie nodded. "Yeah. That all sounds fine. Clean break. Have him send me the papers. I'll give them to an attorney to look over. I get the dogs, right?"

"Of course," Aaron said. "They're yours anyway." He stood to leave.

"How long, Aaron?" Dodie asked, as he was about to go out the door.

"How long what?"

"How long have you been cheating on me?" she asked.

He shook his head.

"That's what I thought," she said, and he left without another word.

JOEY

The anticipation of the new school week—and the new student—hung a shroud over Joey's weekend. Despite Craig's assurances that it would all be "just fine," the unknown weighed on her shoulders. On Monday morning, all four of the FISH teachers were forty-five minutes earlier to school than usual.

"Guess we all had the same idea," Johnson said. "Enjoy the peace and quiet while we can."

"I'm glad you all are here," Mrs. Dunne said. "We can go over some last-minute details. In the mornings, I will wait outside at the curb for Adam. Mom is supposed to drop him off."

"He was expelled from the bus, right?" Tam said.

"Yes. For now. I don't know if the attorney will try and force the district to let him back on the bus," Dunne said. "Until that happens, Mom or Dad will bring him and pick up."

Tam whistled. "Ooooh. The bus driver will have a fit if they let him back on that bus." Tam looked at Joey. "He hit her over the head with a plastic lunchbox. It forced her to swerve, and she nearly lost control of the bus. She'll probably quit if they make her drive him again."

"We don't know what will happen with the bus," Dunne said, changing the subject. "Let's worry about us. For our opening songs and calendar time, I want designated seating on the floor. I went to the carpet outlet over the weekend, and they gave me a dozen carpet squares. We'll spread them out. I drew up a seating chart." She held it up for them to see. Adam was positioned at the back of the carpet, with Joey and Dunne on either side of him. "I even have a rubber square for Gary."

"Good idea," Johnson said. "I hope it works."

Tam spread the carpet squares around the floor to match the picture Dunne had made. They wrote the students' names in large black letters on notecards to indicate where each child should sit. Then the teachers took seats around one of the tables.

Dunne continued with her instructions. "After carpet time, we'll still split into groups for the morning. Adam will become a part of Russo's group—with me as a second teacher to the group. This way we can show we are allowing him to interact with his peers, but we maintain the one-to-one contact if needed. We'll move Lucas to Tam's group. Lucas rubbed Adam the wrong way last time he was here. I don't want to do anything to potentially aggravate either of them."

Joey was disappointed to lose Lucas. She felt like she'd made some gains with him in math and reading. But having one less student in a group that now had Adam seemed like a wise move.

"What if he gets violent?" Joey asked. It was the question that plagued her since she learned about Adam.

"If he even appears to be losing control, our first concern must be for the other students. I've unlocked the door to the adjacent room. We move the kids out as calmly as possible. If Adam is closest to the door, then move him out, not the other kids. Isolation is the name of the game. Of course, we'll push the call button. I'll do my best to restrain Adam if necessary. I've got the jacket if we need it."

"The jacket?" Joey asked.

"It's kind of like a modified straitjacket," Dunne said. Joey's face registered her shock. "We use it as a last resort for everyone's protection. It's like a body wrap to hold his arms in until help gets here."

"Believe me, if we need it, you'll be glad for it," Johnson said. "We keep it in that corner closet." She indicated to a narrow door behind Mrs. Dunne's desk.

"This is so absurd," Joey said. "I can't believe these are possibilities."

"Yeah, well, we don't get to pick the kids we get," Dunne said. "We have to take them all."

"Even the broken crayons," Joey said to herself.

"What's that?" Johnson asked.

"Oh," she spoke with nervousness in her voice, unsure of how much to share. "I teach Sunday

School at our church. Kindergartners." Johnson groaned and rolled her eyes at the mention of five-year-olds. Tam and Dunne looked at Joey, expectant for her story. "A couple of years ago, I had a student come in one Sunday very upset. His name was Bobby. He went to the corner of the room, sat on the floor, and just sobbed. He didn't want to talk to me, he didn't want to play—he didn't want to do anything. I didn't push him to participate, I let him be. Sometimes kids have rough mornings, you know?" They all nodded. "When we gathered at the table to color, I put out six boxes of brand-new crayons I had just purchased. His head perked up when he saw the new crayons. But he wasn't happy. He got up and began snatching the new crayons from the other kids and snapping them in two. He broke as many as he could grab and threw them on the floor. Kids were yelling, he started yelling, it was a mess. When he broke them all, he stamped his foot and yelled, 'There! Now you're all broken!'"

Tam clucked her tongue in disapproval.

"I hushed the other kids and went to him. I kneeled down and asked why he did that. He had the angriest little face you ever saw on a kindergartner. He said with a pout, 'My daddy moved away last week. Grammy said our family was broken.' He started to bawl. He leaned into me and whispered, 'I don't want to be broken.'" Joey's voice choked as she remembered. "I gave him a hug, then gathered up the crayons and put them all back on the table. I sat down, took a piece of paper, and began to color.

"The other kids didn't say anything. They just picked up the broken crayons and also began to color. Eventually they started talking and laughing together and everything went back to normal. Bobby watched for a bit. Then he sat down next to me and picked up a broken yellow crayon.

"I said to him, 'You know, I think that broken crayons make the prettiest pictures.' I showed him my picture. He nodded and colored with the broken crayons. When his mom came by the Sunday School room to pick him up, he handed her his picture. Her eyes were puffy—obviously she'd been having a rough week too. He said to her, 'Guess what, Mommy? Broken crayons make the prettiest pictures.' She didn't answer, but she took his hand, and they left. They never came back. I heard that the mom and Bobby moved to Detroit. It was after that I knew I wanted to go into teaching."

Joey's captive audience was quiet. It was the most she'd revealed about herself since coming to the FISH room, and for a moment her brazenness embarrassed her.

Tam raised her eyebrows. "That's a great story, Russo. You've got a big heart."

Dunne stood. "We better get ready for this day." Joey saw her dab at her eyes as she headed for the door.

All of the other students had arrived and there was no sign yet of Adam. Joey had just gotten her hopes up that maybe the parents changed their minds when Dunne's phone buzzed with a text message.

"They're here," she said, and she left the room. Joey and Johnson got the other students seated at their carpet squares. The students were all really excited for the change. Katie scooched her carpet square a little closer to the edge of the carpet, closer to where Gary and his rubber square sat off to the side. Gary surprised them all by picking up his square and putting it on the carpet, next to Katie's. He sat on it, unperturbed at the fact that the cuff of his pants and shoes were touching the carpet.

Tam and Joey looked at each other.

"Well! Okay then, Gary. You joined us on the carpet." Joey said, giving him a high five.

"Yeah," Gary said. "I can sit on the rubber carpet."

The door to the room opened. The child Joey had been picturing in her mind was at least seven feet tall, shadowy like a boogieman—with long stringy hair and wild eyes that never stopped moving as he scanned for his next victim. The child who walked into the classroom however wasn't even five feet tall, was scrawny, and had strawberry blonde hair that was closely cut to his scalp and blue eyes that looked at no one.

"Put your backpack over here, Adam," Mrs. Dunne instructed, pointing to the cubbies where the students stored their things. Joey noticed that Dunne had labeled the cubby at the very end of the row of hooks for Adam. He hung up his backpack, then slowly walked to the carpet. He saw the square that bore his name, looked at the other students, then sat on his carpet square, running his fingers through the fibers.

"Hi Adam. I'm Mrs. Russo," Joey leaned over and said quietly to the boy who presented a complete paradox to her expectations. He lifted a hand hello in reply. He crossed his legs and faced Tam.

Carpet time and the morning stations happened without incident. Adam was quiet. Compliant. He did what was asked, went where he was told, and answered verbally when prompted. He ate his lunch at the very end of the cafeteria table—by himself—and none of the teachers pushed to encourage him to eat with the others. At recess he took one of the playground balls and kicked it repeatedly against the brick of the school building. No one bothered him. He bothered no one. At the end of the day, Mr. Matthews visited the room to debrief.

"The day went smoothly," Dunne reported. "Not a thing went wrong."

"Good." The relief clearly showed on his face. "I've been on pins and needles all day. Every time my phone rang, I jumped." They all laughed at that. "I guess his meds are working?"

"I suppose so," Dunne concurred.

"I hope he keeps taking them," Johnson said doubtfully.

"His medication is a requirement for his probation," Mr. Matthews reminded. "If he shows up and hasn't taken it, you call Mom and send him home. Immediately."

"See? I told you it would be fine," Craig said knowingly as Joey recounted her day.

"I expected this monster of a kid," she said incredulously, "but he was so—unobtrusive."

"Unobtrusive?" Craig laughed.

"He was!" she insisted. "He didn't bother a single person. You know what's weird, though? The other kids are all clearly special needs students. You can tell that they have a developmental delay of some sort, but Adam didn't seem to have any visible disability. He could read. He did the worksheets— and got the answers correct—and when he did talk, he talked in proper sentences."

"Is his disability related only to the violence?" Craig wondered.

"Perhaps," she said thoughtfully.

The next two days of that week went just like the first. Adam defied the expectations by keeping to himself and doing everything that was asked of him. He didn't interact positively with the others, but he didn't try and injure them either, so everyone chalked it up to success.

"Mrs. Dunne, can I make a request?" It was Thursday, and Joey had a special idea for Friday's activities.

"What is it, Russo?"

"I'd like to bring in some paints and have the students paint some decorations for the walls." Dunne looked like she was about to protest, but Joey quickly continued. "I thought maybe I could set the paints up on a table in the room next door. I'll bring the kids over one at a time. I'll keep it controlled. I'll clean up any mess that we make. I've even bought all the supplies."

"What kind of decorations?" Dunne was skeptical. "It's fine in here."

"The walls are the color of mustard! It's the worst color in the world!" Joey protested. "I just want to make it prettier in here."

"Okay, Russo. Let them paint," she said. "Just don't wreck the floor. The custodian will have a fit."

"Really? Thank you!" Joey couldn't believe Dunne said yes. "I'll keep it clean. I promise!" She gathered her things and left before Mrs. Dunne could change her mind.

Joey selected Ivan as her first painting customer. He followed her to the painting room and allowed her to put a large plastic smock over his clothing.

"Like a raincoat," he said, fascinated.

"Yup! Like a raincoat!"

"Ooh! Pretty!" He reached to put his fingers in the array of paints laid out on the table.

"No, Ivan. Look!" She handed him a paintbrush, and with her hand over top of his, dipped it in the turquoise blue. Together they painted long strokes on the ocean scene that Joey had sketched in black marker on a sheet of large white craft paper.

"Blue," Ivan said. "Blue water." Joey continued to help him procure the paint on the brush, but she released his hand to create the scene on the paper.

"Painting," he said proudly.

"You are painting," Joey was just as proud.

He then switched to yellow and made dabs of color to fill the scales on a grinning ocean fish that Joey had sketched. She thought they were done, but then he pointed to purple. Joey watched as he made a starshaped purply-blue creature next to the yellow one. He dipped the paintbrush in black and drew a smiling face in the center of the starfish.

"Friends," he said. He dipped his paintbrush in green and drew green swirls in the blue water.

After his picture was saturated with magnificence that only he could create, Joey helped him paint his name in the lower corner of the page.

"Good job, Ivan," she said, removing the smock.

"Thank you, teacher," Ivan responded.

Throughout the rest of the day, each of the other students took their turn to paint a masterpiece. Not all of them had the stamina to finish a whole picture, but between them all, they had eight vibrant underwater scenes that, when dry, would adorn the mustard walls of the classroom, bringing life to the FISH room.

"Nice work, Russo," Johnson said appreciatively, studying the murals spread across the tables drying. "I didn't think you'd be able to pull it off."

It was a rare compliment. "Thanks. They really did well, didn't they?"

Joey stayed late at school that Friday to hang the students' artwork on the walls of the classroom. The looks on the kids' faces on Monday morning would be well worth it. She gave Ivan's painting the prime spot, centered above the bookshelf.

Joey knew something was wrong. As she walked past the front office on her way to class Monday morning, she saw the principal talking with Mrs. Dunne, who was dabbing her eyes with a tissue. The sight brought a skip to Joey's heart, though she did not know why. Ten minutes later, Mrs. Dunne came into the classroom, where Joey was preparing the activity centers. Tam and Johnson arrived right behind her.

"Ladies, I need to talk to you," Dunne said, sitting at the table they usually gathered around.

Her eyes were puffy, and she carried a box of Kleenex. After all were seated, she looked at each of their faces before speaking, stopping with special attention to Joey's. She looked right into Joey's concerned eyes as she said, "Ivan passed away over the weekend."

Joey blinked, not processing this information. Johnson was the first to find the words to ask what happened.

"He had a seizure sometime Saturday night while he slept. His parents didn't find him until Sunday morning. By then it was too late to revive him. The Medical Examiner figured it was quick and there wouldn't have been much they could do even if they'd heard him struggling." Mrs. Dunne took a tissue and held it to her eyes.

"Poor kid," Tam said. "That's awful."

Joey couldn't speak. Ivan was gone? The information didn't—couldn't—get through.

"It's going to be a hard day for us," Mrs. Dunne said. "But we cannot say anything about this to the students. If they ask, we say Ivan isn't here today. I am going to spend part of the morning calling all the parents. We will let them tell their children at their homes, if they even choose to. They might not. And of course, the district counsellors are available for us. If we didn't have Adam, I'd give us a bit of a breather today, but unfortunately, I think we need to stick to the schedule."

Johnson and Tam nodded and solemnly continued preparing the room for the morning activities. Joey sat, dumbfounded, until Tam finally said, "Come on, Russo, the bus will be here soon."

DODIE

Dodie's attorneys were extremely pleased at the divorce settlement sent over by Aaron's lawyer. They summed it up for her four days after Aaron's visit.

"Apparently Aaron was more concerned with getting stuck paying high hospital bills than he may have been to consider anything might have been amiss with your hysterectomy," Jerry explained. "You don't have any personal credit cards together?"

Dodie shook her head. "We haven't been married that long. We each had our own car loan from before our marriage. I have a credit card with a $5,000 limit, but if I put anything on it, I pay it every month. Honestly, I have no idea what Aaron's credit card—or cards—have owing. We've each continued to take care of our own stuff from our own bank accounts. I never even officially changed my last name."

"And neither of you are on the other person's insurance?" Rene asked.

Again, Dodie shook her head. "Nope. We each maintained our own insurance through the companies we work for."

Jerry shrugged. "This will be simple. Paperwork, speaking. I know it isn't simple emotionally," he said with a sympathetic smile. "The one thing his lawyer clearly spelled out was that any bills resulting from your hospital visits will be covered either by your insurance or by you personally. He stipulates that Aaron is not to be held responsible for any hospital bills resulting from this accident."

"Bastard," Sherry muttered.

Rene smirked. "I agree. His attorney probably expects us to balk at that. We must be careful how we word our reply. We don't want to raise any red flags. But we do need to adjust the wording slightly to include that Aaron is severed from any financial dealings related to this matter. This way we include any possible financial gain that could be in the future."

Dodie detested Aaron in that moment. "What next?"

Jerry and Rene stood. "We'll give this to our legal team," Jerry said. "They'll know how it needs to be worded. Don't worry. Once they make some adjustments, I'll bring it back here for you to look at. If you approve, we'll have you sign it, and we'll return it to their lawyers for review."

Dodie nodded. "Okay."

"Any update on a release date?" Rene asked.

"Physical therapy is going well. I'm meeting with a home care worker to discuss prepping my home for my release. It could happen by the end of the week."

"That's great!" Rene said. "I bet you are ready to be out of here."

"You have no idea," Dodie agreed.

Anne came by the hospital for Dodie's meeting with the home care worker. Anne was twenty-eight, single, and lived with her parents. She offered to move in with Dodie while she got settled in her new normal. Dodie wouldn't be able to drive for a little bit, so Anne would also be Dodie's chauffeur.

"You sure you want to do this?" Dodie asked Anne, after the worker explained the many scenarios in which Dodie would require assistance. "I can Uber where I need to go."

"Are you kidding? My parents are driving me crazy. This will be like a vacation for all of us," she joked. "Seriously. It's my pleasure to help you. Besides, someone's got to make sure you get back to work! We need you around there."

"Ha. I'm sure things have gone just fine without me," Dodie said. "Like Chris always has said, 'No one is indispensable.'"

"Yeah, well, it certainly hasn't been as much fun," Anne said. "It'll be good to have you back."

"It'll be good to be back. I'm ready."

The following Friday, Dodie was released from the hospital. It took Anne and Sherry two trips to the car to pack all of the things she'd accumulated over the past five weeks. Kelly, Dodie's favorite nurse, had the honor of wheeling Dodie to the lobby doors.

"Good luck, Dodie," Kelly said, as Dodie stood from the chair and made her way slowly to the car. "I'm proud of you."

"Thanks," Dodie answered. "And thank you for all your help. And for the extra pudding."

"Keep up with your physical therapy," Kelly advised.

"Don't worry! She will," Anne promised.

Anne had taken the care to remove any sign of Aaron from the townhouse. She replaced any photos of the two of them with pictures of Dodie or of her puppies, and threw any stray t-shirts, toiletries, or books Aaron had left behind into a box which she carted off to her parents' garage for storage. He'd taken the office furniture—which he claimed he purchased even though Dodie knew otherwise—but Dodie didn't fight him on it, as it just made it all the easier to turn that room into Anne's bedroom. From the hospital, Dodie had ordered a new double bed and a small dresser from IKEA.

"Home, sweet home," Dodie said as she crossed the threshold. She reclined on her couch, hugging her giant panda bear while her friends unpacked her things. "I don't remember my couch being so comfortable." After Sherry said goodbye, with promises to see Dodie on Monday at work, she and Anne ordered Chinese food for dinner. Dodie couldn't decide if she felt excited or bleak about this new chapter of her life. As she drifted off to sleep in the bed she had planned to share with her husband for many years, she decided it was a solid mix of both.

"Ta-da! We got you a new desk chair!" Chris made a big presentation as Dodie made her way to her desk after missing it for the last month and a half. A vase of flowers perched on the corner and a gathering of "Welcome Back" balloons rose proudly from the back of her new chair. "It is supposed to be the latest ergonomically-designed chair and will reduce back and hip pain by up to eighty percent. Or so say the marketing materials," he explained.

Dodie sat tenderly into the chair while her coworkers applauded. "Oooh, this is nice," she agreed. "Thank you all. And Walt, I better not catch you sitting in my new chair!" she jibed.

Walt grinned and patted her gently on the back. "You won't catch me."

It was good to be back. Donna, the woman who replaced Amy, was a good twenty years older than Dodie. She had reorganized Amy's files and made an order-processing procedure that was actually quite efficient. She was smart, capable, and had picked up quickly on the way things worked. Dodie had asked her twice that morning for updates on the open orders and Donna brushed her off as if Dodie was insignificant in the process. By lunchtime, Dodie realized that they really could continue to get along without her. She expressed as much to Chris over lunch. It had been their Monday tradition to eat lunch together whenever Chris was in town so Dodie could catch him up on everything around the office. Their favorite spot was a Mom and Pop diner near the office.

"Don't be ridiculous," Chris said, taking a bite of his Reuben sandwich. "You are far from insignificant."

"I am so out of touch," she said. "It's like I've been gone for a century."

"You'll be back in the swing of things in no time. I want you, Donna, and I to sit down this afternoon so she can review all of the outstanding orders for you." Dodie raised an eyebrow at him. "I heard her dismiss your request for information. It won't happen again. I will establish you as her boss and her main go-to. I need you to continue to make business decisions when I am not around. I've refrained from travelling over these past few weeks and now that you're back, I can do the rounds with the North American offices. How are you feeling?"

"Physically, I feel great. Mentally? Ups and downs."

"It'll take time. Suzy said she'll bring you over dinner on Wednesday when we bring the dogs back home. I leave on Thursday for Dallas. Any update from Jerry?"

"They sent the revisions to the divorce

agreement over to Aaron's lawyer. If he signs it, then it should be pretty much a done deal. They can file it with the courts."

"Any update on the medical part?"

"I am meeting with them tomorrow after work. Jerry said they have a lot to tell me."

Rene and Jerry met Dodie at her townhouse Tuesday evening promptly at six. Anne served tea and they took seats around Dodie's dining room table.

"Do you want the good news or the bad news first?" Jerry asked.

"There's bad news?" Dodie said. "I wasn't expecting bad news."

Rene gave a sympathetic smile. "We've been investigating the hospital's procedures regarding your treatment following the accident, but we've also done some probing into the causes of your accident. That's where the bad news lies."

"Okay. Hit me with it. Bad news first," Dodie said. She looked to Anne for support. Anne reached over and put her hand over Dodie's.

Rene looked to Jerry. Apparently, he was the chosen one to deliver this part of the update. "An accident of your magnitude was bound to have been caught on social media. We scoured the internet and sure enough found several videos of your fall and of the rescue and evacuation."

"Oh my God!" Dodie said. "My fall is on the

internet?"

Jerry shook his head rapidly. "Trust me, don't look for it. You do not want to see it. Here's the thing. As we were searching for photos and videos tagged at Bastille Crack, I found something disturbing." He paused.

Dodie's stomach suddenly hurt. She pulled her hand from Anne's and crossed her arms in front of her gut, holding it to still the brewing storm. "What? What did you find?"

"The couple who was waiting to climb after your group were making a video diary of sorts leading up to their climb. They were standing behind Aaron and Lucy. The husband had the camera on his wife, but Aaron's and Lucy's voices could be heard in the background. When I saw them in the video, I asked the couple for a copy, and we enhanced the background to hear their conversation. I am assuming Lucy's husband was not around."

"The bastard!" Anne said. "Unbelievable!"

Dodie couldn't speak.

Jerry continued. "That's not all. At one point you can hear Lucy remark at how far up you are. Aaron says, 'Oh shit, I forgot to call out.' You then hear him give you a 'halfway' call.

"He and Lucy resume their conversation. A little while later, Lucy stops talking and asks Aaron what you just said. He replies that you must have anchored off. He then says something very

derogatory about you and calls out, 'Belay off.'"
Jerry paused.

"He—he took me off belay?" Dodie couldn't
believe it. She didn't recall hearing him say that.

Jerry took a deep breath. "When he noticed
you were actually climbing down, he realized his
mistake and quickly tries to fix it. Right about then
the crowd starts screaming."

Dodie pushed back from the table, got herself
to the bathroom, and threw up her tea. The heaves
hurt her pelvis, and the information hurt her heart.
Anne knocked gently on the door and let herself in.
She rubbed Dodie's back while she cried, with her
head resting on her arms folded on the toilet seat.

"Come on, let's go hear the good news," Anne
encouraged after letting Dodie weep for a few
minutes.

Jerry and Rene were waiting patiently, sadness
and sympathy on their faces.

"Sorry," Dodie said, resuming her seat.

"Please. Don't apologize. I'm so sorry we had to
tell you this," Rene said. "Dodie, you can sue him if
you want. He is clearly at fault for your accident."

Dodie shook her head. "He has nothing I want.
He can't give me back the thing that means the
most to me. The thing I lost through this."

Rene nodded in understanding. "We just want
you to know your options. If there is any upside to
it, it would be that Aaron does not have a leg to
stand on if he were to ever come after you for any

of the money you will get from the hospital. With this video, we've got him by the nuts."

Dodie wanted to chuckle at that, but it was too horrid. Instead, she sighed. "So, what is the good news?"

"Remember we had you sign a medical records release?" Rene asked. "We took that release, as well as the copy of the audio recording from the cafeteria, to a judge who is also a good friend of mine. I asked him the best way to proceed, expressing our concern that if we simply request the records from the hospital, that they may be tampered with prior to their delivery to our offices. I said that we would like to interview under oath the nurses who were involved with the surgery, as well as review any video or other records of what happened during both of your surgeries, if there are any."

"And the judge agreed?" Dodie asked.

"Even better," Rene continued. "He sent a sheriff to accompany us to the hospital. The chief administrator met with us. We explained what we wanted. As soon as we handed her the order for the records, the administrator put two and two together. She asked outright what we were looking for. The sheriff explicated their need to comply with the court request to hand over the items immediately under his supervision. The sheriff waited for two hours while they gathered the video footage and notes. He watched while their administration and investigative staff pored over it all and catalogued it.

"We took it back to our offices and our investigator went through it. The video footage does not have sound, so we reviewed it in conjunction with the written notes. The report glosses over an incident where it reads that your right iliac artery and your bladder were damaged. In the video, there is a moment where the surgeon and nurses are working steadily, but suddenly activity increases in intensity."

Dodie cut in, "I'm sorry to interrupt, I had damage to an artery? And my bladder?"

Rene nodded. "It does not appear that they were damaged prior to the surgery, but rather something happened during the surgery. They were nicked during the repair to the laceration in the cervix and uterus. A hysterectomy wasn't the original plan. That night, when your bladder became infected, the uterus became infected, and you started going septic. Then the artery started leaking blood. Basically, the second surgery and the hysterectomy came about because the surgeon made an error in the initial surgery. We are going to have our own hired surgeon review it all, but I rather expect we will hear from them before we ever file anything. That administrator is smart. I am sure she reviewed everything before we even got back to the offices. They've probably already spoken to their insurance company and attorneys. And when they hear we have a recording of the doctors talking, well, that will be that. Which reminds me, I have reported our intent to file suit to your insurance company. They'll be glad that we are asking for all your medical bills to be covered in the suit."

Dodie nodded. "That is all good news. Right?" she said uncertainly.

"It's awful what has happened to you," Jerry said. "The only good part is that we might be able to get you some help for your future. It's a small comfort, I know."

"Yeah," Dodie agreed.

Aaron's attorney filed the divorce paperwork the following day. Following a standard 90-day waiting period, it would be complete.

By the end of the month, Dodie and her attorneys had come to an agreement with the hospital. The subsequent infection and hysterectomy were a result of a surgical error from the initial surgery, not from the original fall. Had the doctor come clean from the get-go, it may have gone better for the hospital. But he tried to whitewash it and made no mention to the chief of staff, as was protocol. He knew he was in the wrong, as the recorded conversation clearly showed, which all tipped the scales way in Dodie's favor.

Dodie would receive her attorney and medical bills covered, plus any future medical bills that arise related to the hysterectomy, plus the sum of four million dollars.

JOEY

Craig gently shook Joey, while she pretended to be asleep. "Joey," he whispered. "Come on, sweetie. Time to get ready for church."

"I don't want to go," Joey said, pulling the covers over her head.

"I know. But it would be good to get back in your routine," he argued. "You've missed for two weeks now."

"I'm sick of having to follow the routine!" Joey said angrily. "Ivan followed the routine and look where it got him." She knew how immature she sounded.

"Joey. Ivan was a sweet little boy with a lot of health problems. When we talked to his mom at the funeral, she said it was a miracle he'd lived to be twelve. You got to share in a piece of his life. That was a blessing for him. You helped him read. You saw the joy when he painted. His mom said that all he could talk about at dinner that Friday night was how much he loved to paint. She said all day Saturday he painted pictures, laughing and talking more than she'd ever heard him talk. You did that for him. Don't let those memories be tarnished."

Joey rolled over and looked at her husband through swollen, sad eyes. "I had so many great ideas for other things I could teach him," she said dolefully.

"Guess what?" Craig said. "There are a lot of other kids there who can benefit from your passion."

Joey wanted to remain in her wretched state, but she knew Craig was right. She'd not been much good for the other kids over these past two weeks. She'd lost her "What's best for the kids?" attitude and was just trying to function day-by-day. Putting one foot in front of the other, she eased herself out of bed, went to church, and even managed a bit of small talk. By the end of the day her heart felt like it might want to heal. Not for herself, though. For the other kids.

And then Monday came along. If she could have rewound the clock, Joey would have called in sick. The poor judgement of other people often dictates our days, and this Monday brought it in droves. Mrs. Dunne must have had psychic foresight that Joey didn't possess because she called in sick. Unfortunately, this created the first problem, as there was no substitute to be had on short notice. The ladies decided that since Adam had been doing so well in Joey's group of students, and since Joey's group was one student short following Ivan's passing, that Joey would be able to handle both Adam and Katie. This was the second problem. Tam went out to the curb to meet Adam's mother, who was running so late that she didn't even talk to Tam, she just let Adam out of the car and sped away before Tam could verify that Adam had his meds. Third problem.

When Tam brought Adam into the classroom, he threw his backpack at the wall.

"Adam, please hang your backpack up on the hook," Tam requested. In reply, Adam looked at her, turned away, and went to his carpet square. He sat on it with folded arms and a scowl.

Joey picked up the backpack. It was extremely heavy. She hung it on Adam's hook and then encouraged the other kids to find their spots on the carpet to get the day started. Adam turned his back during the singing, and when Matt hit his usual high note in the "Days of the Week" song, Adam covered his ears and yelled, "Stop it, idiot!"

"Let's get a drink of water, Adam," Johnson suggested, holding her hand out to Adam to help him stand. In reply, Adam slapped Mrs. Johnson's hand away. He refolded his arms.

Johnson looked at Joey; clearly, they were facing a different Adam today. "Did his mother say if he took his meds?" Johnson asked Tam.

"She didn't say nothin'. She zoomed away as soon as he was out of the car," Tam answered.

"Adam, sweetie, did your mom give you your medication today?" Joey asked in as gentle of a voice as she could.

Adam narrowed his eyes at Joey. She hadn't felt fear around him before, but it was starting to bubble up. Adam didn't reply.

Johnson chewed on her lower lip as she thought about what they should do. "I'm going to guess that he didn't take his meds. I'll call Mom to confirm. She'll have to come back and get him if he hasn't had them."

Johnson went to Dunne's desk, where Adam's parents' phone numbers were prominently displayed on a yellow sticky note. When his mom didn't answer, Johnson left a pointed message for her to call the school immediately. When his dad didn't answer either, she left the same message, adding that she was very concerned that it appeared Adam hadn't had his medication that day.

The other students had broken themselves into their groups and went happily to their first activity centers. Every Monday began the same way, so the students would know what to expect. Adam hadn't yet moved from his carpet square, so Joey kept one eye on him as she went to the math table with Katie. Joey was certain she could hear his breathing becoming heavier and heavier—almost like a dog panting. Or a wolf.

Johnson called Mr. Matthews and informed him that Adam was out of sorts. Upon hearing that Adam was sitting on his carpet square relatively calmly, Mr. Matthews advised them to try and keep him relaxed while they waited for Mom or Dad to call back. This was the final mistake.

"But he doesn't appear relaxed," Johnson

explained. "He seems agitated. Can't someone come get him? Put him in isolation until we know for sure what's up?" Johnson asked.

Mr. Matthews's reply was that Adam wasn't being disruptive, so he had no cause for removal.

"I guess we'll wait until he gets disruptive then," Johnson said with frustration, and hung the phone up with a smack. "Okay, ladies. We wait for a phone call. In the meantime–" Her phone rang. "Hello? Yes, ma'am. He seems out of sorts. Did he take his medication today?" Pause. A frown. "I'm sorry, but you will have to come pick him up. He is not allowed to be here unmedicated." Another pause. A deeper frown. "No, that will not do! You need to come get him, now!" Johnson looked at Joey. "She hung up on me. She said she had to work until one and could not get here before then. Can you believe that?"

"Call Matthews," Tam called from the math table. "Now he has to come get him."

Mr. Matthews was in the middle of a parent meeting but promised to be there as soon as possible. Johnson requested the SRO and was told he was dealing with a drunken eighth grader, who was caught with a water bottle full of tequila. The eighth grader had started a fight in the locker room and the SRO was needed for crowd control. The secretary promised to send him there as soon as the fight deescalated. It was little comfort to the teachers in the FISH room. Adam had stood from the carpet and walked over to his backpack. He unzipped it, reached inside, and pulled out a very large rock.

"Adam, sweetie, please put the rock back into your bag," Joey requested.

"I'm going to get the other kids out of here," Tam said.

The other students were oblivious to Adam. They allowed themselves to be corralled into the adjoining classroom with no fuss. Adam, meanwhile, was studying his rock with intense focus, turning it round in his hands to examine it from all angles. Joey watched as he traced his fingers over the surface. Tam grabbed some books and a large Rubbermaid container full of Legos and shut the door behind her, leaving Johnson and Joey with Adam.

"I'll wait in here with him until Mr. Matthews arrives," Johnson said. "You go help Tam."

"I don't really want to leave you in here alone," Joey said.

"If Tam has a problem, we need more hands in there," Johnson said.

"You go. I'll wait here. He's in my group," Joey said, suspecting that she should have taken the chance to get out while she had it. Johnson nodded and left the room. She knew to take a way out when offered.

Adam remained near his backpack, staring eerily at the weapon in his hands. Joey took a seat in one of the chairs, so as not to appear threatening to Adam. Joey had an idea. "Adam, have you ever seen a rock that's been painted?" she asked. "They look so pretty. We can paint your rock, if you want to."

He looked up at her. "No."

"No, what? No, you've never seen a rock that's been painted? Or no you don't want to paint your rock?"

His eyes twitched back and forth as he stared at Joey. "No," he said again.

"Why don't you put your rock in your backpack to keep it safe while we wait for your mommy?"

"No Mommy!" Adam suddenly shouted. He raised his arm back and hurled the rock at Joey. Joey was far enough away that she had time to lean out of the way—barely—but she fell out of the chair in the process. The rock sailed past her with alarming power and smashed into the jar of pens on Mrs. Dunne's desk, sending them flying and making a horrible noise."

Johnson opened the door. "What happened? Are you okay?"

Adam had reached in the backpack and had another rock in his hand. He aimed this one at Johnson, who turned, but the rock connected with her shoulder. Even Joey heard the thud.

"Adam! Stop it!" Johnson yelled.

Adam had no more rocks in his pack, but he

began running around the room grabbing anything that was loose and throwing things alternatively at Joey and Johnson.

"Imma grab the jacket," Johnson said, heading for the closet. She pushed the call button on the way.

"Adam! Please stop!" Joey begged, ducking as he threw a large wooden block her way. "You're going to hurt us, and that's not nice!" Joey yelled. It was like trying to reason with a tornado.

The closet door was locked. "What the hell? I gotta find the key," Johnson said. She began a frantic search through Dunne's desk drawers.

At nearly the same time, Joey and Adam both noticed the rock on the floor near Mrs. Dunne's desk. They each made a run for it, Adam getting there a hair ahead of Joey. He snatched it and before Joey could stop him, flung it at the wall above the bookshelf, where it tore into Ivan's drawing.

"No! Adam! Stop it right now!" Joey screamed loudly. The sharp raise in her tone gave him pause for a split second, and she was able to grab his wrists, fury coursing through her. She held him tightly while Johnson, who finally found the key and unlocked the closet, wrapped the straitjacket around his body. He squirmed and kicked at them while they wrestled him to the ground. Over and over he repeated, "No! No! No!"

Joey sat on his legs so Johnson could fasten

the strap at the back of the wrap. Joey looked up. Mr. Matthews and the SRO were standing over them.

"A little trouble here?" Mr. Matthews said wryly.

"It's about time. Look around!" Johnson yelled. "I told you he was gonna explode!"

They climbed off Adam and helped him sit up. He flopped himself back to the ground as soon as Johnson let go of him. He lay, facedown into the carpet, screaming incoherently.

"No meds?" the SRO asked.

"Mom was running late and said she'd forgotten to give him his pill. Then she said she couldn't get here until one o'clock."

"Jeez," he said.

"What do we do?" Johnson asked.

"I'll sit with him until Mom arrives," the SRO said. "I'm not sure we can keep him in that jacket, though. If anyone were to see that, we'll be on the news."

"Look around," Johnson said again. "He was destroying the room and throwing things at us. He hit me with this." She held up the rock.

"Where'd he get rocks?" Mr. Matthews demanded almost accusingly at the teachers.

"His backpack," Joey said. "He brought them with him."

Mr. Matthews rolled his eyes. "Unbelievable. Are you okay?" he asked Johnson.

"My shoulder is gonna have a whopper of a bruise," she said. "But I'll be fine."

"Go to the nurse and get an ice bag," he instructed. "And tell her what's going on here."

Johnson gave Mr. Matthews a look that said, "I told you so," and left the room.

Joey inspected the damage to Ivan's picture, infuriated that he destroyed the one thing in the room that meant something to her. Up close it looked like she could repair it with her clear box tape. She felt tears well up from stress and disappointment.

"Are you okay?" Mr. Matthews asked.

"Yes. And no," Joey said. "I've never seen anything like that."

Adam lay face down on the rug. Mercifully he stopped screaming and now just looked like a burrito.

"Go get a drink of water or go to the break room and take a breather. I sent a para in with Tam. When you're ready, come back. We'll take him down to the office and he can wait there for his mom."

The SRO removed the jacket from Adam, who was now limp and listless. His energy was spent. He offered no struggle as the officer guided him from the room. Mr. Matthews followed, with Adam's backpack. Johnson returned as they were leaving, sporting an ice pack wrapped to her shoulder by an Ace bandage.

"Don't forget the rocks," Johnson called after them, and she handed off the two rocks.

Once the classroom door closed, Johnson's phone rang. She looked at the screen. "It's Adam's father." With more than a little aggravation in her tone, she informed him that he could find his son in the SRO's office awaiting pickup. There was satisfaction to be found in clicking off without saying goodbye. How could those parents let him go into the world without his meds? It was unfair to everyone.

Johnson and Joey quickly tidied up the classroom so the other students could return. Then Joey went to the break room and cried for ten straight minutes.

Adam did not return the next day. Nor the next. Mrs. Dunne was relieved that she could resume her supervisory duties from the comfort of her desk and told the teachers how sorry she was that she wasn't there for Adam's outburst. Joey didn't think she sounded all that sorry.

They got word on Thursday that Adam would be returning after the Thanksgiving Break, which was the following week. Everyone breathed a sigh of relief until they learned that Mrs. Rodriguez would be by with the district's attorneys for a debriefing on what happened.

After school, the attorney interviewed each teacher individually to take her statement.

"Why does it feel like we are the ones at

fault?" Joey asked Johnson, while they waited for their turns.

"Cause they gonna try and make it our fault," she replied. "They always do."

After each of the three teachers had been questioned, the attorney and Mrs. Rodriguez brought them all together.

"It is extremely unfortunate that Adam's mother did not administer his medication," the attorney began. "In the future, to prevent this from happening, we must stress that it is imperative that you ask the mother for verbal verification of medication before she drives away. If you had done that, we would have known right off the bat that he was unmedicated."

"You do realize that she sped off without saying a word to me?" Tam asked the haughty attorney.

"We just can't let that happen. You *must* ask her," the attorney said, placing a heavy and accusatory emphasis on "must."

"Are you gonna tell her that rule as well?" Johnson said. "Cause if she don't abide by the rules, we can't do anything about it. You want us to grab the bumper of the car and hold her there till she talks?"

"We will communicate this requirement to his parents as well," the attorney said. "Secondly, those rocks should never have been allowed in the classroom. They posed a great danger to everyone."

"Ya think?" Johnson cut in. Mr. Matthews gave her a scowl.

"His backpack must be inspected. Every day," Mrs. Rodriguez said.

Mrs. Dunne pursed her lips. "We are allowed to go through his backpack?"

"We'll get parent permission. We'll require it," Mrs. Rodriguez said.

"Hm," Mrs. Dunne said. "Anything else?"

"Um, yes," Mrs. Rodriguez continued. "Between now and next Monday, when he returns, we will be making some modifications to the classrooms at the end of your hall. The classrooms connected to 618 and the room across the hall will be remodeled. We are still working out some of the details, so we will fill you in when we know what it will look like."

"What kind of modifications?" Mrs. Dunne asked.

"Again, we are working out the details," Mrs. Rodriguez stressed. "We'll let you know."

"Adam will be back on his meds on Monday. His parents have to bring him into the office to meet with me first," Mr. Matthews said. "So, we know he will be calm on Monday. We will plan an after-school meeting Monday to discuss the changes and what they mean for your schedules."

"I don't like the sound of any of this," Johnson said, as they were dismissed from the meeting.

In past years, around this time of year, Joey

would chuckle at the funny memes posted on social media about how much teachers needed the Thanksgiving week to recuperate. Pictures of teachers racing from the school building to their cars, exhausted teachers slumped on their sofas, short rap songs poking fun at the many demands of teacher-life. She didn't give these expressions much thought, though, and had certainly never realized just how many of her classmates and other "friends" were in education. This year was different. She not only felt every teacher meme out there, but she was also shocked at how universal the problems of teachers were. Friends in Arizona, Texas, Michigan, and even Canada all faced the same struggles in the classroom.

"I can't believe how tired I am," she moaned to Craig on Friday night when school was finally over for nine whole days.

"You've got a nice break ahead of you," Craig promised. "What are you going to do with it?"

"Clean this house, for one thing," she noted. "I've really slacked off."

Craig gave her a squeeze. "Nope. I hired a company to come in and do a deep clean. They'll be here Monday. I want you to take a book, or your journal, and spend some time at Biltmore."

Joey gratefully looked up at her husband. "You always know what I need."

"What's the picture on the table?" Craig asked.

"I brought home Ivan's painting," Joey

confessed. "I'm going to try and repair it."

"Why don't you have it laminated?" Craig suggested. "Or framed? That'll preserve it better."

"Yes!" Joey said excitedly. "That's exactly what I'll do."

Joey's Thanksgiving week was filled with hours wandering the grounds of Biltmore, drinking coffee, decorating her house for the holidays, and cuddling with her husband on the couch. Craig's sister hosted Thanksgiving dinner, so she didn't even need to dirty her newly cleaned kitchen, except to make her famous banana pudding. By the time Sunday night rolled around, she was refreshed and ready for the stretch between Thanksgiving and Christmas.

"What on earth−?" she couldn't believe the sight before her when she walked into the classroom on Monday morning.

The two side-by-side classrooms had been turned into three. Mrs. Dunne's desk, four worktables, and the backpack storage cubbies were now the only things in the space that would have been their previous class. The other classroom had been reconfigured into an activity center space. The bookshelf, a new carpet, the toy bins, and other math and science manipulatives were there. Sandwiched between the two classrooms was now a third space, with doors that opened on either side.

The floor of the third space was not the standard classroom linoleum. It was a hard rubber surface. The walls were not cinderblock—nor even drywall—but were padded with one-inch folding mats like you see bolted to the walls in a gymnasium to keep basketball players from injuring themselves on wild plays. Four large foam blocks lined the wall, big enough to sit on or even lay across. Two giant rubber yoga balls were in the corner, and a swinging hammock-style chair hung from the ceiling.

"So what's all this?" Johnson said, coming up behind Joey. "The solution to our problems?"

"A padded room?" Tam said, incredulously. "Seriously? Who's this for? Them or us?"

Johnson snorted. "I hope us."

Mrs. Dunne came in with an armload of photocopies. "Not my idea," she said, heading off any questions. "Also, they've made a break room of sorts for us across the hall. It's got a refrigerator and microwave. So, we don't need to go far at lunchtime in case there is a problem."

"How's this going to work?" Johnson demanded.

"We have a meeting after school to find out. In the meantime, we'll run today like we normally would. We'll keep the doors to the padded room closed and take the kids around through the hallway to get to the centers."

"And Adam?" Tam asked.

"They're going to call when he gets here."

The phone on Mrs. Dunne's desk rang. "Fish room," she answered. She listened for a moment. "I'm sorry, what?" She looked at the other teachers. "Okay. Be right there."

"Adam's here?" Tam asked.

"No. Our new student is here," she replied, heading for the door.

"What new student?" Joey asked.

"Good question," Dunne replied.

DODIE

Anne's parents bought a cabin in Telluride when they were newly married, and it proved a profitable investment. Major holidays could be spent enjoying Colorado's favorite sport—skiing—with plenty of room for guests. This Thanksgiving, they invited Dodie and her pooches to spend the holiday there with their large and raucous bunch. Dodie wasn't able to ski, but she enjoyed lounging by the fireplace with Benny and Joon at her feet and a stack of books by her side while the rest of the family hit the slopes. In the evenings, they played board games and watched movies. She helped Anne's mom with the cooking, and when it was time to head back to Boulder, she realized she hadn't enjoyed a Thanksgiving so much since her grandma had died.

"So have you decided what you are going to do about the settlement?" Anne asked on the long drive back to Boulder.

"You mean, what to do with the money?" Dodie asked. Anne nodded. "I talked to a financial adviser—a guy Chris knows—and he suggested I don't rush into any big decisions. We're going to put the bulk of it in a money market account while I seek to understand my options. I'm going to keep working; keep being me."

"Good. I'd hate to lose you!" Anne said.

Dodie smiled. No one else at the office knew about the settlement, so it would be easy enough to continue with her life as she sought her emotional healing. She wondered how slow that would be in coming. Dodie was finding it increasingly difficult to sleep at night. Physical therapy was going fine; she was able to lift increasingly heavier things and could manage the pull on the leashes to take the dogs for short walks. Her bladder still caused some trouble, but it seemed to be heading the right direction. Anne would be moving back to her parents' house the following weekend. Physically, she was healing. However, her mind often wandered to imagining the children she would never carry. As a girl, she imagined having a home full of kids—siblings to care for one another. She appreciated all her grandma did for her, but orphan life was lonely. Now it seemed even lonelier. Being around Anne's three brothers these past few days reminded her of what she didn't have growing up, and what she would never experience moving forward. Sure, there were things that could possibly be done with her eggs, she still had her ovaries, but she'd never carry kids, never feel the weight of a baby on her hips. And it broke her heart.

"Whatcha thinking about, friend?" Anne asked with a worried look on her face.

"Honestly? My uterus," she answered.

"Interesting choice," Anne replied.

"Do you realize I am *barren*?" Dodie stretched out the word for emphasis. "Barren. I heard that word the other day on the Discovery Channel. It's such an ugly term. I am barren."

"It is an ugly word," Anne agreed. "Barren means unfertile, though, Dodes. They haven't said that you were not fertile."

Dodie brushed that comment away. "I'm not going to get my hopes up. The therapist that the hospital is paying for me to see keeps wanting me to paint a picture of my future. The trouble is, I can't. Every picture I want to paint has kids in it. When I think about my future, you know what I see? I see me—in the middle of a desert. And it isn't one of those cool deserts, like in Star Wars, with me bravely and determinedly facing the wind and the sandstorms of life. My desert is dry, cracked, and—barren. And I am in the middle of it—stagnant. I'm planted there with nothing around me."

"I know you, Dodes. That may be where you feel right now. But you won't stay there. And you aren't alone. You might feel alone. Your picture may not have anyone else in it right now. But we're there, standing just out of view of your frame of vision, and we're cheering you on. Believe me, you're in my picture."

Monday's back to work routine brought with it the first snow of the year. Feathery crystals rested gently everywhere, transforming the city into a white dreamland. Dodie had just refreshed her mug of coffee and settled into a stack of invoices which needed reconciling when her phone buzzed.

"Dodie, you have a visitor," the receptionist said.

Dodie grabbed her coffee mug. When she rounded the corner and saw who stood waiting for her, she nearly dropped it.

"Jason?" she queried. "What are you doing here?" She hadn't seen him since he checked her equipment prior to her fateful climb.

"Hey, Dodie. Is there somewhere we can talk?" he asked.

"I'm kinda at work right now," she opened the arm that didn't hold the coffee to indicate the office activity going on around her.

"Yeah. It's just—I don't—know—" he started to sob. Ridiculously. He covered his face with his hands.

The receptionist and Dodie looked at each other, shocked.

"Okay, Jason, come on in here." Dodie ushered him into the conference room and closed the door. He flopped into one of the chairs.

He reached over and snatched three tissues from the box on the conference table. He blew his nose so loudly Dodie was sure the entire lobby could hear. He honked twice more and still said nothing.

"Jason, what's going on?" she finally asked.

She chose a chair across from him. Dang, he was an ugly crier.

"Dodie, I don't know how to tell you this—" he began. Dodie had a pretty good idea what he was about to say, but she let him go through the motions. "Lucy left me about four weeks ago. She didn't give me any reason. Just said, 'I need a break.' I didn't push her too hard for answers. We'd been talking about having a baby, and I figured she just got spooked. I gave her some space, you know, to feel her freedom before being tied down with a baby."

Dodie's whole body tensed. *Did this idiot not understand what happened to her?* She bit her lip and felt her hands ball into fists.

Oblivious, Jason continued. "I hadn't been able to get a hold of her lately. She told me not to contact her—said she'll call me when she's ready to talk. She's not returning my texts. So, I waited outside her work and followed her yesterday. You know, she teaches three spin classes at the Fitness Palace," he added needlessly.

I don't give a crap about any of this, Dodie nearly said aloud. "What's your point, Jason?" There was more than a little irritation in her voice. It was lost on him.

He blew his nose again and dabbed his eyes before continuing. "I followed her to her new apartment. The car parked in the space next to hers was," he paused, either for effect or because he was afraid that saying aloud would make it real, "Aaron's."

Dodie didn't react. *So Lucy is the tramp he's living with. No big surprise*, she thought.

"Didn't you hear me?" Jason said incredulously. "I'm pretty sure Lucy and Aaron are living together."

"I knew he moved in with someone," Dodie said. "But he and I split up after my accident. My horrible accident." Dodie's anger kicked in, and Jason was about to feel the weight of it. "You do remember my accident, don't you, Jason? The one in which I nearly died? The one in which I lost my ability to ever carry children?"

He didn't seem to hear her. "I followed them to a sushi place. She always said she hated sushi."

"Jason!" she said sharply. He blinked dumbly. "I am so sorry you and Lucy won't be able to have kids. But, hey, you'll be able to find another wife and she can bear you some little Jasons, who hopefully won't be as clueless or as inconsiderate as you are. Lucy and Aaron deserve each other. Please get out of my office and do not come back here." As she spoke, she'd stood and moved her way to the conference room door.

Jason's face showed how stunned he was. "That's it? I'm supposed to just give up?"

Dodie opened the door. She pointed. "The depth of your stupidity is mind-boggling. Out."

He took his fistful of tissues and left.

Dodie returned to her desk. She hadn't been on social media much since the accident. She had posted some pictures of Benny and Joon, but that was about it. Now, she went to Jason's page. His profile picture was of he and Lucy on their honeymoon. A sapphire blue sky and golden beach surrounded their tanned, loving embrace. She tried to find Lucy's account but Lucy apparently blocked Dodie sometime over the last weeks. *Slut*, Dodie thought. She and Aaron deserved each other. Then she made the mistake of Googling her accident.

By the end of the day, Dodie was in an emotional slump. She felt useless, alone, and unwanted. She was snappy with Donna, Walt, and even avoided Anne in the break room. She left work without a goodbye to anyone.

That night, Dodie opened a bottle of pinot grigio and continued trolling the internet for signs of Aaron's life. He'd blocked her, too.

"I need some new friends, Joonie-girl," Dodie said with a bit of a slur from the wine. "I don't want to be stuck like Jason." Joon thumped her tail in reply.

She started scrolling through different social sites, looking for old friends from high school. She more she sipped her pinot, the more she determined that she needed to get some other people in her life, and behind the computer screen was as good a place as any to start, wasn't it?

A former friend from her high school soccer

team was the first to reply to her IMs.

Jules: Dodie! So good to hear from you. Whatcha up to?
Dodie: Not much. Work. Sleep. Repeat.
Jules: LOL! Me too. How's married life?
Dodie: Not married anymore. Didn't work out.
Jules: Damn! I'm sorry. What happened?
Dodie: Long story. He doesn't deserve me.
Jules: Jerk
Dodie: IK. How r u?
Jules: Really good. Livin the dream
Dodie: LOL. Nice. Want to get together sometime?
Jules: Would love that! Let's go out for drinks Friday.
Dodie: Kk. Text me.

Dodie's whole body relaxed into the mattress when she laid down that night. Jason can stay screwed up if he wants to. His visit heightened her confidence that she had indeed made the right decision. Now she just needed to find her purpose for the next chapter in her life. Cloudy-headed, she drifted off to sleep.

Dodie and Jules met up at a dimly lit bar known for playing alternative music from the 90s—Dodie's favorite genre. They sat together at a small metal table with a clear view of the dance floor, sipped their drinks—rum and Coke for Dodie and vodka with cranberry for Jules–and laughed as they reflected on their high school days.

"And then there was that time Pete Gomez broke into the girls' locker room and stole Jemma Phillips's bra from her locker while she was in the shower–remember that?" Jules snorted with amusement.

"She was so mad," Dodie recalled. "If I remember, Jemma was not a little girl." Dodie held her hands in front of her chest to indicate large breasts. "She walked the halls holding her books in front of her all day to hide the fact that she had no bra on."

"I still remember the look on Mr. Moody's face when she walked into chemistry class." Jules made a mock shocked face to mimic their old teacher. They giggled.

"Man, it's good to catch up with you. Feels like no time at all has passed," Jules slammed back the remainder of her drink. "I'll go grab a couple more."

The rum was already swimming around Dodie's head, but she didn't object to Jules's offer to get another. "Losing My Religion" blared from the speakers and her thoughts were starting to feel thick.

Catching up with Jules brought some laughs, but they were laughing about things from a lifetime ago. Did she really think Jemma Phillips going through the school day with no bra ten years ago was something to laugh about now? Dodie was a different person than she was in high school, wasn't she?

"What next?" Jules asked, setting a drink in front of her.

"High school was so long ago. Tell me what you're up to now. What do you do for a living?"

Jules shrugged. "Shit, I don't do much. I work at Whole Foods. The one on Pearl Street. It sucks, and my boss is a dick. But what are you gonna do? Hey, do you smoke?"

Dodie shook her head. "No, cigarettes make my stomach churn."

"No, girl. I mean weed," Jules laughed.

"Oh!" Dodie felt stupid and took a big swig of her drink. "Not really. I've never gotten into it."

"Well, what do you do for fun then?" Jules challenged.

"I go to work. I take my dogs on hikes. I used to rock climb and kayak quite a bit—but it's been a while." Jules didn't look impressed; Dodie suddenly felt pathetic. Here she was, 26 years old, no family, drinking in a bar with a person she hadn't seen in more than eight years. Someone she didn't even really know. What did they really have in common?

Dodie was just about to make an excuse to leave, but Jules broke into her thoughts. "Hey, Smoke Club's just down the block, you want to go?"

"Smoke Club?"

"Yeah," Jules clarified. "Come on, let's go. It'll be dope. You look like you need a little fun."

She got up and turned to go. Grandma's face flashed in Dodie's mind's eye. Grandma was furious when cannabis was legalized in Colorado and made no small secret that she didn't want Dodie to ever think smoking pot was something to be recreational about.

"It alters your mind and your mood," Grandma would say. *"And that's dangerous, no matter which way you look at it. Stay in control of who you are, Dodie. Promise me."*

But Grandma wasn't here now. Grandma left her. Rum-buzzed Dodie spoke back to Grandma. "Sorry, Grandma. I need some mind and mood alteration. I don't like either at the moment." Dodie downed the rest of her drink and followed Jules.

Dodie was flying again with the green dragon, but it was raining. Her cheeks were wet, and a foul odor filled her nostrils. She blinked her eyes. A golden retriever blinked back at her. *Benny?* No, not Benny. Then he licked her cheek. She scrunched her face. "Who are you?" she asked the dog. He whimpered and licked her cheek again.

Awareness came upon her, like a dimmer switch being slowly cut on. She was lying in a strange room on a bed she did not know. Panic jerked her upright, but a throbbing pain in her head forced her back down.

"Woah. Ouch," she muttered. She sat up again, more slowly. Her alarm increased. The room was plain. White painted walls. A window covered in sad beige miniblinds revealed that wherever she was, she was on the second floor. She did not recognize the street below. A dark wooden dresser held an assortment of personal grooming products that looked like—men's products? Then she noticed the sound of a shower running from behind a closed door.

"Where the hell am I?" she said aloud. She was dressed, but her clothes were disheveled. Her leggings and panties were intact, a good sign. Her bra was undone under her t-shirt, but not off. She stood, hooking her bra and straightening her clothes. She left the bedroom, finding herself in a small living room that had a pitifully small galley kitchen in the corner. Clearly, she was in an apartment. But whose?

The water in the shower cut off. She saw her purse on the narrow ledge that separated the living room from the kitchen and her shoes on the ground near the door. Snatching up her purse, she checked inside. Phone and wallet both there. So were her keys. She looked at the golden retriever. "What did I do?" she asked it while slipping on her shoes. He yawned in reply. She quietly opened the apartment door and escaped before learning who was in the bathroom.

She was on the middle floor of a three-flat. She trotted gingerly down the stairs and out the front door into the sunlight. No sign of her car. She scampered around the corner to get out of sight of the apartment before looking at her phone's GPS to figure out where she was. It was a neighborhood she didn't know. "How the hell did I get here?" she wondered. And like a bucket of water had been thrown in her face she suddenly realized she'd been out all night, it was morning, and Benny and Joon were at home waiting for her.

"Oh, no!" she yelled. There was a coffee shop on the corner. She noted the address and called an Uber. She'd have to find her car after she took care of her babies. She wanted to smack herself for being so careless.

After feeding Benny and Joon and cleaning up the inevitable poop they couldn't hold in, she allowed herself to replay what she could remember. She and Jules walked down the block from the bar to the smoking club. It was loud. The air was thick, permeated with marijuana smoke. *Did she smoke?* She remembered Jules getting them a couple of draft beers from the bar. Then Jules took out a joint and lit it. She handed it to Dodie.

"Ah, crap, I smoked pot," she confessed to Benny, who had his head on her knee. He sensed her despondency and hadn't left her side. "I am such a jerk. I'm so sorry, baby," she said. "I shouldn't have been so irresponsible when I had you guys waiting here for me." She rubbed his head. For the life of her though, she couldn't remember anything past smoking with Jules. What would have possessed her to leave the bar with a stranger?

In hopes that her car was still near the first bar where she originally met Jules, she called another Uber. She breathed a sigh of relief when her Jeep came into view right where she'd left it. Once safely back in her townhouse with her Jeep tucked in the garage, she decided it was time to see what happened to Jules.

Dodie: Hey - are you alright?

Two hours later, Jules finally replied.

Jules: Girl, I just got up. That was some good shit!
Dodie: WDYM?
Jules: The dope. From the bartender. lol.
Dodie: ??
Jules: In our drinks. 2 enhance the high.
Dodie: There was something in our beer?
Jules: oc - didn't you feel it?
Dodie: Who'd I leave with?
Jules: Didn't get his name? lol! Hot guy. Nice ass.
Dodie: Why'd you let me go?
Jules: I ain't your momma. lol
Dodie: What'd you do?
Jules: Went 2 another club. Hooked up with the DJ. Thanks for a fun time. We should totally do it again next weekend. lol

Dodie wanted to take Jules's LOLs and shove them up her—Wait. *Jules drugged her? Then let her leave with an unknown guy?*

Now that Jules was awake, she took it upon herself to post to her 472 followers the worst picture Dodie could have imagined. Dodie looked spaced out and had one arm thrown across the shoulders of a guy who was clearly holding a joint. The caption read: "Took my new BFF out for a good time! #smokeclub #legalizedpot #hellya"

Dodie wanted to die.

JOEY

In the five minutes it took Mrs. Dunn to retrieve the new student from the office, Tam and Johnson roller coastered through a variety of emotions, all negative.

Outrage: "How can they dump a new student on us when we have so much going on?"

Fear: "What if this one is worse than Adam?"

Hopelessness: "It's just one more kid we won't be able to do nothin' with."

Resignation: "Figures."

Joey, after listening to their diatribe against the system, decided to be a voice of hope. "What if this student is a sweet kid who is a joy to teach?"

They looked at her like her hair was on fire. "Russo, you keep living with your head in the sky, you gonna fall into a hole," Johnson shook her head in pity.

"I just don't want to decide this student is all bad before we've even met him. Or her."

"You always looking for the sunshine and rainbows, girl," Johnson said.

Before they could say more, the classroom door opened. Mrs. Dunne shuffled in, followed by a boy holding the hand of a man who Joey presumed was the boy's dad. The boy was small—not nearly as tiny as Travis—but small for a sixth-grader. He was slender, with blonde hair and blue eyes that looked cautiously around the room. Joey could see the boy squeezing Dad's hand more tightly as they came further into the class. In his other hand he held a green water bottle.

"Mrs. Tam, Mrs. Johnson, Mrs. Russo, this is Evan and his dad, Mr. Rivers," Mrs. Dunne made introductions to which the ladies all smiled politely.

"Please, call me Jeremy," the dad said, offering his hand in greeting to each of the women. Evan grabbed it again quickly when he was done.

"It's okay, buddy," Jeremy said, "these nice ladies are going to take care of you here at school. I'll come back and get you at 3:45."

Evan turned to his dad, burying his face into Jeremy's flannel shirt. A muffled, "No, Daddy, peeze, no," nearly broke Joey's heart.

Joey set her coffee mug down and stooped in front of Evan. "Hi Evan. I'm Mrs. Russo. But you can call me Joey if you'd like. Can I hold your hand for a while until your dad comes back?"

Evan eyed her coffee mug then turned his face toward Joey and studied her with his wet blue eyes. He released his grasp of Jeremy's shirt and offered one hand to Joey. The other still clutched the water bottle. But he didn't move.

"Transitions are really difficult for Evan," Jeremy explained. "As I was telling Mrs. Dunne, he has trouble letting go of one thing to move on to another, even if it's something he really enjoys. It's a condition of his autism that I haven't been able to help him through."

"What can we do to help him?" Joey asked.

At that moment the phone shrilled from Mrs. Dunne's desk. She scooted over to answer it, learning the news they least wanted to hear. Adam had arrived. She left the room again.

Joey looked at Jeremy, waiting for an answer. He looked at Evan, hesitantly. "Evan, can you please go sit over there for a minute so I can talk with your teacher?"

Evan nodded sadly. He released his hold on Joey and walked to the bookshelf. He picked up one of the Arthur books and sat on the ground. He hugged it to his chest along with the water bottle, shut his eyes and began to rock back and forth, humming.

Jeremy lowered his voice. "Evan's mom passed away recently. We moved here from Wilmington to be closer to my parents. He was very attached to her. The water bottle—it was hers—and he won't let it out of his sight. He gets very distressed if he can't find it. Like I said, he always has struggled with going from one thing to another—or one place to another—but it's been worse since Hallie died. She knew how to help him work through transitions. She could count him down, prepare him. I'm trying, but it's hard, you know?" He ran a hand through his brown hair. His own blue eyes were tired. Joey guessed he was probably no more than thirty-five. He'd clearly come into his "good-looking grown-up" years, and Joey wondered if he and his wife were high school sweethearts, like she and Craig had been. She couldn't imagine losing Craig—but then she stopped her thought. She *had been* on the losing end of a deep love. But instead of her spouse, she'd lost her child. Was one easier than the other? She imagined not. All loss brought pain.

"Mrs. Russo? Are you okay?" Tam said.

Joey realized they were all looking at her. She had tears in her eyes. "Sorry," she said, she grabbed a tissue and wiped her eyes. "I got lost in my thoughts there for a minute. I, too, have lost someone who meant the world to me," she explained.

Jeremy locked eyes with her and nodded. She determined then that she would do everything she could to help Evan.

Joey was just taking a meatloaf from the oven when Craig arrived home from work.

"Meatloaf?" Craig said enthusiastically, wrapping his arms around Joey from behind. "You must have had a very good day. Or you've crashed the car again."

Joey turned and hugged him. "I did not crash the car. Someone backed into me. And that was once. When I was twenty-seven."

After they filled their plates with meatloaf, mashed potatoes, and biscuits and said grace, Craig asked, "So was it a good day?"

She took a big bite of her dinner before answering. "It was a very good day. Adam was medicated. And we got a new student. Craig, he is so sweet. His mom passed away recently, and he is hurting. But he let me hold his hand. He has a speech impairment, and the others have trouble understanding him, but I'm figuring it out. For example, his R sounds come out like W sounds. And he doesn't do well with Ls. He calls me, 'Woffey.' I don't know if that's a cross between Russo and Joey or what. I think I'll be able to teach him things once he relaxes a bit and gets used to the routine. Keeping to a strict routine is going to be so important for him because he struggles with transitions. I downloaded a countdown clock for my iPad, so he can see how long until−" she stopped.

"What's wrong, babe?" Craig asked.

"I'm an idiot," she set down her fork and put her head in her hands. "I'm a complete idiot."

"Joey. What is it?"

"The routine! I've spent all this time complaining about the routine. But it is exactly what Evan needs. The routine helps him understand the parts to his day. I'm a horrible teacher."

Craig laughed. "You are only an idiot if you believe that. Joey, you have used your passion to figure out how to help these students learn. What is it you told me you ask yourself every day−what is best for the kids?" She nodded. "You realized that no one believed in these students. The routine did need changing. Not the existence of routine, but what the routine stood for. You're doing that. Don't be so hard on yourself."

Late into the night Joey laid awake thinking about what Craig said. The existence of routine was necessary. But what the routine consisted of needed adjusting. She envisioned the different activities she could plan for Evan, while giving him clarity in his routine and considered how to make transitions between the activities easier for him. She felt hope rise in her chest again; hope that hadn't been there since Ivan died. She drifted off to sleep and dreamt that she was painting a large ocean themed mural on the wall of a coffee shop.

That Friday, Joey pulled out the paint during free time. She showed Evan the pictures of the fish on the wall and asked if he wanted to paint his own fish picture.

"Yes, Woffey," he said. He looked like he wanted to, but something held him back. For inspiration, Joey placed a large picture book filled with ocean creatures before him. He took the book and sat in the beanbag chair, turning pages determinedly, as if looking for something. When he got to the end, he set the book down and began to cry.

"What's wrong, Evan?" Joey asked. "What are

you looking for?"

"Heart fish," Evan said through his tears. It came out more like "Ard fish," but Joey tried to hear him through the speech impediment.

"Heart fish?" Joey repeated. "Is that what you said? What's a heart fish?"

Evan closed his eyes and grabbed his water bottle. He hugged it tightly and repeated, "Heart fish, heart fish, heart fish," until he fell asleep.

That night, Joey scoured the internet looking for a heart fish. She thought she hit the jackpot when she found some cute pictures of goldfish shaped like hearts, but when she showed them to Evan on Monday, he shook his head and cried.

The teachers had to admit, the new configuration for the FISH room did add variety to the students' schedule. The padded room was used as a space where a student with too much energy for classroom activities could have some alone time to let off steam. They could literally bounce off the walls without hurting themselves or anyone else. In their discussions with district personnel, it was suggested that if Adam became violent again, the teachers should corral him into the padded room, closing him inside until help could arrive.

"You mean lock him in there alone?" Tam asked.

"Have someone watch him from the window, but we would rather you isolate him there than wrestle him into the jacket," Mrs. Rodriguez explained.

"And what if he refuses to go into to room?" Johnson had asked.

Mr. Matthews had sighed loudly. "Just do your best to get him in there as opposed to sitting on him."

But it was the other students who used the room daily. On his medication, Adam was lethargic. He barely had the energy to get through the day, much less bounce anywhere. He completed all his work quickly and when he was done, he napped.

"Do you think we should let him sleep so much?" Joey asked Tam one day. Adam was curled up in a beanbag chair snoring softly.

"Haven't you heard the saying, 'let sleeping dogs lie'?" Tam responded.

"He's not a dog, though, he's a boy. And this is school. I don't know what he can possibly be learning here," Joey countered.

"Learning? Are you kidding me? We just need to survive with this one."

"But he hasn't been violent, not even once since he came back. A what point do we treat him like the others?" As frightened as she'd been of Adam, and as angry as he'd made her when he tore Ivan's painting, she felt he was being done a disservice. The sleepy, compliant boy who showed up every day deserved something more than what he was getting.

"Look, Russo," Tam said firmly. "When you've been around a few years, then come talk to me. Trust me. Kids like this need more than we can give them. His parents are thrilled that he can stay here all day and we ain't callin' them to come pick him up. That's all they want. They don't care if he learns anything. He's gonna be on medication probably forever."

"Forever?" Joey asked. "Don't they do any other therapy with him to help him with his violence?"

Tam shrugged. "Who knows? It's not our business. I guess we do have to wake him for lunch, though. It's almost time to go to the cafeteria. C'mon."

Joey couldn't shake what Tam said. On medication forever? It made sense, though. He was at school all day. Both of his parents worked. When would they have time to take him to therapy?

The first week of December brought Katie's birthday. Her mom had sent gluten-free, dairy-free, peanut-free, everything-free cupcakes to school to celebrate, and she wore a new headband with Hello Kitty ears sprouting up from red plastic. The teachers decided to give the cupcakes to the students in the cafeteria after lunch. While the FISH room kids finished up their meals and Joey cleared their garbage away, Johnson set a drab brown cupcake cradled in a pink foil wrapper in front of each student. Since frosting was not an option, Katie's mom printed images of Hello Kitty in various playful poses, cut them out, and taped them onto toothpicks which rose up out of the top of each one.

"Sing?" Katie asked.

"Okay, Katie, just a minute. We'll sing before eating our cupcakes. Lucas – don't lick your cupcake until we sing!" Johnson scolded. She placed the last one in front of Evan, who eagerly set his water bottle down and grabbed up the cupcake.

"We'll sing Happy Birthday on the count of three. One, two, three," Tam said.

Even though the kids rarely participated in the "Days of the Week" song, they sure knew how to belt out Happy Birthday. Joey couldn't help but smile, her heart warmed at the sound. Just then, though, general ed students started filing into the cafeteria for the next wave of lunches.

"Hey, I didn't know retards can sing," Joey heard someone say. Her head whipped around. She caught the eye of a tall red-haired boy wearing a grey "Polk Athletics" hoodie with the number 21 and the name "Miller" sloppily scrawled in black Sharpie on the front. He grinned at Joey and began his own version of the happy birthday song, singing as if he had a speech impediment. Joey fumed.

"What's your first name?" she demanded of the kid. He finished the last line of the song extra loudly and opened his arms for emphasis. He laughed in Joey's face and kept walking. She started after him, but Tam called her back.

"You can't leave your group," she said. "Let him go. They won't do nothin' to him anyway."

"He used the 'r' word!" Joey was outraged. "Did you hear him? He can't use that word. He can't make fun of our kids."

Katie, Evan, and Lucas were looking at her.

"Woffey? More?" Evan asked, holding up his empty wrapper.

"Only one for now, Evan," Joey said. He nodded and picked up his water bottle.

"He sang happy birthday to me," Katie said. She seemed proud to have been noticed, oblivious of the mockery. "It's my birthday." She smiled and popped the last bite of cupcake in her mouth.

Joey took in their sweet faces. She gazed across the cafeteria at the kid, whose attention was now elsewhere. She sighed.

Joey found her feet taking her down the athletics hallway on her way to her car after school. She didn't know who she was going to talk to or what she was going to say, but her body was on a trajectory toward the gym, and she guessed she'd figure it out when she got there. She could hear the pounding of gym shoes on the floor as she pulled open the heavy orange door to the large gym. Twenty or so male students were engaged in basketball drills, while the coaches looked on from various spots around the court. The Black Bear Creek cheerleaders were practicing their chants on the sidelines. It was a stereotypical middle school gym scene. Young teens doing the things young teens do. Joey's heart hurt a bit as she looked around, realizing these were the kinds of things her students would never get to do. She blew out a big puff of air. *You can do this,* she told herself.

A quick size up told her which of the three coaches scattered around the room was in charge. Only one had a clipboard. She figured he was a good place to start. She walked to him with purposeful strides.

"Coach. Got a minute?" she asked. Firm, but kind.

"Um, sure, Mrs.—"

"Russo. Joey Russo," she held out her hand and they shook. His hand was thick and hot.

"What can I do for you?" he queried, shifting his clipboard to underneath his armpit and crossing his arms in front of his chest protectively. It was almost as if he anticipated she was there to say something he didn't want to hear.

"I am one of the teachers of the exceptional students," she began. "I'm in room 618. The FISH room. Today at lunch, one of your athletes—number 21—made an extremely derogatory remark to one of our students."

"Hm. What he did say?" the coach asked skeptically.

"We were celebrating one of the student's birthdays. As he came into the cafeteria, the kids were singing. He rudely called out, 'I didn't know *blank* could sing,'" Joey paused for his reaction.

"Blank? What's that mean?" the coach asked.

"No. He didn't say the word blank. He said the 'r' word," Joey clarified.

"The 'r' word?" the coach asked. "What's that?"

"The 'r' word," Joey huffed. Then she whispered, "Retards."

The coach scrunched up his mouth and Joey was pretty sure he was trying not to smile. She narrowed her eyes, challenging him.

He nodded slowly. "You're telling me you are upset because Tray said the word 'retards.'"

"I'm telling you that one of your athletes disrespected a fellow student, and it is not okay." She put extra emphasis on the word "not."

"Did he push anyone or do any damage?"

Joey sensed his impatience. Clearly, he wanted this conversation to be over.

"No, he didn't push anyone. Was there damage? I am sure the special needs students emotionally do not like hearing themselves referred to in that way," Joey's voice was getting louder.

"I will talk with Tray; would that make you happy?" the coach asked.

"Would that make me happy?" Joey's voice was starting to shake. "It depends. What are you going to say?"

"I'll tell him to not talk loud like that around those kids." The coach nodded, actually thinking this was taking care of the problem. Joey was sick to her stomach.

"*Those kids*? Seriously?" she was incredulous. "Unbelievable." She turned on her heel and stomped from the gym, slamming the orange door with all her might on the way out.

The next morning, Mrs. Dunne pulled Joey aside. "Hey, next time you have a problem with another teacher, come tell me first."

"Are you talking about my conversation with the coach?" Joey asked, shocked. "How did you even hear about that?"

Mrs. Dunne smirked. "I'm married to that old fart. He couldn't wait to tell me about you chewing him out on the basketball court. Don't do that again."

Joey's eyes widened. "Are you kidding me? He seemed to think it was okay to call our kids, you know. What would you do if it were your son being made fun of?"

Mrs. Dunne's smile faded. "Look. We can't police everybody. We just do our jobs. Just do your job."

"I thought my job included protecting our students," Joey said quietly. Dunne had no reply. As she walked away, Dunne's hand protectively rubbed her shoulder, where Joey had seen the tattoo.

DODIE

Dodie laid on the couch for the better part of Saturday, getting up only to feed the dogs and let them out. She was embarrassed at her behavior and disappointed in herself. It was small consolation that she was 99 percent sure that she didn't have intercourse with the pot-smoking stranger. She thought with horror that she didn't even know if it was okay to have intercourse. How long do you wait after a hysterectomy? She made a note to ask at her next appointment, not that she planned to put herself in that position again.

Just after seven, she got a text from Jules.

Jules: Hot band playing 2nite at Club SFX. U in?

Dodie left her on read while she tried to figure how to respond. Jules allowed Dodie to be drugged, and then—Dodie stopped the thought. *No, I allowed myself to be drugged.*

"Darn it, Benny," she said aloud. "It's my own damn fault." Benny cocked his head at her expletive. He jumped off the couch and sought out Joon. Dodie typed back to Jules:

Dodie: Sorry. I can't. I have plans.

It wasn't true, but she didn't want to be completely rude. Lesson learned. No more clubbing with Jules. She opened Instagram. Dodie had an inbox message from another friend from high school she'd contacted earlier in the week but hadn't heard back from.

Alison: hi dodie! great to hear from u.

Dodie stared at the screen for a minute. Alison was decent enough in high school. Smart, athletic, kind to others. Dodie thought about clicking off without answering, but she was the one who first reached out. It would be bad manners to ghost off without responding. Dodie looked at Alison's Instagram posts, which were scarce. She hadn't posted since before the COVID pandemic.

Dodie: Hey there Ali. Great to hear back. How are u? Still in Boulder?
Alison: sure am. i work at chautauqua park.
Dodie: I love that place! What do u do?
Alison: im a rec team member – we do all kinds of outdoor stuff. i love it.

Dodie smiled. Maybe this was a good idea after all. If Ali worked for the city parks department, maybe they had some things in common. They chatted back and forth for a bit, Dodie telling Ali about her job, Ali telling Dodie about the city park and also about some other friends she'd kept in touch with from high school. Then Ali asked the question Dodie knew would come.

Alison: so r u married? kids?
Dodie: Not married. I have my dogs. We do a lot of hiking.

The hiking part wasn't exactly true as of late, but she wanted to start up again. The snow and cooler temps drive some people indoors, but Dodie was always lured to spend more time outside as winter set in.

Dodie: We could meet up on a trail sometime?
Alison: yaaas! how about tmw?

Dodie had no Sunday plans. Assumedly she'd be past the hangover which was causing her head to still pound, despite the Tylenol and Gatorade she'd been gulping all day. Did she have a reason not to go? No chance of being drugged while hiking the trails of Chautauqua Park. She glanced at Benny and Joon, who were now curled up yin-yang style by the patio door. Yup. She'd go.

Dodie: Sounds great!

They exchanged text numbers and agreed to meet in the morning at a popular trail Dodie knew well. Dodie hoped this attempt to make a new friend would go better than her meet up with Jules.

Benny whimpered as Dodie leashed up Joon and packed a small sling bag with water, peanuts, and a couple of dog poop bags. He was the bigger and stronger of the two, and for her first long hike since the accident, Dodie thought it would be better to have Joon accompany her.

"Sorry, boy." She patted him on the head. He sulked away, knowing he was not going. She watched him settle down in a patch of sunlight streaming in from the kitchen window and then headed out, Joon at her side.

"Hey, Dodie," a male voice came from behind her as she was locking the front door.

"Jeez!" she jumped out of her skin as she turned around. Joon let out a low growl, causing Benny to start barking from inside the house. When Dodie saw that it was only Jason, she shushed Joon. "It's okay, girl. Jason, what are you doing here? I'm on my way out."

The stubble on Jason's face and shaggy, unkempt hair may have been attractive on some men, but it gave Jason the haggard look of a man who had seen better days. He stuffed his hands in his coat pockets. "I was wondering if maybe we could talk," he said meekly. He reeked of pot.

Dodie pushed past him, heading toward her car. Did he not remember that the last time she saw him, she called him stupid? "I can't right now. I'm meeting a friend. See you later, Jason." She didn't pause for him to reply. Joon leapt up in the driver's side ahead of Dodie and hopped over to the front passenger seat. Dodie gave Jason a half-hearted wave as she backed out of the driveway.

"What was that about, girl?" she mused to Joon. Joon growled again. She sincerely hoped Jason showing up at her house would not become a regular thing. She had nothing to say to him and couldn't possibly imagine what they had to talk about. The past weekend's behavior aside, she knew she was in a better place without Aaron. A small stab in her heart reminded her, though, that she was likely never going to have a baby to share her life with, and that thought caused her stomach to tighten and a sob to escape her throat. She choked it back and drove to the park.

As she turned in, Dodie saw Ali's described navy Trailblazer and pulled into the parking spot beside it. There was no sign of Ali, and Dodie assumed maybe she'd gone inside the small restroom station off to the right. She unloaded Joon from the car, tightened the laces on her sneakers, and slung her bag over her shoulder. A minute later a woman emerged from the restrooms.

"Oh!" Dodie said aloud.

Ali smiled when she saw Dodie and walked toward her. But Dodie was frozen in spot. Ali wore an adorable mint green parka and black leggings.

With her white knit cap and matching scarf casually looped around her neck, she looked like she belonged in a magazine. A maternity magazine. Ali was noticeably pregnant.

"Dodie! Hi!" Ali gave her a hug, which Dodie did not return. Dodie felt her whole body tense up as Ali's belly brushed against her. She clutched tightly to Joon's leash. "I'm sorry, I'm a hugger," Ali gushed. "After COVID and all, you never know who you can hug and who you can't. I should have asked."

"Oh. No, it's fine," Dodie said, scrambling to make her brain work. "I just, um, don't want to hurt you." It sounded more like a question.

Ali laughed easily and placed a mittened hand on her stomach. "Oh, I'm fine! I'm barely six months along, if you can believe it. I look like I'm ready to pop, but baby has about 12 weeks to go."

Dodie bit her lip and nodded. "That's great." Again, it sounded more like a question. *What were these feelings she was having?*

They started walking the nearby trail. Ali took a water bottle from her pocket and gave a swig. She talked faster than Dodie's thoughts could keep up.

"Yeah, the doctor said hiking and exercise are just fine, and staying in shape will make delivery easier when the time comes. My husband is home with our other baby, but he usually brings the trail stroller and comes with me. I told him, though, not today! I'm getting reacquainted with an old friend. He pouted a little; he hates leaving me. I know he'll worry continually until I get back home, but he'll get over it. I'll let him massage my feet or something later." She laughed, pausing for a breath.

"Other baby?" Dodie managed to ask. This felt like a nightmare.

"Yes! Bradley junior was just three months old when we found out I was pregnant again. For some reason I didn't think you could get pregnant while breastfeeding, but apparently that is a myth. So, keep that in mind when it's your turn!"

Dodie didn't know what to say. How'd she miss in their chat over IM that Ali was married, had a baby, and was pregnant? She realized she didn't ask those kinds of questions when they chatted. Was that a conscious decision or gross oversight? Well, she certainly didn't know she'd feel this way.

They walked a three-mile loop through the park, sticking to the marked trail and watching for slick spots. Ali talked incessantly about her life with Brad, who, for all intents and purposes, was the quintessential husband. Dodie made active listening noises with her mouth, but her mind was disconnected. The more Ali talked, the worse Dodie felt. She couldn't describe what was going on inside of her, but she knew it wasn't good. By the time they headed into the last half mile, Dodie was balancing a fine line between holding it together and falling completely apart. She didn't want to fall apart in front of Ali.

"Um, I didn't see any family pictures on

Instagram," Dodie said.

"Oh goodness, I never use that account anymore," Ali explained. "I only noticed your message notification because I had seen this amazing sushi chef on Good Morning America, and they gave out her Instagram account. She posted the recipes that she shared on the show, and I thought it would be a wonderful surprise to make fresh homemade sushi for Brad. That's when I noticed your message."

"Fresh homemade sushi for Brad? How wonderful," Dodie said dryly. Uh-oh. She heard an ugly tone in her voice.

"Um, yeah," Ali said, a touch of hesitation in her words. Apparently, she heard the tone too. "Are you okay?"

Dodie felt the tears coming. *No, no, no.* She willed them to stay down. "I'm fine," she said. "I, um, had a bad sushi experience once." She took a big drink of her water, hoping to distract her brain and stabilize her emotions.

They finished the hike in silence. Ali didn't attempt another hug as they said goodbye, and she made what Dodie knew was an empty promise to "do this again sometime." Dodie watched Ali drive away. She looked at Joon, who sat happily in the passenger seat.

"Oh, girl," she said, before bursting into tears.

Later that day, Dodie recognized the emotion

she'd been fighting since seeing Ali's perfect pregnant figure and hearing about her perfect married life. When Dodie was growing up, whenever she wanted something that someone else had—the latest Nikes or the newest iPhone—Grandma would say, *"You know, Dodie, more men die of jealousy than of cancer."*

Dodie always hated when Grandma said that because she knew it meant she was not going to get whatever it was that she wanted. But as she stroked Benny's head absently while watching last week's Chicago PD on Peacock, she knew that's what she felt. Bitter. Jealous. Resentful. Neither Anne nor Sherry had kids. Yet. When they did, would she feel this way around them, too?

She watched as Jay Halstead sat alone at the end of a bar, drinking away the pain from his latest relationship. She went to the kitchen and poured herself a glass of wine. One glass became two, and before she knew it, it was Monday morning, and she was about to be late for work.

"Sorry, sorry, sorry," Dodie uttered as she slipped into the Monday morning meeting, which was well underway in the conference room. Everyone was at their usual spot around the large wooden table. She frowned as she plunked heavily in her seat near the front of the table to the right of Chris. Walt was in the process of giving an update on the orders scheduled for installation that week, with sales reps lending insight as needed. Dodie pretended to listen as she got her thoughts together for her part of the Monday meeting. Her head was pounding. When called upon, Dodie gave a respectable update on orders scheduled for invoicing that week and recapped the customers who were more than 90 days past due. She silently gave thanks that she'd run all her reports Friday before leaving the office and thought she made a good show of contributing her part.

After the meeting though, Anne followed Dodie back to her desk. "Hey, are you okay?"

Dodie tried to sound casual, but she felt like she'd been hit by a train. "I'm good. Why?"

"You look pale. Like you do when you are about to get sick." Anne paid too much attention sometimes.

"Annie, I'm fine. I took something to help me sleep last night and I didn't hear my alarm," she brushed off Anne's concerns. Her response was partly true. She just left out the part that it was a bottle of wine that helped her sleep.

Anne gave her friend a hug. "You know, if you ever need to call me, even if it is two in the morning, I am here for you. Your phone number always rings through."

Dodie nodded thoughtfully and watched her friend walk away. It was not a weekend to be proud of. But something inside of her hurt, and she wasn't sure what to do about it.

JOEY

Evan's ARD meeting is on Wednesday," Mrs. Dunne informed Joey. "You'll need to prepare some notes on the kind of support you are giving him in the classroom. You'll be asked to give an update on his progress in his short time here."

"You want me to do it?" she asked with surprise. She didn't think Mrs. Dunne would trust her with something so important.

"He's in your group. You've been working with him," Mrs. Dunne shrugged.

My group, Joey thought. She loved her little group. Joey's group included Evan, Katie, and Leah. Adam was an unofficial part of Joey's group with Mrs. Dunne "helping." She didn't need Dunne's help, though. The girls were happy and did whatever Joey asked of them. Evan stayed close by her side. He, too, did whatever Joey asked, except for the times when he was overwhelmed or unable to make a transition. Then he curled into a ball and rocked back and forth crying, "Heart fish, heart fish," over and over until the feeling passed.

"Oh, we received an update from the nurse," Dunne said, breaking into Joey's thoughts. "Adam's doctor adjusted his medication. His parents felt he was too sleepy all the time on whatever they had him on, so they switched up what they were giving him. The notes are in his file."

Joey nodded. She took in what Mrs. Dunne said about Adam but at the moment was concerned about Evan's ARD. Joey was familiar with the purpose of an ARD meeting, but having never attended one, she had some questions. She asked her coworkers about it at recess.

"Look, just make some notes about Evan and let the diag do all the talking," Tam responded in answer to Joey's query as to what she needed to prepare.

"The die ag?" Joey was confused by the term.

"Diag. The district diagnostician. She attends all ARDs and runs the show," Tam responded. To which Johnson gave a snort.

Tam and Joey looked at Johnson. She huffed with annoyance. "That woman bugs the crap out of me. She sits in those meetings all high and mighty like she knows these kids. She don't know these kids. She wouldn't even recognize them on the street. But she acts like she's got all the answers to what's best for them in the classroom. She fools the parents, but she doesn't fool me."

Joey was shocked. "What do you mean? Doesn't she want what's best for the kids?"

"She does. She *thinks* she knows what's best. She says all kinds of words that sound real good. But her knowledge is all book knowledge. She's nice enough as a person. But she's never even worked in a special education classroom. She doesn't get it. She thinks she's better than the teachers."

Johnson's opinions were strong, and Joey found them hard to believe. Until Wednesday came along.

Joey stayed up late Tuesday night, making notes on her laptop regarding Evan's first couple of weeks at Black Bear Creek. She'd read the IEP that his previous school had in place for him, and there were some things she disagreed with. It listed him at a kindergarten-level for math, needing manipulatives for basic functions. However, with Joey, he was able to complete a sheet of multiplication tables at nearly a third-grade level.

For his reading goals, they listed him as needing work on basic sight words, with a goal of reading 60% of the Dolch sight words by the end of sixth grade. However, when Joey spread the cards out and said a word, he identified by pointing to the correct word every time. He had no reading comprehension goals listed in his IEP, yet when Joey read short stories to him, he showed he could point to the correct multiple-choice answers if she supported him by reading the questions aloud.

His writing was pretty low, but he could copy words and Joey thought that if she gave him some sentence starters, he'd be able to complete the sentences on his own. He needed writing goals built into his IEP as well. She crafted some suggestions.

Her notes and examples of Evan's work were neatly displayed in a folder, and she felt confident as she went into the conference room for Evan's ARD.

The district diagnostician, Beverly West, was already in the room, along with one of the assistant principals. Joey introduced herself and took a seat. They were just awaiting Evan's dad.

"I know you are new, so don't worry about contributing. We can just refer to the IEP from Evan's other school and implement it here," Mrs. West said to Joey.

"Actually, Mrs. West," Joey replied, "I looked over the previous IEP, and I am not sure the goals they have listed are reflective of his abilities."

Mrs. West raised her eyebrows, but before she could respond, the door opened and Mr. Matthews brought Evan's dad, Jeremy, into the room. Introductions were made and Mrs. West started the meeting by reading the considerations. Joey thought Jeremy's eyes looked glassed over; he was listening but not listening. Going through the motions.

"Do you have any questions, Mr. Rivers, before we talk about Evan's accommodations?"

Jeremy shook his head. "I don't even know what to ask. My wife had always come to these meetings."

Mrs. West smiled sympathetically. "We are going to talk about the support Evan needs during the school day. We'd placed Evan in our fully individualized setting until we could have this meeting. I suspect it isn't quite the right placement for him, but until we'd had the chance to talk to you formally, I didn't want to give him a general education schedule."

"A general education schedule?" Joey blurted. "You want to move him from our classroom?"

Mrs. West's eyes narrowed at Joey. "Mrs. Russo. As you know, our job is to place Evan in the educational setting that is the least restrictive environment for him. He was in a general education classroom at his previous school."

Joey opened her folder. "Yes, and I am not sure the teachers working with him were as in tune with his needs as they could have been. I noticed his previous goals—"

"Hang on, Mrs. Russo," Mrs. West cut her off. "We'll get to that. Mr. Rivers, would you have an objection to Evan being in a general education classroom with the support of a classroom aide? It aligns with his plan from Wilmington."

Joey looked at Evan's dad, who glanced briefly at her. She gave her head a slow shake, hoping to convey how she felt. He looked at Mrs. West. "I don't really know if we should change it. If my wife thought that was best, I guess it is?"

"Mrs. West, could I please share my findings for Evan's goals?" Joey begged.

"Please. Go ahead," Mrs. West leaned forward on her elbows to listen.

Joey proceeded to recount the past two weeks with Evan. She showed the previous IEP goals along with the work he had done so far. When considered side by side, it was glaringly obvious that the goals were misaligned with his performance. Joey felt she was building a strong case for individualized education. Her efforts, however, had the opposite effect of what she'd intended.

"It does appear Evan has come a long way since those goals were written," Mrs. West noted. "Great work, Mrs. Russo."

"Thank you," Joey said. "He's such a great kid. He is extremely quiet, so I would recommend we develop some goals around his speech."

Mrs. West nodded enthusiastically. "Yes, we should definitely have our SLP—that's our speech-language pathologist," she clarified for Mr. Rivers, "schedule an assessment and begin working with Evan immediately."

"I don't mind working with him on his speech goals," Joey said. "I've developed a comfortable rapport with him."

Mrs. West brushed her off. "No, Mrs. Russo. That's a job for the SLP. You have your hands full with the students in the FISC room."

"Evan IS one of my students," Joey replied.

Mrs. West turned to Mr. Rivers. "With this kind of potential for Evan academically," she indicated Joey's report, "I would strongly suggest we continue the same kind of placement he had in Wilmington. He will be in a general education setting with his peers. For his core classes—English, math, social studies, and science—there will be either an extra teacher in the classroom or an aide to assist Evan with his learning."

"I'm afraid I disagree," Joey cut in. "Emotionally, Evan is very shy. When he gets upset, he sometimes cries, and he doesn't always know how to ask for what he needs. I help him through by reading his body language and sometimes things go by trial and error. They may not notice what he needs in a general education room." She thought of Tray and his friends. *They would eat him up,* she thought.

Mrs. West was not swayed. "Then we will put some social-emotional accommodations in place to help him. For example, Evan can request a break. To go for a walk down the hall or get a drink of water when he feels overstimulated."

"He doesn't always know when he needs a break," Joey countered.

"It is part of the learning process," Mrs. West was insistent. "He managed it in Wilmington, he'll manage it here. We certainly don't want to give him a more restrictive placement than he had at his old school."

Mr. Matthews finally spoke. "I must agree with Mrs. West. She's been doing this a long time, Mrs. Russo. We do not want the records to show a more restrictive placement without good cause."

"He's gone through a lot emotionally," Joey could hear her voice waver. "The major life changes he's experienced are a pretty cause, in my opinion. I just think he should be in a safer emotional space for a while."

"Mr. Rivers, what do you say on the matter?" Mrs. West asked. "Do you want him to continue the path he was on in Wilmington, or take a backward step to a more isolated classroom?"

Joey was furious. *Backward step?* Of course, when Mrs. West put it like that, Evan's dad opted to keep Evan in general education, even though they clearly were not challenging him nor setting appropriate learning goals. Even though they didn't seem to know him at all. She lost that battle. But she did not quit the ARD. She did her best to ensure Evan had realistic goals and accommodations that would help him in the general education classrooms. At the end of the ARD, she politely said goodbye to Evan's dad, but deliberately turned a cold shoulder to Mrs. West as she left. She found the nearest staff restroom and pounded the sink in frustration.

Mr. Matthews was waiting for her when she exited.

"Are you okay?" he asked, noting her flushed cheeks.

"General ed is not the right environment for that little boy." Joey knew she was right.

"Look. Your passion for your students is admirable. I'm extremely impressed with the work you've done so far. But Mrs. West is our district diagnostician. She knows her stuff."

"She's never even met Evan," Joey said. "She doesn't have the full picture."

"His father was part of the decision process

too," Mr. Matthews reminded.

"Respectfully, sir, you heard how it was presented to him," Joey cocked her head to the side and raised her eyebrows.

Mr. Matthews sighed. "We will have another meeting at the end of the year. If we see he is not thriving, we'll review his placement."

Joey shook her head. "I hope he makes it that long."

She cried recounting the day's events to Craig that evening. She sat next to him on the couch, her head on his shoulder. He had an arm around her and rubbed her arm while she vented. He listened quietly, knowing there wasn't anything he could say to help.

"This job has put quite the emotional strain on you," he noted.

"I didn't even realize losing him out of my class would be an option," Joey said. "If I'd known she was going to do that, I−" She stopped. She didn't know what she'd have done.

"You would have done just what you did," Craig said. "You gave an accurate report on his progress. It's okay. I'm sure the other teachers in the school will work just as hard with him. He'll be alright."

"Honestly, it's not the teachers I'm worried about. It's the other kids. Boys like Tray. They see him as different. They aren't going to befriend him. The other day Katie sat and read two Arthur books to Evan. He won't get a friend like Katie in the other classrooms."

They sat for a while longer, lost in their thoughts: Joey fretting over Evan, Craig praying for Joey.

The following Monday was Evan's first day following the general education schedule. His absence from the room left a tangible void for Joey. She tried not to think about him as she worked with Adam, Katie, and Leah. On his new medication, Adam was a model student. As far as Joey could tell, he was nearly at grade-level for his ability to read and work math equations. He was very good with fractions and simple word problems. Academically, Adam did not need exceptional student services. Joey said as much to Mrs. Rodriguez when she popped in that afternoon to see how Adam was doing.

"I'm glad to hear he's participating," Mrs. Rodriguez said.

"On his medication, you would never know he had any problems," Joey said.

"Could you email me your documentation on his support?" Mrs. Rodriguez asked.

"Yes, I've got it all on my laptop. I'll send it over after school," Joey promised.

When school was over, it took Joey an extra few minutes to finish updating Adam's support schedule and send it to Mrs. Rodriguez, copying Mr.

Matthews and Mrs. Dunne. By the time she walked out to the staff parking lot, most of the students and staff had cleared the building and were gone. As she walked past the athletic hall, she saw a small figure sitting against the wall, in an alcove by the boys' locker room.

"Evan?" she asked. He was rocking back and forth and crying quietly. She rushed over to him and squatted down. His eyes were closed tightly, and he was humming.

"Heart fish. Heart fish. Heart fish," his soft voice murmured over and again.

"Sweet boy. Where are you supposed to be?" she wondered, knowing he wouldn't answer.

"Come with me, Evan," she said, gently taking his arm to pull him to his feet.

"No, no, no," Evan shook his head even though he allowed her to help him stand. "Heart fish." He pointed to the locker room. She tried the door. It was locked.

"It's locked, Evan. We can't go in there."

Evan began to cry more loudly. Just then, one of the custodians turned the corner.

"Miss!" Joey called. "Could you come here please? Could you let us in the locker room? This student needs something."

"Students are not allowed in the locker rooms after school," she chided.

"I understand. This is a special education student. He needs to get in here for a moment.

Please." Joey was ready to grab the keys and unlock the door herself if need be.

The custodian unlocked the door. As soon as Joey pulled it open, Evan ran inside. He came back immediately hugging his green water bottle.

"Oh!" Joey felt stupid for not realizing he didn't have it. "Your water bottle!"

Evan took off running toward the front office. Joey followed. As they neared the front, Joey saw Jeremy, talking animatedly with Mr. Matthews. When he saw Evan, relief flooded his face. He bent down and held out his arms. Evan ran into them and hugged his dad.

"Mrs. Russo! Was he with you?" Mr. Matthew asked harshly.

"No, sir. I found him crying outside the boys' locker room. I was on my way to the parking lot. His water bottle was inside," she explained.

"Oh, Evan," Jeremy said. "Come on, buddy, let's go home." Jeremy gave Joey a nod of thanks, and Joey and Mr. Matthews watched them go.

"I guess we need to outline some after-school procedures," Mr. Matthew said.

"I can review his schedule and talk with his eighth period teacher," Joey said. "I'm guessing though, that it is P.E.?"

Mr. Matthews nodded. "Yes, that would be Coach Dunne. If you could talk to him, that would be great."

"Will do, sir," Joey promised.

Joey got to school early the next morning and waited outside the boys' locker room for Coach Dunne. When he saw Joey in the hallway, she was sure she heard him mutter something under his breath.

"Good morning, Coach Dunne," Joey said.

"How can I help you?" he asked gruffly, unlocking the locker room and going inside. Joey followed him to his office.

"You got a new student in your eighth period yesterday, a boy named Evan," Joey started.

"Yeah, I did. He wouldn't dress out. Wouldn't do anything. Sat in the bleachers crying the whole class."

"You just let him cry?" Joey asked.

"I have fifty students in P.E. that class period and one classroom aide. I can't babysit."

Joey bit the inside of her mouth to tame her anger before replying. "That boy has autism. He has accommodations for support during class. Did you even look at them?"

"Don't get bossy with me. I got the email with his IEP. I have not had a chance to read it yet," he said defensively.

"Mr. Matthews asked me to talk with you to suggest a procedure for making sure he gets to his dad after school," Joey said. "I'm not trying to be bossy. This boy needs extra support."

He didn't reply, but crossed his arms as if to say, "So?"

"Can you or your classroom aide help him gather his belongings, including his green water bottle, and ensure he makes it to his dad after school? His dad picks him up at door 11—which is just at the end of the hallway."

"If that's what we have to do, then I guess that's what we'll do," Coach Dunne said unenthusiastically.

"Thank you. That green water bottle is very important to him. It's like an emotional security blanket. I am sure Evan will appreciate your help," Joey said dryly. "I'll be following up to make sure things are going smoothly." She knew that last part sounded threatening, but she no longer cared. She raised an eyebrow before leaving. She refrained from slamming the door this time on her way out.

As the end of the day drew near, Joey found herself watching the clock, wondering how Evan was doing. She determined that as soon as her students were safely on the bus, she would high tail it to the athletic hallway to ensure Evan made it safely to his dad.

As she rushed toward the gym, she spotted Evan walking with a teacher who Joey assumed was the aide. She saw that Evan held his green water bottle, and they were heading toward the correct door. She breathed a sigh of relief. Christmas break could not come soon enough.

DODIE

Evertor Technologies closed their offices between Christmas Eve and New Year's Day each year. Most of their customers were shut down during this time, and productivity among the sales and engineering teams declined to nearly zero. On the Friday night before Christmas Eve, Dodie was two glasses into a box of wine when she heard a knock on her front door. She had taken to lying in the dark with her wine lately, so the lights in her townhouse were off. With her car in the garage, she figured whoever it was would just go away, thinking she wasn't there. Unless of course it was Anne, but then again, Anne had a key.

Benny and Joon barked protectively, and when there came another knock, Dodie figured she better see who it was. She went quietly into the office-now-spare-bedroom and peeked through the blinds. Jason stood on the stoop, shifting from one foot to the other to fend off the cold. He knocked again, and the dogs continued to let him know they did not approve.

"Jeez, Jason," she whispered to herself. "Go away."

It was a full five more minutes before he walked sullenly back to his car. He got in and sat in his car for another fifteen minutes before driving away. It was long enough for Dodie to down a third glass of wine. Shaky, she called Anne.

"Hi Dodes," Anne answered right away. "What's up?"

"He was here again," Dodie said. "Jason. He showed up here again."

"What did he want?"

Dodie was still standing at the window. "I don't know. I didn't answer the door. Annie, he sat in his car forever. I don't want him coming around here. He's a reminder of—" she stopped.

"Want me to come over?" Anne asked. "I can be there in fifteen. We can have a movie night."

Dodie thought perhaps she just needed another glass of wine to calm her nerves.

"No thanks, I'll be okay. I was just freaked out a bit. He's gone now. It's going to be a long Christmas holiday." Dodie didn't want to be alone in her house for nearly two weeks. She'd started drinking when she got home from work—it made her less anxious. But more nights than not, her one or two glasses ended up with her passed out on the couch come morning. She knew the cycle was not healthy but didn't know how to break it. If only she could go away for a while. She got an idea.

"Hey!" she exclaimed. "You said you will be home during Christmas, right?"

"Yeah," Anne said. "I'll be around. Why?"

"Why don't we go on a girls' trip? Like a cruise or something? My treat." She had kept a small amount of the money from her settlement accessible in a savings account. She could think of nothing she'd rather spend some of it on than a cruise with Anne and Sherry.

"A cruise!" Anne squealed. "Yes! That is a fabulous idea. Let's call Sherry."

They conference-called Sherry into the conversation. Sherry loved the idea, but Anne and Sherry both agreed that they would buy their own tickets. Anne, expert at all things Google, was elected as the trip coordinator. She promised to find them the perfect last-minute cruise.

Annie came through. The girls decided on a 7-day Western Caribbean cruise that left on December 23 from Galveston, Texas. The early morning flight from Denver to Houston was a bit of a blur for Dodie, who'd stayed up late packing the night before. Chris and his wife were watching Benny and Joon, and it was lonely in her townhouse without them. She was proud of herself, though, for only having one glass of wine as she packed. Anne's brother had picked her up at 4:30 a.m., with Anne and Sherry already in the car. They all napped on the plane, declining even the coffee service.

They'd prebooked a shuttle from Houston to Galveston, and everything went smoothly. When they arrived at the port, they joined the queue and within forty-five minutes they were boarding.

Dodie always wanted to go on a cruise. She and Grandma had talked about going "someday," but someday never came.

Brent, the slimy sales manager from the office, cruised regularly with his wife. His desk displayed a framed photo of the two of them holding sparkling tropical drinks in front of a deck railing adorned with a yellow life ring bearing the name S.S. Nova. She always noted that picture when she walked past his desk. Oddly, she thought of that photo now as they crossed the gangplank. She wondered if Brent's wife knew what a scum ball he was. The company holiday party was just two nights earlier, and Brent flirted shamelessly with one of the cocktail waitresses serving the hors d'oeuvres. Dodie had turned down a wrong hallway looking for the restroom and stumbled across Brent, who had the cocktail waitress backed against the wall. He was leaning in, toying with the neckline on her dress. He looked over at Dodie and grinned; she rolled her eyes and left him to his lecherousness.

As she recalled it now, Dodie felt anger and disgust rise in her gut. *Did Brent take his wife on cruises to ease his guilty conscience? Was that why Aaron wanted to take her rock climbing that Saturday? To ease his conscience?* She gave her head a shake. *Why were these negative thoughts creeping in?* She didn't want to think of cheating husbands or guilty consciences. She wanted to enjoy her much-earned vacation. She suddenly wanted a drink.

"So, what do you think, Dodes?" Sherry and Anne were looking at her.

"Mm. Sorry, I missed the question," Dodie replied. "Lost in thought."

"Do you want to find some deck chairs and margaritas while we wait for the boat to shove off?" Anne grinned.

Dodie smiled. "That sounds super!"

They located the perfect spot on an upper deck and, margaritas in hand, laughed and enjoyed the glorious view as the S.S. Excalibur sailed off into the Gulf of Mexico.

The first three days of the cruise were restful, relaxing, and rewarding. All three days were spent at sea as they sailed toward their first stop, Mahogany Bay. Between lounging in a deck chair, trying her hand at the slot machines in the casino, or relaxing in the hot tub, Dodie felt she was made for cruise life. More than once, she wondered how many consecutive cruises her four million dollars could keep her on before she'd have to return to land. She had brought along a couple of novels she'd been intending to read—the latest by Richard Osman and an Agatha Christie—and for the first time in a while, she wasn't anxious. She slept when she wanted, read when she felt like it, and ate when she was hungry. She always had a drink at her side.

Anne and Sherry were excellent travel mates. They gave her space, and when they were going to the comedy club or to play pool or to the spa, if Dodie didn't want to go, they didn't push her.

On Day 4 of the cruise, they disembarked at 8 a.m. to see the sights of Mahogany Bay. Even though they could afford it if they wanted, the girls felt the cruise ship excursions were overpriced and they didn't really want to spend their free time herded around with other tourists. Instead, they took a taxi to the other side of the island toward Sandy Bay and brunched at a place Anne had found on the internet called The Salty Mango. They placed an order for coconut shrimp, ceviche, and garlic steamed sea bass. Anne ordered a raspberry iced tea to drink, Sherry a bottled water, and when the waitress looked at Dodie, she glanced briefly at her friends before asking for a drink menu. The waitress stepped away to get it.

"What?" Dodie questioned Anne's and Sherry's stares.

"Dodes, it's not even ten in the morning," Anne observed.

"We are on vacation!" Dodie declared. "I thought there were no rules on vacation."

"No rules, but sweetie, we are going to be outside in the hot sun all day. If you start drinking now, you can get dehydrated," Sherry warned.

Dodie felt frustration creeping in. "Look, I am a grown woman, who would like a cocktail with her sea bass. Whether it's ten in the morning or ten at night shouldn't make a difference." She paused for a moment then added, "If you don't like it, too damned bad."

Anne's eyes widened. Sherry opened her mouth to say something, then closed it again. Dodie had never said anything remotely like that to them before. When the waitress came back with the drink menu, though, Dodie just asked for a Diet Coke.

"I'm sorry, Dodie," Sherry said quietly after the waitress walked away. "I didn't mean to upset you." Sherry and Anne looked at each other.

"What is it?" Dodie asked. "I know that look."

"There's no look," Anne said.

"Yes. There was a look. It's the same look we give one another in the office when something is going on that we don't want to talk about. Go ahead. Out with it," Dodie waved her hands in a "come at me" way, encouraging them to speak what was on their minds.

"We don't want to upset you," Anne said.

"Upset me? About what?" Dodie demanded. "You talking about me behind my back?"

"No, Dodes. We are worried about you," Sherry reached for Dodie's hand, but she yanked it away.

"What for?"

"Dodie, there's no easy way to say this, and we've never kept things from one another," Anne started. "And we certainly did not want to do this here." She indicated the surroundings. "You are drinking an awful lot."

Dodie spoke calmly. "Well, we are on vacation," she said.

Sherri shook her head. "Not just on vacation, Dodie. You're coming in to work late, sometimes smelling a bit like last night's wine."

Dodie shook her head and looked down at her placemat.

"And Dodie, have you started drinking at lunchtime?" Anne asked as gently as she could.

Dodie raised her eyes to Anne's. "So what? What if I have a beer at lunch? Is that a crime? The reps have drinks at lunch all the freaking time with clients."

"This is different. I think you know that," Anne said.

Dodie's eyes filled with tears. She refused to look at Anne or Sherry. Her Coke sat, untouched. When the food came, they ate mostly in silence, despite how delicious everything tasted. Anne and Sherry sensed Dodie's need for space; they sensed she was processing what they'd said. Sherry paid the restaurant bill. Their original plan was to spend the rest of the day on the beach, soaking up the Honduran sun. Anne flagged down a taxi.

"Where to?" the driver asked.

Anne looked to Dodie. "Do you want to still go to the beach?"

Dodie shrugged. "We might as well," she

replied. Even though she was hurt, she didn't want to ruin the trip.

"Is there a nearby beach?" Anne asked the driver.

"Yes, yes. Sandy Beach. Very close," he replied.

After couple of miles winding along Carretera Principal, he pulled over and indicated an area where they could access the beach. Anne gave him a few dollars. She bought several bottled waters from a small refreshment booth, and they claimed a spot on the butterscotch-colored sand. Sherri played music from her iPhone, and they spent the next hour laying out on their towels, absorbing the warmth, deep in their own thoughts.

Dodie didn't want to be mad at her friends. She knew she shouldn't be because they were right; she just wasn't yet ready to admit it. Admitting it meant she'd have to do something about it, and she didn't know what that "something" was. No one could change the past. She despised her present. She didn't have a vision for her future. So, what then?

The sudden sound of children laughing and yelling to one another caused all of them to open their eyes and sit up. Down the beach, a group of fifteen or so children and a handful of adults were scattered about. The kids were working in groups of two or three. It took the girls a minute to realize what they were doing.

"Oh!" Anne exclaimed. "They've got kites!"

"That's so cool," Sherry said. "I wonder if they

are from a school or something? They are all wearing the same yellow shirts."

"Let's go see what they're doing!" Anne jumped up, wrapped her purple beach coverup around her waist, and trotted toward the kids.

Sherry looked at Dodie. "Want to go see?"

Dodie shook her head. "You go. I'll watch the stuff."

She watched as Anne and Sherry approached the group and began making friends. Anne talked with one of the adult women, laughing and talking animatedly with her hands. The woman seemed very friendly. At one point they looked over at Dodie and gave a wave. Dodie waved back. Anne indicated that Dodie should come over. Dodie shook her head. But Anne was insistent. She waved wildly, leaving Dodie no choice. Dodie looked around. There really wasn't anyone else near them on the beach to disturb their things. She sighed heavily and stood, pulling her cotton dress over her head. She slipped her phone into her pocket and went over.

"Dodie, this is Ms. Angelique," Anne introduced her. "These kids are with a local school. Sandy Bay World School."

"It is very nice to meet you," Ms. Angelique said, her Spanish accent heavy, but her English very clear.

"Hello," Dodie said.

"These are special needs kids from the school

over there," Anne explained, pointing to a pink building across the road.

"Our school *only* has children with special needs," Ms. Angelique clarified. "Here in Honduras, kids with disabilities get no help from other schools. The schools won't take them."

"Oh," Dodie said. "That's so sad."

Ms. Angelique smiled. "Honduras is a poor, poor country, miss. Educación Especial programs like ours help these children to have a chance. Many of these kids are orphans, and if we don't teach them, they won't survive on the streets."

"Orphans?" Anne looked at the students. "I'm sorry for my ignorance; are there a lot of orphans in Honduras? I know countries like Haiti have very high numbers, I never even thought about Honduras."

Ms. Angelique smiled. She was not offended at the question. "My dear, yes. More than forty percent of our children do not live with their parents. The reasons are many, but the root is poverty."

They watched the other adults help the children with their kites. Sherry had joined in the fun. The kids were laughing and happy, even though the kites did not much like to cooperate. Dodie felt a tug on her dress. A small girl smiled up at her.

"Muy bonita," she said, rubbing the sea blue cotton fabric of Dodie's dress between her fingers.

"Gracias," Dodie said, smiling down at her.

The girl took Dodie's hand. "Ven conmigo," she insisted, pulling Dodie away.

Dodie looked at Ms. Angelique for permission

"Sí," she said. "It's okay. That's Emilie."

The girl led Dodie to the water. There was a small patch of seaweed peeking up through the waves. Dodie could tell that the water was very shallow.

"Mira," Emilie said, pointing into the weeds.

Dodie looked, but all she saw were the green blades swaying gently to and fro. "Mm-hmm," Dodie said thoughtfully, as if she knew what she was looking at.

"Mira, mira!" Emilie demanded, pointing at a very specific spot in the water.

Dodie squinted her eyes to see more closely. Laying in the sand at the stipe of the seaweed was a small green lump.

"Oh! I see it," she said.

"Estrella del mar verde!" Emilie said. "Estrella del mar verde!" Her excitement was contagious, and Dodie smiled. She wasn't sure what she was looking at, but she nodded appreciatively. Emilie pointed out a few more green lumps barely visible in the weeds. Dodie took her phone out of her pocket and clicked a few pictures of the pretty seaweed and the green lumps. That made Emilie happy. She ran off to play with her classmates.

Dodie stood with her feet in the warm water,

watching her toes squish the sand. She knew she was fortunate to be alive, to have her health, to be independent. When she was one, she was orphaned, just like many of these children. But she had her grandma. These kids had much more stacked against them than she ever did.

As she watched the students working so hard to fly their kites, for the first time in months she was able to see past her grief. She wasn't mad at Anne or Sherry. Having people to speak truth to you is more valuable than any amount of money. It was what she missed about her grandma. The hard part was going to be figuring out how to get around the mountain that was in front of her.

"I'm sorry Grandma," she whispered.

Sherry noticed Dodie and walked over to her. They embraced, and Dodie sobbed on Sherry's shoulder. Anne came over and joined them. Soon, all the students had also come over to get in on the group hug. Ms. Angelique was so touched; she snapped a picture and immediately posted it on the school's Facebook page. She showed it to Anne, Sherry, and Dodie.

"Emilie pointed out these little green lumps in the seaweed over there," Dodie said, showing Ms. Angelique the pictures she took. "What are they?"

"Oh! Those are green starfish!" Ms. Angelique said happily. "Unusual to see, but very special."

"Green starfish!" Anne said. "I didn't know starfish came in different colors. I thought they were all orange."

"Starfish come in many shapes, colors, and sizes. Just like people. Hundreds of different kinds," Ms. Angelique hugged Emilie, who had come over to see the pictures. "All different. All special."

That evening, Anne, Sherry, and Dodie got dressed up to have dinner in the formal dining room. They dined on melt-in-your-mouth steak Oscar with asparagus and garlic mashed potatoes. If there was one thing they all agreed on, it was that the food situation on the ship was amazing. You could find anything, anytime, day or night.

As they ate, they recounted their time with the students from the Sandy Bay World School. They'd stayed on the beach flying kites—well, trying to—and playing games with the kids right up until they had to return to the ship. There were hugs and smiles and promises to stay in touch when they left. Ms. Angelique had even gone back to the school and got them each a yellow t-shirt that matched the students. Dodie, Anne, and Sherry pooled the cash they had in their wallets (saving a few dollars for the taxi back to the ship) and made a nice donation to the school.

"Ms. Angelique was pretty incredible," Sherry noted. "She's got to be ranked up there with the saints. Anyone who takes care of special needs children like that has got to automatically get one of the best spots in heaven."

Anne took a bite of potatoes. "I found their Facebook page and also had a look at their website. You can sponsor a child at their school for $19 a month. I'm going to sign up to sponsor when we get home."

"We should do an office presentation about it and see if we can get a bunch of signups," Sherry suggested.

"Oh my gosh—I love that idea!" Anne said. "It'll be a great way to start the new year."

Dodie knew it was going to be rough, but she felt they needed to revisit the conversation that was started before they went to the beach.

"Guys, can we talk about what happened at brunch today?" she asked.

"Of course, Dodie," Anne said. "Only if you're sure you feel like talking."

"I'm not sure I feel like it. But I know I need to," she said. She took a drink from the bottle of Perrier she'd requested from the waiter. Anne and Sherry waited patiently.

"I've not been doing so great," Dodie confessed. "When I get home from work, I hardly move off the couch. You're right. I've been drinking wine to help myself fall asleep. Some mornings I don't even remember going to bed. One night I'd left Benny and Joon out in the yard all night." She dabbed at her eyes with her napkin. "I know I've been drinking too much. Without it, I lay there and think about all the things I don't have, and it hurts. I don't know what to do. I hate being alone."

Anne reached out and took Dodie's hand. "What does the therapist say?"

Dodie shrugged.

"You haven't told her about the drinking," Anne correctly guessed.

Dodie shook her head. "I don't like failing. I'm failing at life." She proceeded to tell Anne and Sherry about her night out with Jules and the follow up catastrophe with Ali. They were shocked.

"Oh, Dodie! You could have been raped! Or worse!" Anne was horrified for her friend. "How dare that dumb—"

"Anne!" Sherry stopped her. "You're getting loud."

Anne looked around, the couple at the next table were staring. "I'm sorry," she said to them.

Dodie gave a small smile. "I'm okay. I learned my lesson about going out with people I don't know."

"But you've been closet drinking at home since then, and that's not okay," Sherry said.

"I know," Dodie said, "I don't know what to do with myself when I'm home. I know that sounds ridiculous, I used to be home alone all the time when I was with Aaron. But it's different now. I hate it," she said again.

"Can I suggest something?" Anne asked. "Maybe part of the problem is your home."

"What do you mean?" Dodie wondered.

"I mean, your townhouse. Even though it is yours, it reminds you of Aaron. Maybe you need a change of living space?"

Dodie started to protest, but then thought about it. Maybe a fresh start, in a fresh place, was what she needed to feel new.

"Breaking bad habits is hard. Breaking negative thought patterns is really hard," Sherry acknowledged. "You've got us, Dodie. We'll help you find your way."

The last three days of the cruise seemingly flew by. They wandered the shops in Costa Maya, they played in the beach in Cozumel, and they enjoyed all the entertainment the ship had to offer.

They also made a plan. Anne would move back in with Dodie while she put her townhouse up for sale and began looking for a new place to live.

JOEY

The first week of the Christmas break, Joey rarely left the couch. She'd come down with strep throat and for once followed her doctor's orders and rested. Craig took care of her in the evenings with warm dinners and snuggles while they watched all the top shows and movies on Netflix.

By the second week of the break, Joey was restless. After binge watching two seasons of *The Great British Bake Off*, she threw on some sweatpants and sneakers and headed to Ingles. The urge to bake didn't surface often, but when it did, she leaned into it. Her sugar cookies were the best around, and she was in the mood to make them, but she was out of flour, sugar, butter, and almond extract. Nearly everything.

She zipped around the store, gathering the things she needed and several things she didn't. As she rounded the corner on the last aisle, she nearly ran her buggy smack into Jeremy and Evan.

"Oh!" she said with a start. "Hello! Hi Mr. Rivers. Hi Evan!"

"Hi Woffey," Evan said.

"Hi Mrs. Russo," Jeremy held out his hand for her to shake. "Remember, call me Jeremy."

She nodded. "Of course, yes. And please, call me Joey."

Jeremy nodded. "Right, Joey."

"Woffey," Evan corrected.

"How are you, Evan?" she asked.

Evan looked at Joey but didn't answer.

"How is Evan doing?" Joey asked Jeremy.

Jeremy shook his head. "It's been difficult. He doesn't like having to change classes every hour. Transitions are tough, you know. But I'm hoping he'll settle into it after the break."

"Well, if you ever want him to return to the FISH room—" she started to offer to help reschedule Evan, but Jeremy cut her off.

"Please, Mrs. Russo—don't say it!" he said roughly. "It's been hard enough at home trying to explain to Evan that this is for the best. I don't want him to even hear that it's an option on the table."

Joey was shocked at the sudden anger. "I'm sorry—I didn't mean to upset you. I just want you to know I want what is best for Evan. I'll help however I can."

Jeremy's voice was hard. "His mother wanted what's best for him, too, and she seemed to feel the general education setting was the right choice. It's where she'd had him in Wilmington, and I will not go against that."

Joey felt like she'd been socked in the gut. Her cheeks flushed. "Yes, of course. I'm sorry."

Jeremy shifted the jug of chocolate milk he held into his other hand. "I'm doing the best I can here. Let me be his parent."

Joey nodded. "I'm sorry. Merry Christmas to you, Jeremy. Merry Christmas, Evan," she said with a catch in her throat.

"Mewwy Chwissmas, Woffey," Evan said softly. He took his dad's hand, and they left her there, tears streaming. Other shoppers eyed her warily, but she didn't care. She stayed in that last aisle until she was sure they'd be long gone from the store.

"I can't do this anymore," Joey declared to Craig that evening. "I've cried more since September than I have in the last five years." She was crying again as she said it. "This job was supposed to help me continue my healing journey, be a fresh start, new challenges and all that garbage. It's brought me nothing but frustration, hurt, and heartache." She had rolled out her dough and was busy pounding the cookie cutter into it with all her might.

"Easy there, slugger," Craig said. "Don't hurt the countertop."

"Craig, this isn't funny," she whined. "Aren't you sick of hearing me cry over this stupid job?"

"So, it's stupid now, is it?" he asked with a raised eyebrow. "Have you talked to God about that?"

"Don't patronize me," Joey said. "You know what I mean. This is hard."

"Baby, where in the Bible does it say that things are ever easy?"

She narrowed her eyes at him. "Craig. Don't

talk Bible to me. I'm really struggling here. I know we will face difficulties in the world. I get it. But my heart hurts for these kids. Every time I try to do what I think is the right thing, it blows up in my face. Don't you think that might mean I am not on the path for God's best for my life?"

"Is that what you think? That God doesn't want you to be a teacher?"

She sighed. "I don't know." She placed a dozen star-shaped cookies on a tray and popped it into the oven, setting her timer for nine minutes. She leaned her elbows on the counter and rested her head in her hands.

Craig came up behind her and began to rub her shoulders.

"Don't try to make me feel better," she warned. "It won't work."

But it did work. A little. He massaged her shoulders for the whole nine minutes, and after she removed the baked cookies, put the next batch on the tray, and safely got the tray back in the oven, he hugged her. "Look, Joey. If you are looking for me to tell you to quit, I won't do it."

She looked up at him. "Why not?"

"The day we buried Emily, it felt like our hearts were buried in the ground with her. The last five years, if I didn't have your love and the Lord's strength, I wouldn't have made it. We've kept each other going." She nodded. "Emily got sick. She died. It happened so quickly, and it was awful. But we don't get a say in it. God left you and I here for a reason. He wouldn't have left us here without her if He didn't have a job for us to do. If our work here was done, He would take us home, too. We are still here. We have work to do. I won't tell you to quit."

"I miss her so much," Joey said softly.

"I know you do, baby. I miss her too. She would be so proud of you," he said. "She'd be smiling at all of your stories and would tell you to keep going."

"Would she?" She didn't feel like Emily would be smiling at her at this moment.

"Yes. She would," Craig hugged her tightly. "A year ago, would you have even imagined you'd be working with special needs students?"

She shook her head.

"You wouldn't have imagined it. You probably didn't even want it. But something whispered to your heart to take the special education certification exam. That's God. He knew you'd have a gift for working with these students because He made you. You are the smartest woman in that whole school. You can see what those kids need because you are looking at it with fresh eyes. You aren't clouded by the way things have always been; you are strong enough to stand up for what's right. Didn't you tell me that one boy, Adam, was doing incredible things?"

"He really is. He is like a whole new kid," she nodded.

"You have helped that to happen. You," he said

poking a finger at her nose.

"I just sometimes feel like I can't handle what's given to me," she said.

"You can handle anything," he said.

"How do you know?"

"Because you've already handled everything."

"That's a quote from that Christmas movie we watched last night," she said accusingly.

"That doesn't make it less true. You have already handled the hardest thing."

The oven timer dinged, and she swapped out the tray once more. She made herself a promise to stop crying so much. Imagining Emily's smile would keep her going.

"Toughen up, Russo," she told herself as she iced her star cookies.

Joey used the remainder of the break to design some interesting new lesson activities on her laptop. She had subscribed to a few publications from Scholastic and attended some webinars on guided reading techniques. She felt that as she grew her own knowledge, she was becoming more and more equipped to help her students. Both Leah and Katie showed real promise with reading, and of course Adam could read, she just needed to challenge him with increasingly harder texts.

When school started up in January, she was ready.

"Kids always take a couple of days to settle down after there's been a break," Tam warned as they waited for the bus to arrive. "It'll be important to follow routine and use all the cues until they get back in the swing of things."

Since her realization of the importance of routine, she heard words like this with fresh ears. She didn't feel threatened by the timers and schedules like she once was. She knew if she kept her focus on "what's best for the kids," she could help them thrive in any environment.

Lucas got off the bus wearing a "Happy New Year" hat, glittery green with gold tinsel trim. Katie had another new pair of cat ears, white fur with blue satin. She also had a new My Little Pony backpack that she was so excited to show Gary. Joey was thrilled to see that the new backpack was larger, and the straps fit her arms easily.

"Same but different," she said proudly to Joey when Joey commented how nice the new backpack was.

"Same but different," Joey agreed. "I love it."

By the end of the first week back, the students had assimilated once again into the classroom routine. Adam was absent the first three days, much to everyone's liking except for Joey, who was anxious to present the new lessons she'd worked on with him. Mrs. Dunne rarely worked with him now that his medication levels were optimal. He was no longer overly lethargic, nor was he aggressive. They'd found the right mix to enable him to make it through the day. Despite this, Tam and Johnson still spoke of him like he was the boy who terrorized the room.

"I see Godzilla's back today," Johnson said, as Tam walked him into the classroom. She gave a thumbs up, which meant she confirmed with mom that he took his medication, and hung his backpack on his hook, after checking inside for dangerous items.

"Aw, come on, Johnson," Joey said. "Give him a break. He's like a completely different boy now."

Johnson snorted. "Give him a break? Girl, you're crazy. It's just a matter of time till he comes at us again. Do not let your guard down. Trust me on that."

Joey shook her head. "For how long will we hold his past crimes against him?"

Johnson looked pointedly at her. "Until he is no longer our problem. I know you think you're the Michelle Pfeiffer of the special needs kids, but believe me, Russo, it will bite you in the butt."

Last month, Johnson's words may have caused Joey to back down or—heaven forbid—cry. But a much tougher Joey knew she had the power of good on her side.

"The Michelle Pfeiffer of special needs kids? How long have you been saving that one?" she asked with a raised eyebrow.

Johnson, surprised at Joey's chutzpah, laughed. "I thought of it over the break. I was telling my husband about how charged up you are to do the right thing for these kids all the time."

"You were?" Joey was shocked.

"Yeah. I was like you once, Russo," Johnson said. "I was ready to save the world."

"What happened?" Joey asked. As if on cue, Mrs. Dunne came into the room with Mr. Matthews behind her.

"We're going to have a quick meeting after school," Mr. Matthews said to them all. "I'll come down after the buses pull out."

Mrs. Dunne rolled her eyes and shook her head. She took up her spot behind her desk and stared at her laptop for most of the day.

The meeting, which unexpectedly included Mrs. Rodriguez, was to inform the teachers that they were doing a less than adequate job with their documentation. The student information system that housed all student data had not been updated all year. Mrs. Rodriguez informed then that the district policy was for teachers to update the SIS weekly with notes on accommodations in use and student progress toward goals.

"Weekly?" Johnson asked flabbergasted.

"I'm sorry, I'm not even sure what you are talking about. How do you get to this information system?" Joey asked.

"You mean you never trained her?" Mr. Matthews asked Mrs. Dunne.

"Excuse me, Mr. Matthews, but when Mrs. Russo started, if you recall, we hit the ground running and have not looked back," Mrs. Dunne said, narrowing her eyes for effect.

Mrs. Rodriguez responded with an arrogant tone that surprised Joey. "Mrs. Dunne, you have been doing this for a long time. You know how important the documentation is. If we are audited by the state and we don't have anything in the system, we'll be non-compliant."

Mrs. Dunne pursed her lips but did not reply.

"Look," Mr. Matthews said. "We know how hard you all work. We know it has been an extremely difficult year so far. But none of those things changes the law. We must do what we are required to do."

"Documentation," Tam stated.

Mr. Matthews nodded. "Yup. Documentation."

Mrs. Dunne stood. "We'll have it updated by the end of next week," she said. "Is there anything else?"

Mrs. Rodriguez looked at Joey. "Will you be able to get the training you need to get this done?"

Joey nodded. "I'll get it done."

The next morning, Mrs. Dunne was there earlier than usual. She informed the team that it was movie day in the FISH room. She borrowed an Apple TV from the library and had a lineup of movies ready to stream from her iPad for the students. They were going to allow the students the option of watching movies and/or free play all day, so they could get the documentation entered into the student information system. "Get your laptops. We can sit around the worktable."

The system was not difficult to use, but it was clunky. Each student entry required ten different clicks before you could type the data. And each student needed at least one entry a week for both English and math. Counting back to the beginning of the school year, this meant each student needed thirty-eight entries.

"Lord, this is tedious," Tam complained, after they'd been at it for an hour.

"My screen keeps freezing up on me," Johnson stated with frustration.

"Mine too," Joey said.

"It's probably because we're all working in it," Mrs. Dunne said. "The system is finicky."

Joey found if she counted to three between each click, she had better success for the next screen to load. If she got ahead of herself it froze up, and she had to log out then log back in. Tedious, indeed.

Needless to say, not much learning took place in the FISH room that day.

It took nearly two days for Joey, Tam, and Johnson to get caught up with the documentation.

Mrs. Dunne only did the entries for Adam, so she finished pretty quickly. Joey wished she'd known about this requirement earlier. She could see the value in keeping up with it each week, and the laboriousness of the SIS didn't help matters. She vowed not to ever get behind on documentation again.

She was happy the following Monday for things to return to normal. One lesson she was really excited to work on with Adam involved poetry. Joey always loved poetry, and she had a hunch that Adam would connect with it.

When they got to the reading station, she gave Adam, Katie, and Leah each a piece of paper. She spread crayons on the desk.

"I'm going to read you a poem," she said. "I want you to draw the pictures that come into your mind while I am reading. Okay?"

"Katie draw?" Katie clarified.

"Yes. Listen to my words and draw whatever my words make you think about," Joey instructed. "Ready?" They each picked up a crayon and looked at Joey expectantly.

"This poem is called Rainbows.

"I wonder, wonder, wonder,

"Where do rainbows go

"When we can't see them in the sky?

"I really want to know.

"I wonder, wonder, wonder,

"What happens to the snow
"When summer comes, and the sun is hot?
"I really want to know.

"I wonder, wonder, wonder,
"How do the flowers grow
"From tiny seeds to blooming buds?
"I really want to know."

Joey finished reading the poem and looked at her students. "Okay. I'm going to read it one more time. You can draw while you listen." She read the poem again, making sure to emphasize the cadence of the lines. Then she watched them draw. Katie drew a rainbow. Leah drew a picture of a flower. Adam, however, drew a picture of a boy. The boy had three question marks over his head. Next to the boy, he drew a house. Behind the house, he drew a snowman, a rainbow, and a flower. He gave the snowman, rainbow, and flower faces that appeared to be laughing, as if they shared a joke. He did this all quickly, without hesitating or pausing.

Joey was amazed. She showed the picture to Mrs. Dunne excitedly after school. "Look at this! He caught the nuances of the poem. Katie and Leah drew an object that was mentioned in the poem—and that was wonderful—but he got the deeper meaning. He drew a boy, thinking. He drew the items in the poem and made it so they were hiding from the boy. Hiding behind a house so they couldn't be seen! And he did all of that in ten minutes after hearing the poem read only twice!"

"Mm-hm," Mrs. Dunne nodded. "That's a great picture."

"Don't you see? His comprehension is more complex. We should be challenging him with more complicated concepts," Joey said.

"You can work with him, just make sure you keep track of what you are doing," Mrs. Dunne responded.

Joey wasn't about to let Mrs. Dunne deflate her. "I will," she said.

After Mrs. Dunne left for the day, Joey, Tam, and Johnson cleaned up the room.

"Why is Mrs. Dunne so negative all the time?" Joey asked while fitting the books neatly back to the shelf. "I'm not trying to gossip; I'm just trying to understand why it's so hard for her to get excited over our students."

Johnson shrugged. "She hasn't been the same since she lost her son."

"I'm sorry, she what?" Joey asked incredulously.

"Two years ago, her boy took his life. He was fifteen," Johnson said. "He was being bullied at school and never told anyone."

Joey gasped. "That's horrible."

Tam nodded. "The world ain't all sunshine and rainbows, Russo."

That night, Joey reflected on what Tam had

said. She and Johnson accused her often of not understanding that things aren't always easy. Emily's death was the first time Joey had to accept that *really* bad things happen to good people. But she couldn't expect them to understand. When children are born, their whole life is full of possibilities. Until it isn't. She knew it well. Being in the FISH room helped her realize that even when things aren't how others think they should be, good can happen. Her students weren't broken crayons, they were whole crayons that colored differently. And her job wasn't to fix them, but to be a part of their lives in a positive way.

Mrs. Dunne's pain spilled into every decision made in the classroom. It became who she was. If she had a joy for teaching, it certainly was gone.

Thinking about Adam, Joey had an idea for a follow up lesson using the same "Rainbows" poem. On her computer, she typed a part of the poem, inserting blanks for some of the words.

I wonder, wonder, wonder,
Where do _____ go
When _____ ?
I really want to know.

She printed copies for Leah, Katie, and Adam. The next day, she gave them each a copy and explained that they were going to write their own poem by filling in the blanks. "What is something you wonder about?" she asked. "That is what we will write on the lines."

Katie and Leah each started drawing flowers and rainbows on their page. Joey was happy that they remembered the objects that the original poem was about. Adam, however, took his paper and wasted no time filling in his blanks, just as Joey suspected he would.

> I wonder, wonder, wonder,
> Where do caterpillars go
> When they fall asleep in their cocoons?
> I really want to know.

He spelled the words correctly and topped it off by drawing a picture of a butterfly, flying off in the opposite direction of the poem.

"That's brilliant, Adam," Joey said, smiling.

Adam rarely spoke unless he was answering a direct question. He never really looked anyone in the eye. Now he did both. His eyes met Joey's and a faint smile crossed his face. "Thank you," he said.

DODIE

No surprise to anyone, Chris's youngest sister, Jeanette, was a real estate agent. Less than 48 hours after Dodie mentioned to him that she wanted to put the townhouse on the market, a For Sale sign was on the lawn. Jeanette had showings scheduled by the weekend.

"This is moving so quickly," she said to Anne. It was Sunday, and they loaded the dogs into her Jeep to vacate the house so prospective buyers could tour.

"That could be a good thing," Anne said optimistically. "Jeanette said it was a seller's market right now, and there aren't too many townhomes out there for sale."

"I just don't know where we are going to go?" Dodie wondered. She'd looked online at a few rental houses but didn't see anything she loved.

"You've got the money, you could buy a place," Anne suggested.

"True. I just don't want to make any big decisions. I'm afraid I'll screw up."

Anne pointed at a coffee drive thru, and Dodie turned in to join the queue. "Dodie, you need to trust your instincts. Don't let what's happened cause you to question your good sense. Did you tell your therapist about it all?"

"I did. Everything. It wasn't as scary as I thought it would be. She's helping me practice replacing my negative thoughts with calming ones. She didn't say this, but I think I used Aaron to fill the void left by my grandma. It makes sense. What would you like?" They'd made it to the speaker box.

Anne said, "Get me a venti matcha latte with cold foam. And a cake pop. Please." She paused the conversation until Dodie placed the order. "Don't overanalyze, Dodie. Everyone makes mistakes. Maybe you got married too quickly, but that's life. We screw up sometimes. But Dodie, you have a chance to start over. I would never wish that accident on you, but if one good thing came from it, you learned what an asshat he really was. He was cheating on you long before the accident."

"I can't believe I didn't realize it," Dodie said.

"I think deep down, you knew," Anne observed.

Dodie paid for their drinks and handed Anne her matcha latte. "You're probably right. On a happy note, I've been researching the work that people like Ms. Angelique do to help orphans—and especially special needs orphans. It's fascinating."

"I signed up to sponsor two kids," Anne said.

"Me too," Dodie answered. She didn't tell Anne that she also made a large donation to the school. "I can't stop thinking about those sweet faces. And Emilie—her joy over finding the green starfish. I want to be like her, excited over the good things around me. You know?"

"I know," Anne agreed.

"The world is such a big place. There's potential everywhere to do good things. I'm going to take opportunities to make a difference whenever they are placed before me."

Anne held her matcha up to toast Dodie's coffee. "To good things!"

They spent an hour or so at Benny and Joon's favorite dog park, then went to Anne's parents' house so Anne could grab some clothes for the week. On the way back to the townhouse, they picked up burgers. When they pulled up at Dodie's place, Jeanette was standing outside talking to someone.

"That's Jason," Dodie said. "What's he doing here?"

Anne and Dodie hopped out, leaving Benny and Joon barking from the car. "Jason!" she called. "What are you doing here?"

"You moving?" he asked, ignoring the question.

"Yeah," she said. "What do you need?"

"I was wondering if we could talk?" he asked.

"Not a good time," Dodie said. "I need to talk with Jeanette here, and then I'm going to eat dinner."

"Can I come in, just for a bit?" he begged.

"No, Jason," Dodie said. "I'm not even sure what we have to talk about."

"I just want to know what you know about

Lucy and Aaron," he said.

"I don't know anything about them," she replied. "And I don't care to. They're moving on with their lives. You need to move on, too."

Jason shook his head. "No. Never. She can't just leave me. We were going to have a family. I put everything I had into our house. Now she wants to sell it? And split the money? It's not right."

"Jason, this is a conversation for your lawyer," Anne said. "Dodie doesn't know anything about your situation."

"That's what Lucy said. That I need to talk to her lawyer. Is that what you think, too, Dodie?"

Dodie kept her anger in check. "Jason. I do not want to talk about this with you. It is none of my business. Yes. Talk to a lawyer. But stop bothering me about it. Please leave."

He looked from Dodie to Anne to Jeanette. He opened his mouth as if to protest, but Dodie pointed toward his car. He furrowed his brow, then turned away. They watched him drive off, then Dodie let the dogs out of the Jeep.

Once they were settled back in the house, Dodie apologized to Jeanette.

"I'm so sorry he bothered you," she said. "It's a long story, but basically he won't leave me alone."

Jeanette wasn't fazed. "I've known his type," she said. "You might need to get a restraining order on him. I would. Especially if he comes around again."

Anne agreed. "Dodie, that's a great idea. Maybe a restraining order will snap him back to reality. He's living in a dream world where he can't possibly imagine his little wifey leaving him."

"One thing after another," Dodie said sadly. "When will this end?"

Anne looked at Jeanette. "So how did it go?"

Jeanette smiled. "We had three showings while you were out. I think all three are strong prospects. We might even have a bidding war."

"After three showings?" Dodie was shocked.

Jeanette nodded. "Like I said, there aren't many townhomes available right now. And yours has a lovely small yard, fenced in, no less. That is a unique feature. Don't be surprised if you hear from me by tomorrow with an offer."

Dodie whistled. "Wow. Does it really happen that fast?"

Jeanette patted Dodie's hand. "Sometimes it does."

"I don't know what I'd do without you," Dodie said. "Thank you."

The next morning, while Dodie sorted through the office mail, she got a text from Jeanette. They had two offers come in, both above Dodie's asking price, however both requested a fifteen-day close. Dodie asked Chris if his sister could join them for their scheduled Monday lunch to go over the details of the offers.

"Which one should I take?" Dodie asked.

"You don't have to take either," Jeanette explained. "It is entirely your decision. They are both above your asking price, which tells me we can hold out and see if we get a higher offer if you wanted. If you want us to ask for more time, we can do that too. Fifteen days is doable, but it is quick."

Dodie shook her head. "The offers are good. Heck, I'd be happy with even the asking price. It's way more than I paid for the townhouse."

Chris cut in. "But Dodie, prices are up everywhere. The extra money you gain will go right back into your new place."

"I hadn't thought about it that way," Dodie said.

"If you want, I can disclose to the potential buyers that we've had competing offers and see what comes of it," Jeanette said.

"That sounds good," Dodie agreed.

Jeanette responded to both buyers' agents that there were two offers on the table and the seller was considering them. Before lunch was over, one of the agents responded back with the offer increased by $15,000. Dodie was ready to accept it, when the other agent responded with a $25,000 increase, all cash.

Dodie chose the higher offer.

With only fifteen days, she and Anne began packing right away after work. Anne's parents had a small studio apartment above their garage. Dodie and the dogs would be moving in there until Dodie could find the perfect place. It had enough room that Dodie didn't even need to get a storage unit for her things; she sold the appliances with the townhouse and decided to get rid of the bedroom furniture and anything else that reminded her of Aaron.

"This is going to be easy-peasy," she said to Anne as they sat on her kitchen floor, wrapping Dodie's favorite coffee mugs and the few dishes she had in newspaper and bubblewrap.

"I'm so glad you'll be close by. I can come hide out in your apartment when my parents are driving me crazy. Which is all the time," Anne said.

"Your parents are the best," Dodie said.

"Yeah, they are pretty great."

"Let's call it quits for now," Dodie suggested. "I'm kind of tired. It's starting to get dark. Feels like movie time!"

"Want me to go get Chinese food?" Anne asked.

"Ooh, yes, please," Dodie's stomach grumbled happily at the thought. "Garlic chicken, fried rice, spring roll. Hot and sour soup. Will you let the dogs out before you go? Just throw them in the yard. I'll get up in a minute and get their supper."

Anne opened the slider, and Benny and Joon trotted out to do their thing. She grabbed her purse and left. Dodie sat for a moment longer, surrounded by boxes and newsprint-wrapped kitchen ware. She was peaceful about the move, but she was exhausted.

I'll close my eyes for just a minute, then I'll get up, she thought. Her head bobbed as she dozed off. A low thud jerked her awake. *Was Anne back?* She could hear Benny and Joon jumping at the sliding glass door, barking wildly.

She stood slowly, achy from sitting on the floor. It was fully dark outside now, so she flipped on the kitchen light. A figure appeared in the dining room. Dodie gave a small scream.

"Hi Dodie."

"Shit. Jason! How'd you get in here?" she demanded.

"Oh, the door was open," he said.

"No, it was not," she retorted.

"It was unlocked. I saw your friend go home for the night, so I knew you were here. I was going to knock, but I knew you'd look out the window and probably not even answer."

Adrenaline pumped through her chest.

"You shouldn't just walk into someone's house, even if the door is unlocked. Why'd you do that, Jason?" she asked, trying to steady her voice. If she could keep him talking, Anne would be back soon. If she could open the slider, Benny and Joon would tear him up.

"I told you, Dodie. I want to talk about what happened. You won't talk to me."

"Let's go sit in the living room," she suggested.

"Fine. But first," he walked to the patio door and flipped the lock. Benny and Joon were going crazy on the other side of the glass. Benny was flinging himself up against it, and Joon was howling ferociously. "Those dogs of yours don't seem to like me very much," he said coolly. He indicated that Dodie should go into the living room.

Dodie's living room boasted a small armchair on either side of the couch. She sat in the one that faced the front door. Jason came around and sat in the other. The dogs continued their frenzy. Dodie studied Jason from across the coffee table; she wanted to keep distance between them. He leaned forward in his chair, placing his forearms on his legs. His hands were fidgety.

"Can't you shut them up?" Jason asked.

"The only way they'll stop is if I let them in," Dodie offered. She started to stand.

"No. Sit," he ordered.

Dodie noticed that the cuff on his jacket had a dark stain on it, as did the heel of his right hand. He caught her staring.

"Is that blood?" she asked cautiously, not sure she wanted the answer.

He shrugged. "Yeah."

"Jason, how can I help you?" she asked, her unease evolving to full-on fear.

He laughed. "Now you want to help me? Now? I tried and tried to get you to help me figure out how to talk sense into Aaron and Lucy. But you wouldn't help me. It's too late now."

"Jason, Aaron wanted to divorce me. There isn't anything I could do about that."

"Maybe if you tried harder to get him back, Lucy would have come back to me," Jason accused. "But you didn't care about that, did you?"

"It hurts like hell that they were cheating on us behind our backs," Dodie said. "I feel like an idiot because I didn't see it coming. I'm sure you do, too. I'm so angry at them both for what they did." Jason was nodding along with her. "But Jason, I don't want Aaron back. Ever. I'm better off without him."

"Dodie, you could have talked sense into him," Jason insisted. "You could have, but you didn't. And now it's too late."

Dodie shook her head. *Why did he keep repeating that?* "It's too late because they both moved on. I've moved on. You need to move on, too. I never wanted him back. And what makes you think if Aaron and Lucy break up that she'd come back to you anyway?"

"Don't you say that!" he yelled. He leapt across the coffee table toward her with his arms outstretched. He grabbed her, enclosing his hands around her neck. At the same time, Anne burst through the front door. He turned as Anne flew toward him, loosening his grip on Dodie. Anne's Glock was in her right hand. She swung it hard at his face, connecting the butt of the gun with his cheek. He released his grip completely on Dodie, who scrambled to the back door to let Benny and Joon inside. They pounced on Jason, driving him to the ground. He curled in a ball on the floor of Dodie's living room and covered his face with his arms while the dogs tore at his jacket.

"Call 9-1-1!" Dodie screamed, but she already heard sirens.

"They're on the way," Anne promised. She stood over Jason with her gun pointed at him. Dodie called Benny and Joon to come to her, which they did. The room started to spin. The last thing Dodie remembered were several uniformed officers racing into her house.

Dodie opened her eyes. She was in the back of an ambulance. Anne and a face she didn't recognize were staring at her. The wail of the siren pierced her head.

"Ma'am, can you hear me?" the paramedic asked.

Dodie nodded. There was an oxygen mark over her nose and mouth. She reached up for it. The paramedic gently removed her hand from her face. "Let's leave that on there, please. We're almost at the hospital. They'll take care of you."

Dodie looked at Anne. Anne knew the question Dodie wanted to ask. "The dogs are fine," she said, patting Dodie's arm. "Perfectly fine. Not a scratch on them. The police took Jason into custody. An officer will meet us at the hospital."

Dodie closed her eyes. Benny and Joon were okay.

The emergency room staff were ready for her when the ambulance arrived. Chris and Sherry were already there, as Anne called them the minute the police arrived at Dodie's house. The doctors thoroughly examined Dodie. They even ran x-rays to ensure there was no new damage to her pelvis. She would have slight bruising around her neck from where Jason grabbed her, but she would be just fine. Her fainting was accounted to the enormous stress of the evening and still being weak from her previous injuries.

After the doctors gave the all-clear for officers to question Dodie, Anne, Sherry, and Chris listened while Dodie relayed the story to the police officers.

"Just as he came at me, Annie busted in the front door and hit him," Dodie finished up. "I don't remember much after that."

"You hit him with your gun?" the officer clarified.

"Yes, sir," Anne said. "The other officer took my gun and permit to check it all out."

"You didn't fire it though, correct?"

"No, sir," Anne said. "I just wanted to get him off of her. It happened really fast."

The officer nodded. "You did a great job," he assured her. He looked at Dodie. "You both did. It was very smart of you to keep him talking as long as you did. The other girl had it a bit rougher."

"Other girl?" Dodie asked.

The officer nodded. "We got to your place so fast because we were already on the way. Before coming to your house, Jason allegedly went to the apartment where his ex is living. When she tried to get rid of him, he stabbed her with a screwdriver. Allegedly."

"Is Lucy–" Dodie couldn't finish the sentence.

"She'll survive the attack. He got her in the side. After he stabbed her, though, he'd said something about you, Dodie, and he left. Lucy called 9-1-1 and told us who he was. She said she was worried he was going to hurt you. So, like I said, we were on the way."

"Unbelievable," Chris said.

Anne then told her story to the officer. "I'd gone out to get supper. When I pulled up to the house and saw his car, I immediately called 9-1-1. The dogs were barking so intensely–almost like they were panicked. I knew something was wrong. I removed my gun from my purse. I entered the house and saw him over top of Dodie. I don't know if I said anything, I just rushed toward him and when he turned this head, I swung at his face."

Sherry gave Anne a hug. "You were so brave! I'm so proud of you."

"Thank you, Anne," Dodie said. "You saved my life."

The hospital kept Dodie overnight for observation. Anne went back to Dodie's to stay with the dogs. Dodie was worried there'd be a mess, but Anne texted to say it all looked pretty good. There was some blood on the hardwood where Jason had been lying on the ground with Benny and Joon on top of him, but it cleaned up easily.

The next day, Anne came by to drive Dodie home. As Dodie and the orderly waited by the curb for Anne to pull up, the hospital doors opened and another orderly pushed out another patient.

"Hi Lucy," Dodie said when she saw who it was.

"Hi Dodie," Lucy replied.

"Are you okay?" Dodie asked.

Lucy nodded. "I'll be okay. Several stitches and I had to get a tetanus shot. My mom is picking me up."

"Where's Aaron?" Dodie asked, surprised.

Lucy shook her head. "I don't know. We aren't seeing each other anymore. He moved out a couple of weeks ago." It was quiet for a moment, then Lucy continued. "I'm so sorry Dodie. For everything."

"Did you tell Jason that you and Aaron weren't together?" Dodie wondered.

Lucy nodded again. "I did. But when I said I didn't want to get back together with him, he flipped out. He said something about it being your fault. He had a screwdriver in his pocket. He pulled it out and stabbed me with it, then he took off."

Lucy's eyes teared up.

Dodie felt a bit sorry for Lucy. "Thanks for sending the police to my place."

"I really am sorry," Lucy said again.

Anne pulled up and helped Dodie into the car. Dodie gave Lucy a small smile as they pulled away.

Dodie stayed home from work that day. And the next. She continued packing her house. On the third day, she came across a box on the upper shelf in her closet that she hadn't gone through in years, some of her parents' things. She took it down gently, and wasn't going to open it, but a small whisper in her heart compelled her to break the tape and look inside.

Her dad's favorite watch. Their passports. Saved birthday and anniversary cards. Her mom's Raggedy Ann dolly. She hugged Raggedy Ann to her chest with a smile. Both of her parents had graduated from Colorado State University, and her mom had gone on to earn a master's degree in sociology. Dodie ran her hand over the embossed diplomas. The plastic anklet from the hospital that identified Dodie as "baby Scherer."

"Oh, Mom. I wish you'd never left me," she said aloud.

A small gold-pressed photo album caught her eye. Her mother's neat printing penned captions on the back of the photos, noting places and dates. In one photo, two teenaged girls grinned hugely at the camera, with their arms around each other's shoulders. Behind them was the largest house Dodie had ever seen. The description on it read: "1983-Me and Dorothy at Biltmore. Besties forever!"

Dodie knew she had been named after her mom's best friend. The last time she saw "Aunt" Dorothy, though, was at her parents' funeral. Being only one year old then, Dodie didn't remember her. Aunt Dorothy lived in another state. She'd sent Dodie Christmas and birthday cards for several years after her parents' death, but eventually, the correspondence had stopped.

Dodie pulled out her laptop and Googled "Biltmore." She saw it was in North Carolina and remembered that was where Aunt Dorothy lived. She spent the next two hours reading about the Biltmore Estate and the beautiful part of the country it was located. She was enthralled. The Blue Ridge Mountains. The French Broad River. The artistry. She didn't realize how amazing that part of the country was.

That night, she laid in bed, staring at the ceiling. Thinking. Wondering. An idea began to play in her brain, but she decided that she would keep it to herself. Until she was sure.

Closing day for the sale of her house came quickly, and things went smoothly. She walked away with a lot more money than she'd bought the place for, and she felt that Grandma would approve.

She was also confident that Grandma would approve of the next big decision Dodie made. She'd been doing a lot of research over the last couple of weeks. She was considering moving to Asheville, North Carolina.

JOEY

Encouraged by the academic progress Adam showed, and the fact that he'd come to school on his medication every single day since returning from the Thanksgiving break, Joey wondered if perhaps Adam should be moved to a general education classroom. She mentioned her idea to Tam and Johnson one morning.

Johnson laughed. "Good luck with that. They'll never move him."

"But it would be what is best for him academically. And socially. Don't you think?" Joey thought they'd be supportive, but they didn't even want to talk about it.

She brought it up later that day with Mrs. Dunne. Mrs. Dunne shook her head. "It won't happen, Russo," she said, not even looking up from her laptop.

"I've done some research, and a lot of students with oppositional defiance disorder are in general education. In fact, most all of them are." Joey had done her homework.

Mrs. Dunne looked up. "His parents didn't know what to do when he started acting out. They held off putting him on medication because they didn't believe in it. He had to be isolated."

"But now they know the medication works,"

Joey argued. "Don't you think they'd want to give him more opportunities?" Joey couldn't imagine how they'd want to keep him in the FISH room.

"Russo," she said with a sigh. "Make up your mind. First you tell me Evan would thrive in here. Now you're telling me Adam isn't thriving in here. You can't have it both ways."

Joey stood firm. "What's best for one student may not be what's best for another. I know you know that."

Mrs. Dunne shook her head and went back to her laptop, ending the conversation, but Joey would not be moved.

"Mrs. Dunne. Look at me please." Mrs. Dunne looked up. "My daughter died when she was five of a rare blood cancer. We didn't even know she had it until she was gone. I couldn't even bear to be around children for a while. I know you don't know me well, but believe me, giving my heart and energy to these kids has given me a new purpose. I'm just trying to do right by them."

Mrs. Dunne considered what Joey said. She acknowledged her with an almost imperceivable nod, then returned to her work.

"I'm going to go to the dean of students," Joey declared to Craig that evening. "I'm going to explain how general education would be the best environment for Adam. His past crimes should not be held against him."

"Shouldn't you ask Mrs. Dunne's opinion on that?" Craig asked.

"She'd tell me not to talk to anyone. She barely wanted to listen to me."

"Joey, you were the one who told me when you try and do what's right, it backfires on you. Are you prepared for that?"

"I have to try, Craig," she said. "If I don't fight for him, no one will. No one wants to fight for him."

"Maybe you should see if his parents want you to fight for him," Craig suggested. "Maybe they don't want him to be in general education."

Joey bit her lip. "I thought about that. It's a double-edged sword. If I get the parents' hopes up, but the dean shoots it down, the parents will be mad. If the dean agrees, but then the parents don't want it, that would be bad, too." She thought about it for a few minutes. "I will talk to his parents first."

After school the next day, she called Adam's mother. After introducing herself, Joey got right to the point. "Since Adam's been on his new medication, I have to say, his academic growth has been incredible. He is reading at his grade level. His math skills are at or even above grade level. And he shows incredible insight for comprehension."

"That's great to hear. I've always known how smart he is. I never receive positive feedback on his schooling," Adam's mother said sadly.

"I'm sorry I hadn't called you sooner with this," Joey said. "Can I ask—have you ever considered whether Adam would be able to handle a general education classroom schedule?"

His mother gasped. "Are you kidding? He's never been able to even manage the individualized environment. It's never been discussed with the school."

"Now that he is on medication, I truly believe he would thrive even more in the general ed classes. I wouldn't even be surprised if he qualified for advanced classes."

"Is the school asking if we want to move him?" his mother asked skeptically.

"Not exactly. I wanted to talk to Ms. Davies, the dean, but I wanted to see what you thought of the idea first."

"I see," his mother said. "It's no secret we've had to get a lawyer to help us deal with the school. I don't know the guidelines regarding his previous probation and what all that entails. But if the school felt that a general education setting would be the best for Adam, I can say that his father and I would be in support of it."

"That's so great," Joey was pleased. "I will talk to Ms. Davies and will get back to you."

Joey gathered a collection of Adam's recent schoolwork. When Ms. Davies arrived at school the next morning, she was surprised to see Joey waiting outside her office.

"Oh, hello, Mrs. -"

"Russo. Joey Russo," Joey said. "I teach in the FISH classroom."

"Ah, right. Mrs. Russo," she said, unlocking her office door. "Come on in. How can I help you?"

"I am sure you are familiar with the student Adam Gonzalez," Joey began.

Ms. Davies nodded. "Oh, yes. Did something happen?" Concern clouded her face.

"No, no," Joey said. "Well, yes, but nothing bad. Several weeks ago, Adam's doctors adjusted his medication. Since that time, he has become the most incredible student." Joey proceeded to show the dean samples of Adam's work and provide examples of how he is proving to be advanced in math and comprehension.

"Yes, this looks great," Ms. Davies said. "So, what do you need?"

"Well, I am wondering if perhaps it would be good for Adam to switch his placement, so he has a general education schedule," Joey said. "He could grow so much more, I believe."

Ms. Davies looked thoughtfully at Joey. "I see. What does Mrs. Dunne say?"

Joey took a breath. "Mrs. Dunne is not confident that I would get the support for moving Adam to general education."

"Support from who?"

"From the school. From you, I suppose. Or Mr. Matthews or Mrs. West. Whosever decision it is."

Ms. Davies did not reply right away. She leaned

back in her chair and interlaced her hands across her stomach as she considered what Joey had said.

"What made you decide to ask about this?" she asked after a long silence.

"I just believe it would be what's best for Adam," Joey said simply. "When he came back to school after his suspension, we were told that the goal was to place him in the least restrictive environment. That's why he was put with the FISH students as opposed to isolation. Now, it seems to me the least restrictive environment would be general ed."

"His behavior was extremely dangerous," Ms. Davies reminded Joey.

"And it has been under control with his new medication. How long will his past crimes be held against him?" Joey asked. "No one wants to see beyond what he did before. It's like he has no chance to redeem himself."

The first bell rang, indicating that there were twenty minutes before school began.

"Thank you for your insight, Mrs. Russo," Ms. Davies said. "I have to get to the cafeteria."

"Will you think about what I've said?" Joey asked.

Ms. Davies nodded. "Oh, definitely."

Later that week, Mrs. Dunne informed Joey that Mr. Matthews wanted to speak to her during the lunch break. Joey could only assume it was about her conversation with Ms. Davies. She was correct. Ms. Davies, Mrs. Rodriguez, and Mrs. West were all in the conference room when Joey and Mrs. Dunne arrived. No one looked happy.

"Mrs. Russo," Mr. Matthews began, "did you call Adam's parents and suggest that they request him to be moved to general education?"

Joey was stunned. "No! I mean, yes, I called his mother, but it wasn't to suggest they make a request. I wanted her to know how well he was doing on his schoolwork. I did ask if they would be open to the idea of general ed placement before I suggested it to Ms. Davies. He's such a smart kid, I feel he would be—"

Mr. Matthews held up a hand for her to stop. "Their lawyer contacted the district. They are demanding a convening of the ARD committee to discuss his placement. His dad wants him placed in general ed immediately. He's wanted him there all along, and your call gave them the fuel they needed to raise the issue again."

"But he belongs in a general ed classroom. He'll do very well there," Joey said defensively.

"It's only recently that has come to be the case," Mr. Matthew said. "It wasn't the best place for him before. You had no business raising the matter."

"So, when? When would it have been raised?" Joey asked.

"Possibly next school year. Possibly not at all," Mrs. Rodriguez interjected.

"But he'd be losing months of learning that way," Joey said, confused. "He's possibly even advanced."

"Are you saying you aren't working with him in the FISH room?" Mrs. Rodriguez asked.

Joey was insulted. "Of course, I am working with him. I can show you all the things he's doing. He needs more."

Mrs. Dunne spoke up. "We all work with Adam from time to time."

Joey looked at her, shocked. She rarely got out from behind her desk.

Mrs. West spoke up. "Mrs. Russo, isn't this your first teaching assignment?"

Joey crossed her arms. "What does that have to do with this?"

"I think you would be better serving the students if you stick to teaching them in the classroom and let those of us more qualified make the placement decisions," Mrs. West's condescending tone could not be missed. "We are now in a very awkward situation."

"Mrs. West, one does not need to have taught in a school for several years to have common sense. This is a matter of common sense." Joey's tone was flat.

Mr. Matthew raised his eyebrows. "Mrs. Russo, there is no doubt you care for your students. Moving forward, we ask that you discuss placement questions with myself or Ms. Davies before you talk to any parents. The student learning environment is an important decision."

Joey nodded. "That's all I was trying to do. Match the student with the right environment."

"You and Mrs. Dunne can return to your class," he said. "Thank you, ladies."

Joey looked at each of them once more before standing up. She pressed her lips together to keep herself from saying anything else, but righteous anger burned inside.

Mrs. Dunne waited until they were well clear of the conference room before speaking. "Holy crap, Russo," she said. "You got big balls."

"I'm so mad I don't even know what to say," Joey replied. "That woman is so—" She didn't know which word she was searching for. The bell sounded and the halls began to fill with students. It was passing period—that time in between classes when the general education students switched from one class to another. Students had four minutes to get to their next class.

Up ahead of them Joey spied Evan, clutching his water bottle, looking timidly around, seemingly uncertain of which direction to go.

"Oh! There's Evan," Joey said, and she quickened her pace. Before she could get to Evan though, a group of boys passed in front of him. Joey saw Tray reach over and snatch the water bottle from Evan's arm. A roar of laughter rose up from the boys, and Tray took off running down the hall.

Joey lost sight of him in the crowd. Evan gave a cry. Joey ran to him.

"Evan, sweetie, it's okay," Joey said. Evan looked at her with terror in his eyes. He dropped to the floor. Worried he'd be trampled, Joey stood over him to create a protective barrier.

"Mrs. Dunne, Tray took Evan's water bottle," Joey said. "Did you see that?"

"What on earth?" Mrs. Dunne said as she came up on where Joey stood. "Evan, stand up," she requested. He scrunched his eyes closed and began to rock back and forth.

"Heart fish. Heart fish," he repeated.

Joey squatted next to him and rubbed his back. "It's okay, Evan. We'll get your water bottle. We'll get it," she promised. To Mrs. Dunne she asked, "Can you find out what class Tray Miller has right now? We need to get Evan's water bottle."

Mrs. Dunne nodded. "I'll be right back."

The tardy bell rang, and the halls cleared. Mrs. Dunne returned shortly to find Evan and Joey exactly how she'd left them.

"Room 712," she said.

"Stay here with Evan?" Joey asked. "I'll go get it." Joey did not want to risk anything else happening to that water bottle. She ran to the 700 hall and knocked urgently on the door. A student opened it for her, and the teacher stopped giving her instructions and turned to Joey.

"Yes?"

Tray was sitting in the back of the room, not even paying attention. Joey said his name sharply. "Tray!" she snapped. He looked up. "Give me the water bottle."

Tray clucked his tongue. "I don't know what you talkin' bout."

Joey walked to where he sat. "I saw you take that boy's water bottle in the hall. I watched you do it. Give me the water bottle."

Kids around them started laughing. Joey snapped her head around. "Quiet. All of you. This is not funny," she barked. "Your classmate stole something that did not belong to him. Stealing is not funny." She looked back at Tray. "I am not going to ask you again."

"I don't have it," he said. "I threw it in the trash."

"You did what?" she asked incredulously. "How dare you! What trash?"

"Boys' bathroom," Tray said.

"Let's go," Joey ordered. She pointed toward the door. Tray skulked out of his desk chair and ambled toward the door. "Pick up the pace," Joey demanded. "There is a boy waiting for his property."

She followed him to the boys' bathroom. He went inside and returned a moment later with the water bottle. He thrust it toward her.

"Go back to class," Joey said. "I'll be dealing with you later."

"You threatenin' me, miss?" Tray asked.

"No, Tray. I am promising you that I will see that you are disciplined for this," Joey said. She turned and ran back to Evan, stopping in the staff washroom to give the bottle a cleaning.

"Here you go, Evan," she said when she returned to where Evan still sat on the floor. Mr. Matthews was now with him.

Evan took the water bottle from her and hugged it. "Thank you, Woffey," he said quietly. His face was red and tear stained.

"Come on, Evan," Mr. Matthews said. "Let's get you to class."

"Class?" Joey said. "Look at him. He can't go to class like that. He needs to calm down."

Mr. Matthews sighed. "I'll take him to the nurse's office and let him rest for a while."

"Tray Miller did this. I watched him snatch it from Evan. Mrs. Dunne saw it too. He threw it in the trash."

Mr. Matthews nodded. "I'll write him up for it. He'll get a day's suspension."

"He should also have to apologize," Joey suggested.

Joey was summoned to the office again the next day. "Russo. Matthews wants to see you," Mrs. Dunne said. "You're becoming quite popular."

"What now?" Joey wondered. When she got to the office, Tray was sitting there, grinning.

"Mrs. Russo," Mr. Matthews began. "Mr. Miller

here says you threatened him yesterday. Is that true?"

"Threatened him?" she looked at Tray. "Threatened you?"

He smiled. "Yeah. You threatened to beat me. And you told me to shut up."

"I most certainly did not," Joey said. "I told you I was going to make sure what you did was dealt with." She looked at Mr. Matthews. "I did deal with it. I told you, and you said you'd take care of it."

Mr. Matthews nodded. "Yes, you did." He looked at Tray. "You can go back to class."

When Tray left the room, Joey said, "Back to class? I thought you were going to suspend him?"

"His mother called this morning. She said that Tray told her that a teacher was harassing him. She said she was going to write a letter to the school board about it."

"Me? Does he mean me?" Joey was astounded. "I'm not harassing him."

"Did you go talk to Coach Dunne about him a few weeks ago?" Mr. Matthews asked.

"I did. He called some of our FISH students a derogatory word," she said. "It was borderline bullying."

"That isn't quite how he told it to his mother. She's up in arms," Mr. Matthews said. "If I suspend him, it'll add fuel to her fire. She's filed complaints against the school before."

"Fuel to her fire? Her kid stole a water bottle

from a boy with autism! How is that okay?" Joey cried. "In which way does my trying to defend a weaker student mean I am harassing someone?"

"I know you're upset," Mr. Matthews said, frustration in his voice. "It's been a trying week. I know your intentions are for the good of the students. Maybe you should take a few days off. We can get a substitute in the class."

"Are you suggesting I take some time off or are you telling me to take time off?" she asked.

"I am telling you. But I think it would be good for you," he said. "Maybe you should think about if this is the right career for you. You seem to be struggling to follow procedures."

Joey had no reply. She finished out the day in a daze, said goodbye to an equally stunned Tam and Johnson, and went home.

Part Two

The Coffee Shop

Craig found Joey in the kitchen nursing a mug of coffee early the next morning. "Do you want to go out for breakfast?" he asked. He'd taken the day off from work. When she conveyed all that had gone on at the school, she did so with such emotional detachment, he feared for her. Her heart was aching, and he knew at some point she would break down; he didn't want her to go through it alone.

"That'd be nice," she answered dully.

"How about Sawhorse? Biscuits and gravy calling your name?"

"Sure," she answered in the same tone. He recognized it. She was trying to sound like everything was fine, but everything was not fine.

She said little over breakfast. There wasn't much to say. She'd been asked to take a two week leave, even though everything she tried to do was for the betterment of the students. She tried to protect Evan. She tried to help Adam. She failed. She didn't want to talk about it.

After breakfast they walked the streets of downtown Asheville. Her favorite bookshop was open, and she bought Matt Haig's latest novel, which she'd been meaning to pick up for a while.

"I think I'll take this to Biltmore tomorrow," she said to Craig.

"That's a great idea," he hugged her. Biltmore therapy would be good for her.

Joey slept in the next morning, stirring only a little when Craig kissed her goodbye, and after she showered, she packed her new book in her bag and set off for Biltmore. The weather was cool, so she strolled through the gardens only briefly before making for the coffee shop.

The cold weather drove more people inside, but Joey secured a table near the bay window. She'd yet to open her book, nibbling on her cranberry scone first, when she saw a familiar face enter.

Craig's sister spotted Joey and gave a wave. Joey waved back. It wasn't unusual for them to bump into one another, his sister also frequented the gardens and the coffee shop as much as her scheduled allowed. Joey's sister-in-law ordered her own large hazelnut brew and a chocolate croissant.

"Hi!" she said, sliding into the chair opposite Joey.

"Dolly!" Joey said. "Fancy meeting you here."

Dolly smiled. "Well, my little brother may have told me to look out for you."

Joey furrowed her brow. "Oh, he did, hm?"

"I called him this morning to see if he wanted to grab lunch. He said he couldn't, as he took yesterday off, but told me you'd be here. So don't be mad at him."

"I couldn't be mad. I love hanging out with

you," Joey smiled.

"He said you've had a rough week," Dolly said.

Joey rolled her eyes. "You have no idea."

Dolly took a sip of coffee. "Well, we don't have to talk about it if you don't want to. Just know I'm here for you."

Dolly had spent twenty years teaching at Asheville School, a prestigious private school where students came from all over the world. She understood the difficulties of being a teacher.

Additionally, her daughter Mary, Joey and Craig's niece, had a six-year-old son who was just diagnosed with autism.

"The last few months have been so hard. I never realized the challenges special education students had in school," Joey said.

"And you want to fix everything for them," Dolly stated.

"There are things that need fixing!" Joey protested. "Important things! There are special ed students in general education settings and no one looks out for them. There's this adorable little boy with autism. He's shy and sweet, and he recently lost his mom. They took him out of our enclosed classroom and threw him to the wolves. He has to get from class to class by himself. Other kids pick on him. And who is there to care about that?"

Dolly shook her head in disgust. "That's terrible."

"Right? And when I tried to have the boy who

bullied him apologize and experience a consequence for his actions, they turned it back on me that I'm picking on the kid. I wasn't picking on him, I was fighting for Evan. No one else was."

"In my experience, people see the special education teachers as being weaker teachers than the general ed teachers. In truth, they are often our best teachers. They have the hardest jobs," Dolly said. She had taught for a few years in public schools before moving to Asheville School. "It isn't like that everywhere, but often our special ed teachers don't get the respect they deserve."

Joey sighed. "I had no idea it was like this. You know, a while back, I wanted to quit. I thought I wasn't made out for teaching. What I think I've realized is I want to teach; I don't think I'm cut out for the system."

"It's okay to see problems in the system," Dolly acknowledged. "Remember when we were on the *John F. Kennedy*?" Dolly's husband was a naval officer and they all got VIP treatment when the new *USS John F. Kennedy* aircraft carrier was christened a couple of years prior.

Joey nodded.

"You know how gigantic those aircraft carriers are, right? They're over a thousand feet long. If it needs to turn around, the whole thing has to turn, and there are a lot of parts that have to work together for that to happen. The school system is like an aircraft carrier. One part of it can't turn a different direction. The whole thing has to go together. And that means a lot of people have to be on board with the movement."

Joey thought about this. "I see your point. How do changes happen, then? It seems impossible."

Dolly smiled. "You turn around one person at a time. You do right by the person in front of you. You simply speak truth. There are few things in life simpler than the truth. You're doing the right things, Joey. The truth may be simple, but it requires thick skin. And the determination to do what's right, no matter what."

"I've never been known for having thick skin," Joey said. "Craig's always been the rock."

"Nonsense," Dolly said. "You've gone through the most difficult thing any parent could go through. You are a rock, too."

"I really care about those kids," Joey said. "If they fire me after this, what'll I do?"

"I don't know, friend," Dolly said. "But I know it'll be great."

Joey and Dolly sat for a while, people-watching and sipping their brews. Joey noticed Dolly was staring at a young woman waiting for her coffee.

"Do you know her?" Joey asked.

"She looks so familiar," Dolly said. "But I have no idea why."

"Maybe you were her teacher," Joey offered.

"Probably," Dolly said. "So many years. So many students."

The barista called out the girl's name to come get her coffee. "Café latte for Dodie!"

Dolly gasped. "Dodie!" she said loudly.

The girl took her coffee from the barista and turned to where Dolly and Joey sat. "Yes? Do I know you?"

"Dodie Scherer?" Dolly asked.

Dodie nodded. "Yes," she said hesitantly.

Dolly stood and wrapped her arms around the surprised woman. "You look just like your mother."

"Aunt Dorothy?" Dodie asked.

"Yes, love," Dolly said. "I can't believe it's you!"

Dodie smiled. "I can't believe it's you! I came here because of you."

Dodie pulled a chair to the table.

"You came because of me? How? Why?" Dolly asked.

Dodie took a deep breath. "I don't know where to begin."

Joey and Dolly waited patiently. Dodie studied her coffee cup.

"It's always best to start at the beginning," Dolly encouraged. "We have all day."

Dodie looked up, a comfortable déjà-vu settled over her. "Okay. Here goes."

It took Dodie nearly an hour to share her story with Joey and Dolly. She left out some of the more embarrassing parts of her struggle; even so, the older women alternated between tears and outrage at what Dodie had endured over the last few months.

"My dear, I am so sorry," Dolly said. She took Dodie's hand in her own. "So, what made you think to come to Asheville? And Biltmore?"

"I found a box of my mom's things. I hadn't looked at it in years. I found this." Dodie took the picture of her mom and Dorothy from her bag.

Dolly took it from her and smiled through tears. "Oh! She kept it."

"What is it, Dolly?" Joey asked. "Let me see."

"Dodie's mom and I met when we were ten years old," Dolly explained to Joey. "My family had taken a ski vacation to Boulder. Lilly and I met on the ski slopes. We were inseparable. After I returned home, we wrote letters and called each other. Each summer, our parents let us visit each other. Sometimes I went to Colorado. Sometimes Lilly came here." She turned the back of the picture over. She chuckled at the caption. "Me and Dorothy. You know, Lilly was the only person who refused to call me 'Dolly'?"

"Why's that?" Dodie asked.

Dolly shrugged. "She had this tattered doll of her own that she called 'dolly.' I think she didn't want to confuse us." Dodie smiled. Raggedy Ann.

Dodie continued. "When I saw this picture, I started Googling about the Biltmore Estate, and Asheville, and I fell in love with what I saw on the internet. I got the crazy idea that maybe what I needed was a fresh start in a new part of the country. I thought I would come for a visit and do some looking around, maybe see if I can find you, Aunt Dorothy, and decide for sure whether I wanted to move."

"God aligned your paths to cross," Joey said.

Dodie smiled. "I suppose so. I couldn't find you on Facebook or anywhere, Aunt Dorothy, but I remembered my grandma telling me you were a teacher at a private school. I was going to start there. But even if I hadn't found you, I am in love with this city. The people are so laid back. The mountains are beautiful. It feels like home."

"Well, then," Dolly said. "Here we are."

"Here we are," Dodie said.

"What will you do for work?" Joey asked.

"I've got some space to decide," Dodie said. "The company I work for has a North Carolina office. They're willing to let me work from home and do their invoicing and purchasing. But I don't really know if I want to keep doing the same thing, you know?"

Joey nodded. "Yes, sometimes a change is good." Joey's phone rang. "It's Adam's mother," she said with confusion. "I'll take it outside." Joey answered her phone and stepped out of the coffee shop.

"Have you thought about where you'll live?" Dolly asked.

"I need a place with a yard. I have two

Labradors," Dodie smiled. "Benny and Joon."

"Like the movie," Dolly smiled too.

Dodie nodded. "Yes. Like the movie. It's one of my favorites."

"There are some wonderful neighborhoods in Asheville," Dolly said. "I'd be happy to show you around?"

"I'd really like that," Dodie said. "I'll be here until next Thursday. I'm staying at the Holiday Inn not too far from here."

"Well, you are family. If you would like to check out of your room, you are welcome to stay with me. My husband Mike is out of town on Navy business, and I'd welcome the company."

"I don't want to impose," Dodie said.

"Not at all. I'd love it."

Joey returned to the table with a heavy sigh. "They'd sent a message home to the parents that I'd be out for a couple of weeks. Adam's mom wanted to know if she'd gotten me in trouble."

"What did you tell her?" Dolly asked.

"I don't want to get in *more* trouble," Joey said. "I told her it was a personal leave."

Dodie didn't ask, but Joey felt she should give her some context. "I teach at a middle school. In a special education class," she explained. "There have been a few things lately that have happened that I've been, well—"

"She got in some trouble for trying to do the right thing," Dolly clarified.

Dodie nodded. "Special education? That's impressive.

Joey shook her head. "Not impressive. I just started this job in September."

"You seem like you'd be really great with kids," Dodie said. "You know, my friends and I went on a cruise over Christmas. While we were in Honduras, we met the most amazing woman. She runs an entire school for special needs children. She told us that Honduran schools have no services to help students with disabilities. Isn't that sad? She said she'd been a teacher in a primary school there and couldn't stand to see kids with disabilities turned away. So, she opened a school for them."

"No kidding?" Dolly said. "A private school for special needs students. Huh." She folded her arms and raised her eyebrows at Joey.

"What's that look?" Joey asked.

Dolly opened her hands as if it were obvious. "Joey, maybe that's what you should do. Maybe that's what we should do!"

"Open a school?" Joey said.

"Yes! Open a school for students with autism and other developmental difficulties," Dolly said.

"Uh-huh. And who would come to our school?" Joey questioned.

"There are so many kids struggling in the school system who don't fit in. I bet we'd fill up quickly," Dolly said.

Joey grinned. "Sure." She looked at Dodie. "My

sister-in-law likes to dream big."

Dolly popped the last of her chocolate croissant into her mouth. "It's the only way to dream."

Dolly's words stuck with Joey. That evening, she read the same page in her book three times, not comprehending what was happening. Craig was watching the news and absently rubbing her feet.

"Joey? Did you hear me?" he asked.

"Hm? Sorry, honey, no. I was just thinking," she said vaguely.

"What are you thinking about?"

"Dolly said something today that I can't shake. She suggested that she and I open a private school for kids with autism."

Craig continued rubbing, pressing into Joey's instep.

"Aren't you going to say anything?" Joey asked.

"About what?"

"Did you hear me?" Joey said.

"Yup. I did. What do you want me to say?" Craig asked.

"Well, I don't know," Joey stuttered. She was offended at his lack of reply but didn't know why. They were both quiet until the next commercial. "I mean, it's a ludicrous idea," she said. "Right?"

"Why would it be ludicrous?" Craig asked.

"People don't just go around opening private

schools. Don't you need, experience, or something?" she asked.

"I don't know, Joey," Craig said. "But I know one thing. You and Dolly have experience."

Joey didn't sleep well that night. She kept wondering about the possibility of opening a school. Around two, she slipped out of bed and opened her laptop. She searched the internet for private schools for students with autism and other disorders. She was surprised to learn that there were private school programs for special needs kids all across the country, but interestingly, there were none locally.

Craig found Joey in the kitchen on her laptop the next morning, jotting notes into a notebook.

"Whatcha doin' babe?" he asked, kissing the top of her head. "How long have you been up?"

"Craig, do you know, there are a handful of private schools for kids with autism in North Carolina, but none are close to us?" she asked.

"I did not know that," Craig said. He poured himself a coffee in his travel mug. He took his lunch from the refrigerator.

"It's true," Joey continued. "I looked at what is required to open a private school. I made a list here," she tapped the notebook. "It's not unreasonable. Once you find a location, you send a letter to the—what?"

Craig was looking at her smiling. "I have to go

to work, babe." He kissed her again. "I'll see you later."

"Craig–" she called.

"Yes?"

"Is it okay that I am getting this information together?"

He walked back over to her and hugged her. "I'm on your side. Always."

As soon as he left, Joey called Dolly. "Got time for a coffee?"

Joey met Dolly and Dodie at the bake shop at Biltmore. They ordered their coffees and an assortment of pastries and settled into a table.

"What did you two do last night?" Joey asked.

"Aunt Dorothy made us a lovely angel hair pasta and we trolled the internet for properties," Dodie said.

"Really? Did you find anything good?" Joey asked.

Dolly smiled. "We found a few things. I called my friend Shannon, who is a real estate agent, and we have a few appointments this afternoon. We can stop by your house first if you want to drop off your car."

Joey shook her head. "I don't want to be a third wheel."

Dolly leaned in toward Joey. "We're going to need you to help us make some decisions. We can't do this without you."

Joey squinted at them. "Decisions about Dodie's house? You don't need me."

"Decisions about the best location for our school," Dolly said. She leaned back in her chair to let the words sink in.

Joey looked from Dolly to Dodie. Both were smiling. "Our school?"

"Our school," Dolly said. "Think about it. I have worked in a private school for over twenty years. My last eight years I was in administration. I know how to run a school. You are a teacher. Together, we would be unstoppable. And we'd do amazing things for kids in this area."

"But, Dolly," Joey protested. "We can't just go get a building and open a school."

"Why not?" Dolly asked. "I'm retired. I have all the time in the world to commit to this. My grandson is going to need a school I trust. I would trust him to no one more than I would to you."

"Oh, Dolly," Joey said. She knew how concerned Dolly had been over Parker's diagnosis. She hesitated a moment, then took her notebook out of her bag. "Actually, I started looking into how to open a school. I couldn't get the idea out of my head last night. I started making a list of what we'd need to do, and I've started outlining the costs."

Dodie spoke up. "Aunt Dorothy?" They looked at Dodie. "I can help. With the school. I'd–like to help."

Dolly took Dodie's hand. "Oh, sweetie. We're

going to need all the help we can get."

Dodie shook her head. "I mean, financially. I can help financially. I'd love to be a part of the hard work, too. But I would like to financially contribute."

"We aren't going to take your money, Dodie," Dolly said. "But we would love to have you be a part of it."

"Wait. So, we're doing this?" Joey said. "Just like that?"

"JoAnn Russo. Would you like to run your own school for special needs kids? One that provides them with what they need? In a loving, caring, supportive environment?" Dolly asked, crossing her arms across her chest.

Joey didn't hesitate. "Yes. I'd love it."

"Okay, then. Let's see if we can do it. We'll take it one step at a time. When you take care of the small things, the big things will work themselves out. And our first step is to see if we can find a location."

"I need to call Craig," Joey said. "Before we go looking at buildings."

Dolly shook her head. "He already knows." Joey raised an eyebrow. "I called him this morning after you asked to meet up. I told him that I really thought we should do this, and I asked him if you'd be open to the idea. I wasn't going to present it to you if Craig thought it would stress you out or would be against it."

Joey grinned. "I guess I know what he said."

The Next Small Step

Dolly's real estate agent friend, Shannon, had three buildings lined up for them.

The first was woefully run-down, and although they knew there would be fixing up needed in whatever building they might find, it had too much structural damage to be a consideration.

The second was better, but as soon as they pulled up to the third building, Joey, Dolly, and Dodie all gasped. It had the look of a bungalow home, as opposed to a boxy, sterile office building. The brick was painted white with welcoming reseda green accents. Flat roof lines provided a contemporary feel, and a classy black wrought iron fence outlined the perimeter of the property. It was the kind of place you wanted to go inside, if for no other reason than to see how it was decorated. They parked in a small, paved lot that separated the building from a neighboring coffee house.

"The coffee shop is a good sign," Joey noted.

"Let's look at the exterior first," Shannon suggested.

The exterior was in pristine shape, and lots of large, tinted windows promised that inside would receive a lot of natural light. Behind the building was a neat, grassed yard that housed a children's play structure, a sandbox, and a small picnic area.

"That's odd," Joey said. "There's a playground?"

"This building was a day care center," Shannon explained. "Quite a large one."

"What happened to it?" Dolly asked.

"The property notes say that the family closed it down just after the pandemic began. The family moved overseas. When businesses started reopening, they just didn't."

"That's sad," Joey said.

"A lot of businesses went the same way," Shannon said. "Want to see inside?"

The three ladies gasped again when they stepped inside the entrance. The reception area was done in river stone accents, with a high ceiling and warm brown tones on the walls. Two small green couches invited visitors to wait comfortably, and the reception desk itself was large with lots of built-in shelves, cabinets, and drawers. To the right of the reception area, a waist-high gate gave access to the school.

"They've left some furniture, which can be negotiated into the price," Shannon stated.

"This is so perfect," Joey noted as they explored. It was designed to be mostly open concept, but there were several variously sized smaller rooms which would provide great flexibility for teaching. Because it had been a daycare, there was a complete kitchen and an area for students to eat.

Dodie began asking the realtor questions

about the square footage, occupancy, and whether the property had a rent-to-own provision available with the lease. Dolly and Joey looked at her quizzically.

"I was the office manager at my company," Dodie explained. "I worked directly for our Regional Controller. He had me deal with property matters and office rental space. Sorry if I overstepped."

"Not at all! Ask anything you think we need to know," Dolly said. She looked at Joey and whistled. "Brilliant!"

Dodie continued to ask important questions about the zoning, inspections, health codes, the condition of the HVAC and electrical equipment, and other elements of renting a commercial property that Joey would have never thought to ask. Joey and Dolly let her do her thing, asking clarifying questions as needed. Joey scribbled it all furiously in her notebook.

"What do you think, ladies?" Shannon asked when they'd exhausted their exploration and took pictures of everything they could.

"I think we need to schedule an inspection and take the next small step," Dolly said. "Joey?"

Joey nodded. "I'd like Craig and Mike to come see it," she said. "And yes, let's take the next step."

That evening, Dodie couldn't wait to call Anne. Benny and Joon were with her, and when Dodie

FaceTimed, Anne was lying in bed with one dog on either side of her. Dodie shared how she'd found Aunt Dorothy at Biltmore the day before and that Dorothy invited her to stay in her home.

"Her house is gorgeous. It's a log cabin style with a huge front porch. I'm sitting out here now." She did a panoramic of the view.

"Your Aunt Dorothy sounds pretty great," Anne said. "I'm so happy you found her."

"She is great," Dodie gushed. "And her sister-in-law, Joey, is the nicest person you'd ever want to meet. She reminds me of how Grandma used to describe my mom. They've just welcomed me into their lives."

"What do you think? Are you going to move?" Anne asked.

Dodie sighed. "I am, Annie. I really am. I haven't found a place to live yet, but I will. I can't describe it. It feels like I'm home. Benny and Joon are going to love it here."

"And I will be visiting you literally all of the time," Anne said.

"I haven't told you the best part," Dodie said. She proceeded to tell Anne about Dolly and Joey's big idea to open a school for special needs students.

"They're going to be just like Ms. Angelique!" Anne said.

"Yup. They're looking into whether they can do it. And if they do it, I'm going to help," Dodie felt proud as she said it.

"Dodie! Yes!" Anne exclaimed. "That's perfect. Simply perfect."

Dolly, Joey, and Dodie met at Joey's home the next day to lay everything out and make lists of the next steps that needed taking. Craig took the morning off to meet a building inspector at the facility to make sure there were no surprises that would prevent the building from passing health, fire, or safety inspections.

Meanwhile, the ladies were researching and outlining the financials. After a long morning, they shared their findings.

"Tuition at most private schools for kids with autism or other special needs ranges from $18,000 to about $25,000 in North Carolina," Joey shared.

"How do parents afford that?" Dodie wondered.

"Good news. There is grant money available from the state and through the Autism Society of North Carolina and other programs. Families have options, and it seems like most families qualify to have the bulk of that cost covered. Which would be good for us, since our money would come directly from the state. In addition, as a private school there are funds and grants we can apply for to help with operating costs," Joey said. "I figure, if we set tuition at $21,000 per student, we would need ten students in order to cover our basic costs. Most school ratios are 1 to 6, but I would strongly suggest we strive for 1 to 5, and maybe even 1 to 4, depending on the needs of the students who enroll."

"Ten students sound like a great start," Dolly said. "What is our maximum?"

"Strictly based on space, we could have up to fifty, maybe more. But we would have to be very strategic with how we plan the space out and structure the learning. For the first two or three years, I would want to keep it around twenty or twenty-five?" Joey suggested.

"Once we know how we want to lay out the floor plan and the classroom needs, I've found a few options for furniture and other equipment. All of it will be driven by the floor plan, though," Dolly said.

Breakfast and lunch food and some of the other costs depended on how many students enrolled, but Joey's plan of $21,000 for tuition would allow for those costs to be easily met.

Craig FaceTimed them from the building and gave a thumbs up. He, too, was impressed with the quality of the space, and the inspector said everything was in good shape. Fire extinguishers needed up-to-date inspections, but there wasn't anything he saw that should prevent them from getting their license to operate. They could proceed with applying for the lease.

Dodie had been on the North Carolina State Board of Education site and the NC Department of Administration site to determine how to officially register their business with the state. The process was surprisingly straightforward.

"Well, then," Dolly said. "It seems to me like we can do this. The question remains, do we want to?"

She looked to Joey for a response.

"Do we really know what we are getting into? I have special education certification for teaching, but I don't have any other credentials. What if I don't know how to care for these kids in the way they need?" Joey said.

"I'm sure there will be a lot of things we don't know," Dolly said. "We will have to become students ourselves. But how have you handled it this year so far when you don't know what to do?"

Joey thought of Rick Lee's advice. "I ask myself, 'What's best for the kids?' and then that's what I do."

"Sounds like a solid philosophy for decision making," Dolly said. "Dodie, what do you think? Would you want to be a part of this adventure?"

"If you'll have me, I would like nothing better," Dodie said. "I know you said you didn't want my money but hear me out on something. I have accounting and office management experience from my job; my degree from CSU is Business Administration with an accounting concentration. If you'd let me, I'd like to be a partner in this with you. I can contribute financially for the startup costs, and when the business allows it, we can work something out? Please?"

Dolly looked to Joey. "What do you think,

Joey?"

Joey took Dodie's hand. "I can think of no better partner. And Dolly, yes, I want to do this. Are you sure *you* want to? You just retired, and this is a big risk. What if no kids come?"

Dolly put her hand over Joey's and Dodie's. "First off, Dodie, I am so sorry we lost touch over these last few years. Secondly, Joey, I've only been retired for six months. I talked to Mary last night. She said she'd love to sign Parker up as our first student."

"One down, nine to go!" Dodie said.

"Yup. Except I doubt we'll charge Parker," Joey said.

Dolly waved them off. "The point is, it's going to be fine, Joey."

"What is this?" Mr. Matthews asked when Joey showed up in his office two days later.

"It's my resignation, Mr. Matthews," Joey said.

"Mrs. Russo, I didn't want you to quit," he said.

"You told me I should think about whether this is the job for me," Joey said. "I've thought about it. I am not sure this is the right place for me."

"You still have another week of your leave," he responded. "Why don't you take it? Don't do anything rash."

Joey shook her head. "No, thank you. I brought my computer and iPad back. Here is my ID and the room key. I am assuming you'll let me out of my contract? This was, after all, your suggestion."

"Mrs. Russo, having you go on leave was just to appease the parent," he explained. "She'll turn her attention elsewhere, and we carry on. It's okay."

"You put me on leave to appease the parent? I'm sorry, but that's *not* okay," Joey said with rising anger. "Here I felt horrible about coming in here and leaving the FISH room kids, but if you pull stunts like this on your staff, I can't believe I felt badly at all!"

"You are leaving us shorthanded," he warned.

"There are three teachers in that classroom. The classroom has nine students now. A one to three ratio is much better than state guidelines," Joey said knowledgeably. "If all three teachers are actively working with students, they should be fine."

He stood from behind his desk. "Mrs. Russo, this is not how I wanted this to go."

"Well, Mr. Matthews, I'm not happy that this is how it is turning out either. But again, I trust you will recommend the board let me out of my contract? It might make you look even better to the parent?" she said in an uncharacteristically sarcastic tone.

"That parent always writes the board," Mr. Matthews said with a wave of his hand. "It never amounts to anything. That's no reason to quit teaching."

"I don't plan to quit teaching," Joey said. "This is clearly not the right environment for me. And this parent's unfounded complaint and your lack of support has amounted to something for me." She said with a hand on her heart.

Mr. Matthews pressed his lips together. "Well, then. Thank you for your candor."

She held out a hand. "Mr. Matthews, I wish you well. I really do." He shook her hand reluctantly. She asked if she could say goodbye to the students, but he advised against it. She was disappointed, but she understood. Maybe her leaving would be the prompt Mrs. Dunne needs to step up and be there for the kids.

That evening, Dolly invited Craig and Joey over for dinner. Mike was back from his trip, and Dodie was scheduled to return to Colorado the next day. Over grilled lemon chicken with new potatoes they shared ideas for the school.

"The real question is this—" Mike asked. "What are you going to name it?"

"I had an idea," Joey said cautiously. "But I don't know if you guys will like it?"

"What is it?" Dolly asked.

Joey got up from the table. "I'll be right back." She ran to Craig's car and returned with a framed picture. She held it up for the others to see.

"That's Ivan's painting," Craig said.

Joey nodded. "It is."

"Who is Ivan?" Dodie asked.

Joey told the story of the day she brought the

paints to school, and how Ivan passed away that weekend. She continued to share how the picture was hanging in the classroom and Adam, before he got the help he needed medically, ripped it by throwing a large rock at the wall.

"I brought the picture home to fix it and laminate it," Joey explained. "But I never brought it back to school. Instead, I framed it and offered it to Ivan's mom. She gave it right back to me."

"What does this have to do with the name of the school?" Mike asked.

"The Ivan Learning Center," Joey said. She looked sheepishly at them all. They all looked at Dolly.

"Brilliant!" she said. "Absolutely brilliant!"

"I called Ivan's mom today. I told her about our school," Joey said.

"And you asked if we could name it after Ivan?" Craig guessed.

She nodded. "I told her I needed to see what my partners thought about it. It's just an idea. We don't have to name it—"

"Joey, stop," Dolly ordered. "It's brilliant. I love it. Dodie?"

Dodie nodded. "I agree."

Goodbye, Colorado

Jason's court appearance was short and uneventful. Dodie sat on the opposite end of the courtroom from Lucy; she didn't really have anything more to say to her. She was there to give testimony, but as it turned out, Dodie wasn't even called to the stand. Jason pleaded guilty to aggravated assault for stabbing Lucy and breaking and entering, false imprisonment, and aggravated assault for his attack on Dodie. He was sentenced to ten years, with the option for parole in seven. He was also ordered to receive psychiatric care.

Much to Anne and Sherry's disappointment, Dodie opted not to have an official goodbye party with people from the office. Instead, they, along with Chris and his wife, Walt, and a couple of the engineers Dodie liked, went to a local Mexican restaurant and enjoyed a long dinner, complete with lots of laughs.

Chris helped Dodie pack her U-Haul, promising that he knew people in North Carolina, in case she ever needed anything. Just like that, less than three weeks after she returned from Asheville, she, Benny, and Joon began the 1,500-mile trek toward her new home.

Two Months Later

Joey pulled into the paved lot of the school, happy to see Dodie's Jeep already there.

"Dodie!" she called as she came through the front door. Benny and Joon came running.

"Hi, guys," she said. "I'd pet you, but my arms are full."

Dodie came around the corner. "Joey! Let me help you with those." She grabbed a couple of bags from Joey. "What is all this stuff?"

"These are for the sensory room," Joey said. "There's more in the car. Wait till you see how amazing it is going to be!"

"I can't wait to see what you've got planned," Dodie said. "I Googled 'sensory rooms' so I could better understand the goal. What an incredible idea to have a room where kids can escape when they are overstimulated."

They walked to the back. Joey smiled. "Actually, we are going to have *two* sensory rooms. We'll use those two—" she pointed to two rooms on the west wall. "One will be done in shades of pinks, blues, and purples. The other will be done in browns, greens, and a more nature-based color scheme."

"Students can choose," Dodie said. "Sweet!"

"Craig is coming tonight after work. He is going to install two hanging egg chairs in each room."

"I love it!" Dodie said. "What can I do to help?"

"Let's set up the rest of the stuff in the rooms."

The floors throughout the center were redone in an industrial wood laminate, the grey planks complementing the soft colors on the wall. They'd had some low walls constructed to create four open classrooms in the large space of the school. Shades of light blues, greys, and light greens created separation.

In the sensory rooms, they covered the floors with soft padded mats. Joey had purchased large, comfortable pillows and bean bags for reclining. Low tables lined the walls, and Joey and Dodie filled baskets on the tables with things that would meet a student's need for touch, sound, and movement. Himalayan salt lamps gave the rooms a warm glow. Joey also bought a wireless speaker for each room to play soothing sounds. The finishing touches were rattan baskets to hold soft blankets and plushies.

"Dolly is going to go nuts when she sees this!" Dodie gushed. "These rooms are fabulous."

"The egg chairs will make them complete," Joey said. "So, what did you work on today while I was shopping?"

"I got the student information system installed on my laptop. When you and Dolly have a minute, we'll get it installed on yours too and I can schedule our training. It's a pretty cool system. It tracks all student data—attendance, health info, IEPs, gradebook, everything. And it manages the tuition and financial aspects as well. It runs all the reports we need to submit to the state for our accountability."

"I'm so glad we have you to help us with that part," Joey said. "You're a godsend."

"Nah," Dodie said. "You and Aunt Dorothy were the godsends."

After a couple of minutes, Joey could tell that Dodie was fighting back tears. She gave her a hug.

"What's wrong, Dodie? Are you regretting your choice to move?"

Dodie shook her head. "Just the opposite. I feel like I've come home. I always thought the meaning of life meant creating the perfect family. I looked forward to my someday, when the family part would work out for me. I couldn't wait for it, you know? Don't get me wrong, my grandma was the most incredible woman in the world—she was my superhero. But I felt like if I could just get married and start having kids, then my life would really mean something. I'd finally get it right.

"I realize now, the meaning of it all isn't for life to be perfect. It's to leave behind something of lasting value. The only way to make that happen is to do the right thing with what's in front of you. If you can't enjoy what you have right now, you'll never enjoy the future."

"You are a wise young woman, Dodie Scherer," Joey said.

Furniture arrived the following week. Individual work pods would give students privacy. Kidney tables in the shared space areas would allow small groups to work together. Giant leather couches were strategically placed throughout the center.

When the portable interactive smartboards arrived, curiosity brought Mike and Craig to the training session.

"This technology is incredible!" Craig said after the trainer left. "We have presentation equipment at work, but this is so much cooler."

"When I was in school, they still had chalkboards," Mike said with a laugh. "We have high tech conference rooms and whatnot in the Navy, but I didn't realize this kind of technology was in schools now. Kids today have everything."

"I think we are about ready to get a photographer in here. What do you think, ladies?" Dolly asked. "Get some photographs for our website and brochures?"

"The signage for out front and above the reception desk will be installed tomorrow," Joey said. "Then we'll be ready for pictures."

"Right," Dolly said. "How could I forget about that?"

Dodie said, "We should do an open house. Invite the press, send invites to the Special Olympics and local autism organizations, that sort of thing."

Dolly hugged her. "What a wonderful idea. We'd budgeted to do some mailings, but an open house would get people in the door!"

Dodie said, "We can create a Facebook event and promote it on Instagram and Twitter."

"Speaking of which, where are we with the website?" Mike asked.

"My friend Sherry is building it for us," Dodie said. "She's used some stock photos as placeholders until we get our own photos. You should have a look. It's www.TheIvanLearningCenter.com."

"Why don't we put it up on one of these smartboards?" Craig suggested. Dodie pulled it up.

"A supportive and welcoming place for neuro-divergent children to grow," Mike read from the home screen. "I like that."

"Every student holds unlimited potential when they feel safe and develop healthy relationships with their peers," Dolly read. "That's so good!"

They went through each page of the site together, giving props and making notes of tweaks and changes to send to Sherry. Overall, it was a site to be proud of.

The installation of the signage for The Ivan Learning Center brought a lump to all their throats. There was a sign near the street, a sign on the building, and a sign above the reception desk. They kept the logo simple, an oval with the words "The Ivan Learning Center" tucked neatly inside. A purple shooting star arced above the oval.

Dolly, Joey, and Dodie stood outside and stared at the sign and the building for nearly thirty minutes.

"It's beautiful!" they all agreed. Ivan's painted picture was also hung in the reception area and next to it, a framed 8 x 10 picture of Ivan.

"I have a surprise for you two. It will be delivered tomorrow," Joey said with a slightly wicked smile. "Don't come in until after lunchtime."

Dolly and Dodie promised, and at precisely twelve-thirty the next day, they pulled up. Joey met them in the reception area and made them close their eyes. She led them by the hands to where she wanted them, and when they opened their eyes, they squealed.

"Ta-da!" Joey said proudly. A thirty-gallon fish tank on a sturdy blue wooden base was filled with sparkling fish. Above the tank were three framed pictures.

"Oh, my word! Joey!" Dolly cried. "Where did you get this?"

"Looking at fish can be calming for children with autism," she explained. "Ivan's mom gave me some of the other paintings he did, so I framed them. I figure once we have some of our own students' artwork, we could use it to decorate the other walls."

"Fabulous," Dolly said. "It's coming together!"

"Now we just need students," Joey said.

The Open House

It's official! We can begin enrolling students!" Dolly called from her office. "I got the approval email from the BOE!"

"Woo-hoo!" Dodie called out. "Just in time for the open house."

It was a bit of a risk scheduling the open house before the approval came back, but moving forward was the only option. The open house needed to be done in May, before local schools let out for summer. Once families began summer vacations, chances of hitting their target number of ten students by August decreased. They picked the Saturday before Mother's Day.

Ten thousand families in the area received the postcard mailer designed by Sherry, and the Facebook event was shared on several local group pages. Joey enjoyed watching the number of people who said they were "Going" to the open house rise. The Autism Society of North Carolina put word in their newsletter as well. Each day they received a handful of phone calls with questions from local parents.

Dodie made up enrollment folders for prospective parents, complete with the forms parents would need to apply for the state grants for tuition. Dolly phoned the three big news stations, and one said they would definitely send a cameraman and reporter to the event.

"How many different kinds of pizza should we do?" Joey asked. She was preparing the catering order.

"Keep it simple," Dolly suggested. "Cheese, pepperoni, and one with veggies."

"I agree," Dodie said. "People will eat it no matter what. At least that's been my experience in event planning from my previous company."

"We'll do bottled water to drink. I am also going to get a couple of cases of small cartons of chocolate milk. The students in my class all loved chocolate milk," Joey said.

"Perfect. And we're getting a big sheet cake, right?" Dodie asked.

"I was looking at the Facebook event page. We might want to get two cakes. Over two hundred people have said they're coming," Dolly said.

"The RSVPs on those events are not super reliable," Dodie explained. "People will say they are 'Going' to an event, much the same way they 'Like' a post. It can be hard to gauge actual potential attendees."

"Hm. Well, we can throw caution to the wind, and if we end up with a lot more food than necessary, we can take it to the homeless shelter?" Dolly proposed. "What are you thinking for decorations, Dodie?"

"Balloons, flowers on the reception desk, a

banner outside that reads, 'Open House Today,' and," she paused for effect, "a bubble machine in the yard out back."

"Bubble machine! Awesome!" Joey said. "Kids love bubbles."

Dodie nodded. "I also had an idea. What if we make small goodie bags to give to the kids? Nothing too fancy, but maybe plastic bags with a couple of sensory toys in them? Pop-its, squishy balls, fidget spinner, that kind of thing?"

"Oh, Dodie! Yes. That's great," Joey said. "How'd you come up with that idea?"

"When we did events at work, we always sent prospects and customers off with a take-away. I know we are giving the enrollment folders, but I was trying to think of something for the kids. I've been reading as much as I can about autism. Meeting their sensory needs is a huge part of supporting their growth. It's fascinating. We can put a sticker on the outside of the bag with our logo and website."

"Okay, you order the stuff, and we'll have a goodie bag making party." Dolly grinned, thankful again that Dodie was a part of the team.

Anne and Sherry planned their first visit to Dodie's new home on the open house weekend to be extra helping hands. They flew in Friday after work, and thanks to Joey's organization and penchant for checklists, the school was ready, which enabled the three friends to go out to dinner then spend the evening relaxing at Dodie's new place. Catching up with Anne and Sherry fueled Dodie's soul, and she realized that although she missed seeing their faces every day, she was affirmed that she was in the right place.

Open house day was bright and sunny. Everyone arrived early to put the finishing touches in place. They wore matching collared shirts that Dodie had ordered with the school logo embroidered on the right breast.

"Oh my, look at us!" Dolly said. "The most professional looking bunch this side of the Appalachians. Come. I have a surprise for you all."

She led them to the conference room, where a framed child's painting hung on the far wall. The building looked like the school, and in front of it, three smiling stick figures wearing matching shirts were obviously meant to look like Dolly, Joey, and Dodie. A shining sun and a rainbow arced over the building across a bright blue sky.

"What is this?" Joey asked. "Who painted it?"

"Parker did!" Dolly said. "Isn't it amazing? It looks just like us."

Anne squealed. "Dodie! It's your future!" When everyone turned to look at Anne, she explained. "Last year, Dodie told me she was having trouble envisioning a picture of her future. But here it is."

Dodie hugged her friend. "Annie, you always

know what to say."

"There are cars already in the lot," Dolly said with a sniffle, looking out the window. "It doesn't start for another hour."

"If we're ready, we can let them in," Joey said. "If they have kids out there, we don't want those kids to have to sit in a car too long."

Craig clapped his hands together. "Let's do this!" He kissed Joey on the cheek and whispered, "I'm so proud of you," and he headed outside. Craig had backyard duty, ensuring safety of the children who wanted to explore the yard and play near the bubble machine. Over the last month, he used his carpentry skills to strengthen the wooden climber and built an extension, creating a bridge and lookout with a winding slide. He removed the sandbox and laid down a small rubber court with an adjustable basketball hoop. The yard was a safe place for kids to burn off energy.

Dodie took up her spot in the reception area to welcome parents, have them sign the guest book, and hand out enrollment packets. Anne's role was kitchen duty, supported by Mike.

Joey and Dolly remained in the teaching areas to explain the learning philosophy, show the curriculum, and answer questions. All three of the smartboards were powered up and displayed a sample schedule of the school day.

Dolly's daughter Mary came to help, too. Parker claimed one of the egg chairs as his own and happily watched movies on his iPad so Mary could monitor the sensory rooms.

Sherry's role for the day was to float around and check on the others, helping however needed. When everyone was in place, Dodie unlocked the front door and indicated to the waiting parents that they could come in.

The first hour was a whirlwind. A steady stream of families came through, keeping everyone on their toes. Some were clearly just curious, others more serious. Joey and Dolly were enthusiastic and passionate, and the more they talked about the program and philosophy driving the school, the greater their confidence in their decision.

"We are limiting our first year enrollment to twenty students," Joey was in the process of saying in response to a parent question, when she noticed a news crew enter. Sherry was walking with them, to make sure they found Joey and Dolly.

"Rylie Robinson, channel thirteen news," a friendly reporter held out her hand. Dolly and Joey shook hands with her and introduced themselves.

"You are the owners of The Ivan Learning Center?" Miss Robinson clarified.

"Yes, we are," Dolly answered. "We're so glad you are here."

"This is a big thing for Asheville. Our first private school for kids with autism," Miss Robinson said. "It's exactly what we need. Can we interview you?"

They moved to the conference room.

"Can you tell me what brought you to deciding to open the school?" Miss Robinson asked Joey.

Joey was ready for this question. "I was a special education teacher in a public school. I saw a need," she said simply. "Public schools are full of wonderful, hardworking teachers. My sister-in-law and I want to support our community by offering options for parents trying to navigate the uncertainties of autism and other developmental challenges."

"My grandson was recently diagnosed with autism," Dolly explained. "I worked for the Asheville School for more than twenty years. I've been both a teacher and an administrator. I could think of no better purpose for this next phase of my life than this."

"Tell me about the program," the reporter stated. Joey explained the concept behind the daily structure. Academic skills would be addressed in the morning, life skills in the afternoons. Students would have structure, but there would be plenty of choice within the structure, so students would have a sense of ownership and control. If students needed occupational therapists or speech therapists, parents could arrange for those to be built into the students' weekly schedule.

"Tell me about the name of the center. The Ivan Learning Center. Where does 'Ivan' come from?" Miss Robinson asked.

The wall separating the conference room from the open area of the school included large glass windows. Joey noticed Ivan's parents had arrived and were out there, watching the interview along with other curious parents. She waved them in.

"Miss Robinson, this is Mr. and Mrs. Green. Their son, Ivan, was one of my students. He inspired me," Joey said with a smile.

"Where is Ivan now?" the reporter asked.

Ivan's dad put an arm around his wife. "Our Ivan passed away a few months ago," he said. "We are so thankful to Mrs. Russo for keeping his memory alive in this way. We came today because we wanted to present her with this donation to the school." From his pocket he removed an envelope. He handed it to Joey.

Joey opened the envelope and blinked in disbelief at the amount on the check. "Mr. Green, this is not necessary."

"Don't worry, we want to do this," Mrs. Green said. "And every year, we want to sponsor a student with a scholarship in Ivan's name. In the short time you taught Ivan, you did more for him than anyone else. We could tell that he loved you."

The reporter looked at the cameraman. "Did you get all that?" He nodded.

The reporter and cameraman allowed Dolly to show them around the school, while Joey stayed to talk to Ivan's parents.

"This check is too much," Joey said. "I'm sure you need this money."

Ivan's mom shook her head. "We don't. We are fine." She hugged Joey. "Can we come by from time to time and visit? I am a teacher, you know."

"You are?" Joey asked. "I didn't know."

She nodded. "I taught first grade. I went on leave after Ivan passed away. I don't know if I'll go back."

Joey smiled. "There will always be a place for you here. Who knows? If we get more than ten students, we'll need another teacher."

"Please let me be your first call," she said.

Joey saw another familiar face through the conference room window. "Excuse me, Mrs. Green, I'll be right back," she said. She left the conference room and worked her way to where a woman was starting to speak to the reporter.

"Excuse me, Mrs. West. What are you doing here?" Joey asked. It was Beverly West, the Black Bear Creek school diagnostician.

"This reporter just asked what I thought about all of this," Mrs. West said sweetly.

"I thought it would be good to capture statements from prospective parents," Miss Robinson said.

"I think that's a great idea," Joey said. "I'm not sure this is a prospective parent, however. Are you, Mrs. West?"

"You are correct, Mrs. Russo," Mrs. West said.

"I'm here as a curious colleague. How does a first-year teacher suddenly decide to open a private school? What makes you think you are in any way qualified?"

Joey was at a loss for words. A voice behind her answered for her. "The state of North Carolina thinks she is qualified. As do I." Joey turned around. Mr. Matthews stood there with a woman Joey recognized from the pictures in his office as his wife.

"And you are?" Miss Robinson asked, holding the microphone toward Mr. Matthews.

"Darryl Matthews. I'm the principal at Black Bear Creek Middle School. Mrs. Russo worked for me. Her heart for kids and integrity to do right by them is admirable. I can think of no one better to run an entire school committed to growing children to reach their full potential." He looked at Mrs. West. "Isn't that right, Mrs. West?"

Mrs. West shook her head. "Best of luck to you, Mrs. Russo. Excuse me." She turned on her heels and made for the exit.

"Can we talk to you, Mrs. Russo?" Mr. Matthews asked. "In private?"

"Of course," Joey said. She looked to the reporter. "You won't–"

"Put that interaction in my report? No," she shook her head. "I can spot sour grapes when I see them. There's no place for that in this story. What you're doing here is a wonderful thing."

The reporter and cameraman went to the yard to capture some shots of students playing for the story. Joey led Mr. and Mrs. Matthews to the conference room, which was now vacant as Mr. and Mrs. Green were exploring the building.

"How can I help you?" she asked.

"First of all, I want to apologize for making you feel that our school was not a place you wanted to work," Mr. Matthews said. "I thought a lot about what you'd said. You are right. I should have stood up for my staff. And my students. I'd like you to know, one of our paras has passed her state exam and has taken the full-time teacher position. She's bright and passionate. Like you. Your intuition for what students need is spot on. And it clearly comes from a good place. My wife and I can think of no one we'd rather have teach our son than you. If you'd have him."

"Your son?" Joey asked, confused.

Mrs. Matthews spoke. "Danny is eleven. He was diagnosed with Asperger's when he was five. He's not exactly struggling in school—he's a good kid—but he isn't. . . happy. He doesn't have many friends. He has little joy in his day."

"We were wondering if you would consider allowing us to enroll him in your school?" Mr. Matthews asked.

Joey was flabbergasted. "You want me to teach your son?" It was a compliment she was not expecting.

He nodded. "I do."

"I'd be honored, Mr. Matthews," Joey said. "We can get an enrollment package for you and schedule an interview and tour with Danny."

Mrs. Matthews stepped forward with glistening eyes. "Can I hug you?" Joey nodded. "As a parent, it is heartbreaking when you look at your child and there is no sparkle. We want to give him a chance for some sparkle."

Joey's heart burst with pride. "I understand."

At five o'clock, after the last few parents left, they locked the doors and surveyed the damage. Half-eaten pieces of cake or pizza were haphazardly left on desks and tables. Dodie and Anne began cleaning them up.

"That can wait," Dolly said. "Let's grab some dinner."

Over fajitas, they debriefed. Dodie counted the registry; a hundred forty families visited the center.

"One forty? Wow! That's amazing," Mike said. "No wonder we had no cake left."

"How many took enrollment packets?" Dolly asked.

"I'd made up two hundred packets. We have about forty or so left," Dodie said.

"Not bad," Craig said. "Did any request an interview?"

Dodie nodded. "Sherry and I set up a Google calendar on our website. Families can go online and schedule interviews. We blocked off space to do one interview at 10 am and one at 2 pm each day. Let's have a look." She pulled the calendar up on her phone. "Oh my gosh. We are booked solid for interviews for the next two weeks."

"What?" Joey said. "That's twenty interviews!"

Dolly nodded. "Brilliant!"

Channel thirteen ran the news story on The Ivan Learning Center the following Wednesday. On Thursday, the phone began ringing at 8:30 am and continued steadily throughout the day. Of the twenty interviews, twelve students enrolled for school in the fall, including Danny Matthews.

"I can't believe it," Joey said. "Twelve students! And we have five more interviews next week."

Dolly nodded. "We better find another teacher."

Joey told her about Ivan's mom.

"Let's call and set up an interview," Dolly said.

Mrs. Green came in the following day. Dolly and Joey talked with her more specifically about the school and their plans for curriculum, the daily schedule, and operations of the school. Mrs. Green talked about her strengths as an educator and where she felt she would be of value. Of the twelve students, five of them were under age eight, and Mrs. Green's primary school experience would fit perfectly for that role.

"And if we get any more students in Pre-K through grade three, we can hire an aide to support you," Dolly explained.

"It sounds perfect," Mrs. Green said. "I'd be honored to come work for you."

Four more students were enrolled by the end of June, requiring Joey and Dolly to hire two qualified paraprofessionals—one to support Mrs. Green with the younger students and another to support Joey with the older students. Dolly would serve as headmaster for the school and Dodie would be the school secretary.

"Take care of the small things, and the big things will work out," Dolly said.

Starfish and Coffee

Throughout the summer, Joey and the other teachers worked to plan the scope and sequence of skills students would develop each week of the school year. She wanted a plan in place before the August.

Working together, they developed curriculum calendars for students in the primary, middle, and upper grades. The schedule left lots of room for adjustment based on students' needs. Joey was pleased.

Two weeks before school was set to start, each student was given a two-hour window to come to the school and set up their desk pods. Parents came too, and they brought family pictures, favorite things, blankets, small fidget toys, or whatever they wanted to personalize their workspace. One tween girl brought a string of pink Christmas lights, and Dodie helped her tape them along the top of her pod.

Pride radiated from the kids' faces as they posed for pictures with their decorated spaces. Before each one left, Joey took them on a walkthrough of what the first day would be like and allowed them to express any concerns or needs. Joey made a list of things that caught their eye, questions they had, or things they avoided. She wanted to get to know her students as quickly as possible.

Dodie gave the parents a printed schedule of what students could expect the first week of school, including the breakfast and lunch options. Parent after parent expressed appreciation for this gesture.

"Preparing Danny for what's going to happen goes a long way towards success. This means so much to us," Mrs. Matthews said following Danny's tour. Danny was looking at the fish tank, a large smile stretched across his face. "After his interview, he has asked every day when he'll get to come back to school."

"We'll do everything we can for him," Joey promised.

Just as Dodie and Joey were closing up for the evening, Joey's phone rang. She looked with surprise at the screen.

"Who is it?" Dodie asked.

Joey held up a hand to Dodie. "Hello," she said cautiously into her phone.

"Hello Mrs. Russo," a male voice said. "This is Jeremy Rivers. Evan's dad," he added needlessly; Joey still had his number in her phone.

"Hello Mr. Rivers," Joey said. "And please, call me Joey."

"Right. Joey," Mr. Rivers said with a nervous laugh. "Um, Joey, would you be able to stop by my house? I'd like to talk to you about something as soon as possible, and Evan is asleep right now. I work during the days, and—"

"It's okay, Mr. Rivers," Joey said. "You don't have to explain. I can come over. I have a friend with me, though. Is that a problem?"

"No, that's fine," he said. "I really appreciate the time. I'll text the address to you."

Joey hung up. She and Dodie had ridden together, as Dodie's Jeep was in the shop. "Do you mind if we make a stop on the way home? The dad of a student I used to teach would like to talk to me."

"Evan?" Dodie asked. "The boy with the water bottle?"

Joey nodded. "Yes, the boy whose mom died last year."

Fifteen minutes later they pulled into Evan's driveway. Jeremy must have been watching for them; he opened the door as they came up the walk.

"Mrs. Ru—Joey—please come in," he said.

"This is my friend Dodie," Joey introduced.

"Call me Jeremy," he said. He showed Joey and Dodie to the living room and invited them to have a seat. They sat next to one another on his couch, and he took a seat across from them. He ran a hand through his hair and looked uncertain how to begin his conversation.

"Jeremy," Joey said, "whatever you have to say, it's okay. Take a deep breath and let us know what you need."

He nodded. "Okay. Joey, I owe you an apology," he began. "Last Christmas, in the grocery store, I was not polite to you. You'd been nothing but kind to Evan, and I snapped at you. I'm sorry."

Joey shook her head. "I overstepped. I had no business talking about Evan's schooling in a grocery store of all places. It was inappropriate."

"But you were right," Jeremy said.

"About what?"

"I assumed his mom had wanted him in general education, and that's why he was in the regular school in Wilmington. I was afraid not to honor her wishes, but it was so stressful because Evan has not settled into the general ed classrooms. I finally worked up the guts to read through Hallie's notebooks. Hallie wrote down everything. I was hoping to find an answer from her what to do. Then I found it. In her diary last year she'd written, 'I only wish Evan didn't have to be in the general education rooms. I feel like he needs more help.' She wanted him in a different place. His school just didn't have that option."

"Evan is a great kid," Joey said.

"He is a great kid," Jeremy agreed. "We barely made it through the school year. He's so smart, but the school is too big for him. After I read Hallie's notes, I asked if we could have another ARD meeting. I asked to have him moved back to the FISH room."

"That's a good thing, right?" Joey asked.

"I thought it would be, but I was told he couldn't move back. They said the room was at capacity for the fall, and due to his academic potential, he needed to remain in the gen ed class. They said it was the least restrictive environment."

"Who told you that?" Joey demanded, fearing she knew the answer.

"Mrs. West," Jeremy said. "I was wondering if you would talk to her for me. Is it true that your classroom is at capacity?"

"Oh! Um, I'm so sorry, I don't work at the school anymore," Joey said.

"You don't?" Jeremy was shocked. "I'm sorry. I didn't know."

"It's okay," Joey said. "Look, maybe I can talk to Mr. Matthews though. See if there is anything I can do? Was he in your meeting?"

"No, he wasn't. He was out sick the day of the ARD. I'd appreciate any help you can give me. I can't stand to see him cry every night after school and every morning before school. Hallie would want Evan to be happy, wouldn't she?"

Joey gave a reassuring smile. "Of course, she would. Every parent wants to see their baby happy. I didn't know Hallie, but I can see how loved Evan is."

Jeremy took a deep breath. "Why'd you leave the school? If you don't mind my asking."

"I left for a new adventure," she said. "Dodie,

my sister-in-law, and I opened a private school for students with autism."

"Really? Wow," Jeremy said. "A private school? That's incredible. Do you think—I mean, would it be the kind of place a boy like Evan could go?"

Joey smiled. "It would be a perfect place for a boy like Evan. Hang on, I have a folder in the car."

When Joey returned to the house, Evan was in the living room, sitting on Jeremy's lap.

"Woffey," Evan said. He hopped down and ran to Joey, startling her with a hug.

"Evan! Hello!" Joey said, hugging him back. "Thank you for the hug."

Evan climbed back up to Jeremy's lap. Joey handed the folder to Jeremy.

"We'll have just under twenty students this first year," Joey said. "Our school building is beautiful with lots of open space, but also plenty of areas where students can have their privacy."

"Each student will have a personalized learning plan," Dodie explained. "They'll work on academics in the morning and life skills in the afternoon."

"We have a safe outdoor yard with a climber and sports court," Joey added. "Oh! And, we have a fish tank."

Evan perked up at this. "Heart fish?" he asked Joey.

"Heart fish?" Joey asked. "I'm so sorry, Evan, I still don't know what kind of fish that is."

"No, he means starfish," Jeremy clarified. "He's wondering if your tank has a starfish. He loves starfish."

"Starfish," Joey said. "Of course. I feel so stupid. This whole time he was saying 'starfish!'"

"What do you mean?" Dodie asked.

"It sounded to me like he was saying *heart fish*," Joey said. "Whenever he would get upset at school, he'd repeat it over and over. I thought he was saying heart fish. I'm sorry, Evan, I could have gotten you a starfish book if I'd have listened a little harder."

"It wouldn't have helped," Jeremy said. "If he was upset, he probably *was* saying heart fish, but he was asking for his mom." Jeremy gently put Evan on the ground and walked to a bookshelf. He retrieved a picture and handed it to Dodie and Joey.

The picture was of Jeremy, Evan, and Evan's mom, Hallie. It was a close up of their faces, together and smiling with blue sky and sunshine behind them.

"Myrtle Beach," Jeremy said. "It was our last family vacation. Look at Hallie's neck."

A silver star fish rested along Hallie's sternum, hanging from a delicate silver chain.

"Heart fish," Evan said, pointing to the necklace.

"We bought that at a jewelry store on the beach during that trip," Jeremy explained. "It hung near

Hallie's heart, so he did call it her heart fish. It was a private joke between them. When he gets upset, he wants his mom. So, he probably was saying heart fish. Except now, all starfish are heart fish."

Joey nodded. "Sweet boy," she said, stroking the back of his hair. "I'm sorry I didn't know." She looked at Jeremy. "Can you come by the school day after tomorrow? We can give you a tour and let you meet Ms. Dolly, she's the principal at our school."

"We'll be there," Jeremy promised.

Joey had called Dolly that evening and asked if they could add one more enrollment to the roster. Dolly was thrilled to learn that Evan's dad was interested in enrolling Evan. She made a suggestion that caused Joey to yell happily into the phone.

"Why don't we offer Evan the first Ivan Green Scholarship?"

When Jeremy and Evan arrived at 10:00 a.m. two days later, the first thing Evan did was to run to the fish tank. He yelled for Jeremy to "Come see, Daddy!"

A large purple starfish rested on the rocks on the bottom of the tank. "Heart fish!" he cried excitedly, pointing.

"It's just a statue, but I thought you'd like it," Joey said. "Thank goodness for Amazon Prime and overnight delivery."

Evan looked at his dad. "Am-zon. Woffey," he said to Jeremy, pointing to Joey.

Jeremy patted Evan on the head. "Okay, okay. We just got here, Evan. But I'll give it to her."

"Give me what?" Joey asked.

Jeremy took a small box from his pocket and gave it to Evan, who gave it to Joey. "Woffey," he said. "For you."

Inside the box was a silver chain with a silver coffee cup pendant. "A coffee cup!" Joey exclaimed. "It's so pretty."

"Woffey," Evan said, and Joey suddenly heard what he was saying.

"Coffee?" Joey smiled. "Have you been calling me 'coffee' this whole time?" Joey laughed.

"He associates people with things they like. He thinks you like coffee," Jeremy explained, "and if I remember, you were holding a coffee tumbler the first time we met you."

"I do like coffee," Joey said. "Thank you, Evan." She put the necklace around her neck.

Jeremy explained. "I showed Evan your website and the brochure for the school. He was so excited, he wanted to get you a present. Like you said, thank goodness for Amazon Prime and overnight delivery. He picked it out himself."

"It's perfect Evan," Joey said.

"Heart fish," he said pointing to the tank. "And woffey." He pointed to Joey.

Just like that, the world was sunshine and rainbows.

EPILOGUE

The Sunday before the first day of school, Joey and Craig went to the cemetery after church. They tried to go every week, but it had been two Sundays since they'd been. They stopped at Ingles and picked up a bouquet of flowers to place on Emily's grave.

Joey cleaned the leaves from around her headstone and wiped it clean. She removed the old flowers from the buried vase and replaced them with the new stems. She filled the vase with bottled water. Once the grave was neatly trimmed and as perfect as it could be, she laid down on top of the grass on her side and rested her head on her elbow. She often laid like this when they visited Emily's grave. She felt closer to Emily that way, especially when she wanted to talk to her.

"Hi baby," she said. "It's me, Mommy. So much has happened in the last couple of weeks. We have seventeen students in our school. Can you believe it? And Em—I found out why Evan called me Woffey. He was saying coffee. Coffee! His dad said Evan often remembered who people are by some feature or something they like. It helps him have context. If you were here, baby, I bet he would call you, 'Strawberry Shortcake' or 'Sparkly Unicorn.'

"School starts tomorrow, Emily. I'm so nervous.

I wasn't even this nervous on your first day of Pre-K. I knew you'd be alright. I remember how confidently you walked from the parking lot to the school, in your purple flowered dress with white Mary Janes. You hated the little white socks with the lace on them. You insisted on wearing Nike socks. You were so ready for school. You marched into that building and right before you went in you turned around and gave me a thumbs up. That's how I remember you, baby. So very brave. I want to be like you when I grow up. I think you would have been a good friend to kids with special needs."

Joey sobbed softly into her arms. Craig laid down next to her.

"What's wrong, baby?" Craig asked.

"I love those kids," Joey said. "I love them, Craig."

"And that's a bad thing because—?"

"When Emily died, I didn't think I ever would love another child. I didn't think I could. But I love these kids who are coming to our school. I want to protect them and take care of them. You don't think Emily will think I've replaced her, do you?" Joey asked. "With other kids?"

"Oh, Joey. Baby. You aren't replacing her. In the brief time we had with Emily, she put so much love in our hearts. You are just giving away the love that Emily put in your heart. Love doesn't die, people do. When the people we love die, we remember them best by giving away the love we had for them to those around us who need it. That's what Emily would want you to do. Hug those other kids and think of Emily. Teach them how to be kind to each other as you would teach Emily. And when all is said and done, you'll leave behind something that will last forever."

"Starfish and coffee," Joey whispered, and she kissed Emily's headstone.

"What, babe?" Craig asked, helping her to her feet. He took her hand as they walked to the car.

"Starfish and coffee," she repeated with a smile, and in that moment she knew without a doubt that Emily would be smiling, too.

A Word from the Author

One of the proudest moments for our family was the day my son graduated high school. Cooper has autism. He had been a "special education" student since the day he entered Pre-K and in eight of the nine schools he attended. However, in his time at Claro Learning Centre in Kelowna, British Columbia, he wasn't considered a "special education student." He was just a student. And that made all the difference.

Claro came along at a time when my son needed a place where he could be himself and still be challenged to learn. I am thankful for the forever friendships that we made with staff, parents, and students. Claro is a private learning center for students with neurodivergent needs. There are centers like Claro in many parts of the world. The Ivan Learning Center in this story was loosely modeled after Claro.

When it comes to learning, what works for one student may not for another. We are all the same in that we need caring people to teach us, but we are all different how that is best accomplished. As such, teaching should not be one-size-fits-all. If you are a parent, I encourage you to be your child's biggest champion. Find what works. I've been both a public school special education teacher and a general education teacher. I've seen students thrive in public school classrooms, thrive in individualized learning environments, and thrive in private schools.

There is no one right answer except for the one that works for your child.

Public and private schools are filled with many wonderful teachers who care deeply for their students. Find the people who fit your child's needs. Find the people who see your child's originality as a gift to the world. Find your child's tribe. They are out there.

The title for this story was inspired by a song by the late musician Prince Rogers Nelson (Prince). If you've never heard Prince's "Starfish and Coffee," give it a Google. Better yet, search YouTube for his performance on Muppets Tonight. I'm sure you'll see the connection with this story.

Thank you for reading my book.

"If you set your mind free, baby, maybe you'd understand. Starfish and coffee, maple syrup and jam."

Kim

Kimberly Soesbee is an author and writing coach.

She is a graduate of Penn State University and also has a Master of Technology and Curriculum degree. She is working toward a doctoral degree in Educational Leadership and Learning.

Her books include: *Maneeya, Made in Haiti, CoCo's Bananas, The Cookie Tree, Radical Love, Roof Cat,* and more.

She is extremely proud of her three children: Cooper, a young man with autism who makes the most amazing animated videos (search OctoCoop on YouTube), Benjamin, who is serving our country in the U.S. Navy, and Kacey, whose raw talent and dynamic personality make you want to be a better person.

Kimberly's husband David is an evangelist and author. His book *What Jesus Did* is one of the best workbooks for learning how to share your faith authentically. David and Kimberly have written a bible study called *Holy Romance,* perfect for couples who want to draw closer to God.

You can connect with Kimberly through her website:
www.KimberlySoesbee.com
Twitter: @AuthorSoesbee